Destiny Decides

Keith Blades

Published by

MELROSE BOOKS

An Imprint of Melrose Press Limited
St Thomas Place, Ely
Cambridgeshire
CB7 4GG, UK
www.melrosebooks.co.uk

FIRST EDITION

Copyright © Keith Blades 2013

The Author asserts his moral right to
be identified as the author of this work

Cover designed by David Pearce

ISBN 978-1-908645-32-6

All rights reserved. No part of this publication may be reproduced, stored in a retrieval system, or transmitted, in any form or by any means electronic, mechanical, photocopying, recording or otherwise, without the prior permission of the publishers.

This book is sold subject to the condition that it shall not, by way of trade or otherwise, be lent, re-sold, hired out or otherwise circulated without the publisher's prior consent in any form of binding or cover other than that in which it is published and without a similar condition including this condition being imposed on the subsequent purchaser.

Printed and bound in Great Britain by:
CPI Group (UK) Ltd, Croydon, CR0 4YY

Acknowledgements

Thanks to Jill de Laat, Gwyn Law, Victoria Potgieter and Ken Darke at Melrose Books for their expertise and guidance.

Appreciation to my wife Wendy and our dear friend Jill for giving the support during the production of this novel.

Disclaimer
Other than mention of real or biblical people, characters in this novel are a figment of the author's imagination. Any resemblance to persons alive or dead is purely coincidental.

CHAPTER ONE
1895

Fifteenth of October – late afternoon
A FISHING boat *Canute* in the North Sea off the east coast of England, nine miles out from its home port of Eastsea. On board a crew of four: Nathan Cartwright the skipper, and deck hands Henry Matthews, Isaac Morris and Peter Smith.

It had been quiet for some time. Nathan Cartwright broke the silence.

'Henry: you and me will make ready to return to port. Isaac, Peter: clear the decks. We've had a good catch, and it's been tiring.'

Nathan and Henry set the sail and fuelled the boiler whilst the other two stored the nets.

'His Lordship should be pleased,' said Henry.

'Hope so. He's been complaining of late about the low catches,' said the skipper.

With the sail set and the steam boiler in operation, they made good progress.

'Don't like the look of those storm clouds, Skipper,' said Isaac.

Nathan looked up at the sky. 'They do look threatening. Be glad when we're back in port,' he said.

Unfortunately, tiredness causes irritability. This seemed to be the case with Henry Matthews.

'What is the matter, Henry?' asked Nathan. 'You've been of good humour, but now you're in a sombre mood.'

Henry Matthews stood on the foredeck.

'Come up here and help me sort this sail, and I'll tell you what's the matter,' he said.

'What beholds you, Henry?' asked Nathan as he stepped onto the foredeck.

Henry began ranting, 'Ever since His Lordship made you skipper you seem to have forgotten your roots and look down on us deck hands, as you were once.'

'That's not true, Henry,' replied Nathan.

Henry went on. 'Seen the way you react when Dick and Mary are together. Suppose my son is not good enough for your daughter.'

Nathan was surprised at Henry's outburst.

'None of this is true, Henry,' argued Nathan.

Henry ranted on, 'Also, tell your son Billy not to drink ale if he cannot keep his mouth shut. Should have heard him in the Cockleshell recently. What he was saying could have been overheard. I told him to shut up.'

'About foreshore activity?' asked Nathan.

'He must have overheard us talking,' replied Henry.

'In future we shall have to be careful,' suggested Nathan.

In the area at the same time, a cargo vessel was under sail and steam power – the *Hollander*, out of Rotterdam. On board were Hugo van Rowhe the skipper, his wife Francis, daughter Helene, and son-in-law Jonas de Smits. They were all in the wheelhouse.

'The storm is getting worse,' said van Rowhe.

'Why did we leave in such a hurry?' asked Francis.

Hugo and Jonas looked at each other for inspiration.

'Tell them, Hugo. We have to some time,' said Jonas.

Hugo began explaining, 'Myself and Jonas have had enough of our bosses Hogmyre and van der Lugen making the most money, when the risks are on the high seas.'

'Have you two stolen the *Hollander*?' asked a horrified Francis.

'Yes, we have,' replied Jonas.

'For goodness sake! The pair of you are crazy! I wondered about the lack of a crew. How could you both think that you would be able to man it?' shouted an angry Helene.

'Helene and me are now innocent parties to this madness,' said an agitated Francis.

There was stony silence.

'What is the cargo and what about when we return to Rotterdam?' asked Helene.

'Those two are probably chasing us now,' said Francis.

'Do not worry. We are not returning,' said Hugo.

'What?' chorused the two women loudly.

On the *Canute* three men panicked; Nathan Cartwright had fallen overboard, Henry Matthews, hung over the side, his legs held by the deckhands, in an attempt to save Nathan. At the time the sea was rough, gale force winds, thunder and lightning.

'Nathan, Nathan,' shouted Henry at the top of his voice, to no avail against the noise of the elements.

'Fortunately, in a few minutes we'll be in the relative safety of the harbour,' said Peter Smith.

'Thank God for that,' said Isaac Morris.

On the *Hollander* the women wanted to know what was going on.

'Not returning?' asked Francis, with anger in her voice.

Helene de Smits then confronted her husband.

'Jonas, is this correct?' she asked.

Jonas looked thoughtfully at Helene.

'Helene, we discovered that Hogmyre and van der Lugen were cheating on us. So Hugo and me guessed the best way to get back at them was this course of action,' he said.

Hugo then interjected, 'Jonas and me found out that the payments they were giving us could have been more. Merchants were complaining to us about the charges for the use of the vessels. We then realised they had been holding back on us.'

The two women looked as though they needed more convincing.

'There are ways they could have been confronted legally. But now they will have the authorities after us,' said Francis.

'They will not involve the authorities. Too many questions will be asked that they would not want to answer,' said Jonas.

'Those two are not what they seem,' said Hugo.

Due to the argument, they had failed to give much attention to the weather.

'While we have been arguing the weather has deteriorated. Look at it,' said Helene.

'We shall have to ride it out,' said Hugo.

The harbour wall at Eastsea was crowded, despite the weather. Men and wagons to load with the catches that would then be taken to ice houses on Eastsea Estate, the ancestral home of Lord St John Courtenay, also the owner of the small fishing fleet now battling through the heavy seas to the harbour. Among those waiting patiently were Henry's wife Susie and the deck hands' wives Hetty Morris and Purdy Smith. Nathan's wife, Amelia, had just arrived. Lord Courtenay mingled with the wives, who were waiting anxiously for the rest of the crews of the fishing fleet. He then approached the women of the *Canute* crew.

'Good evening, ladies,' he said, and then quickly corrected himself. 'Cannot really call it good!'

'Thank you for coming to see them home, My Lord,' replied Amelia Cartwright.

Lord Courtenay looked anxious.

'Least I could do, especially with this storm,' he replied.

The fleet arrived at the harbour wall and took longer than usual to dock and unload due to the waves.

The crew of the *Canute* clambered onto the harbour wall with the help of onlookers.

'Henry, where is Nathan?' asked Amelia Cartwright.

A moment I've been dreading, thought Henry.

He hesitated to find the right words.

'Amelia, I am so sorry. There was an accident. He fell overboard and with the weather…'

Amelia interrupted. 'You're telling me that he has drowned?' she asked.

'Looks that way. So sorry,' said Isaac Morris.

'We tried to save him, but with the weather…' said Peter Smith.

Amelia collapsed in tears.

Lord Courtenay took all this in.

'We must find Inspector Longfield. He's around somewhere,' suggested His Lordship.

There was now a real problem on the *Hollander*.

'The steerage has broken. We are at the mercy of the sea,' shouted Hugo van Rowhe.

'This stupid plan both you and Jonas have cooked up has put us all in danger,' said an anxious Francis van Rowhe.

The storm had worsened.

'We are being driven to that shore,' warned Jonas de Smits.

'Father, the sails are ripping,' said Helene.

I was concerned this might happen, Hugo thought.

He went to a cupboard and took out a rocket gun.

Inspector Archibald Longfield of the Eastsea Constabulary, who lived with his wife Margery and son Dominic in the police house, was organising matters on the harbour wall. The last thing anyone wanted to see was a maroon rocket, especially the crews of the fishing fleet, as some were also members of the lifeboat crew. After a gruelling day at sea, those it concerned rushed to the lifeboat house and donned the relevant gear: sou'westers and waterproofs.

Alec Morse had been on watch.

'Which direction, Alec?' asked Tom Simmons, the coxswain.

'Due north,' he replied.

The boat was prepared, sails set, oars ready, doors open onto the slipway.

'Best winch down. Sea's too rough for us to just hit it,' said Tom.

The shore helpers went about their task.

It would be a difficult manoeuvre. Drop into the water at the wrong moment, release the winch, and the boat could turn over. However, these men were used to launching and the boat went in safely. Going out of the harbour, the boat was tossing about like a cork. It was hard work rowing in these seas but, although weary, these men were strong, and they made progress towards the stricken vessel.

'Someone must have seen the rocket,' said Hugo van Rowhe.

The four of them, Hugo, Jonas, Francis and Helene, were in the wheelhouse. The men were agitated and trying to busy themselves. The women were huddled in a corner.

'I certainly hope so,' said Jonas de Smits.

Hugo walked towards the door.

'Where are you going?' asked Francis.

'To try and get a better view outside,' replied Hugo.

'It's too dangerous, Father,' cried Helene.

Hugo did not heed, and walked outside.

The storm had worsened. High gale force winds, thunder and lightning, black clouds, waves about ten feet high.

Had Hugo heeded Helene's warning he would have lived. But as he walked on the deck, his body laying against the wind, a mast broke and crashed down on him, killing him instantly.

'Oh my God!' cried Francis.

Misfortune did not grant Hugo the chance to see the lifeboat struggling to reach the *Hollander*.

On the harbour wall, Archie Longfield was trying to persuade the crowds to go back to their homes, but they were anxious about the lifeboat.

'We'll get news to you all when we know anything. Get yourselves home,' shouted Longfield.

Captain Percy Baines, Customs and Excise officer, along with constables Alec Palmer, John Dawlish and George Alexander, arrived on the scene.

'You've heard what has happened? asked Longfield.

'Yes we have, and we'll help out with the crowd,' replied Baines.

They moved through the crowd, which then gradually dispersed.

Captain Percy Baines lived with his wife Betsy and two children, Simon and Emma, in the Custom House.

The constables lived in various parts of Eastsea with their wives and families.

Longfield found the Reverend Paul and Mrs Ives comforting various folk.

'Paul, would you both please take Mrs Cartwright home?' asked Longfield.

'Of course we will,' replied the parson.

Sixteenth of October – early hours

Francis van Rowhe and Helene de Smits were hysterical after seeing the mast hit Hugo.

Jonas de Smits was trying to comfort them.

'This is all your fault, Jonas. Hugo won't have survived that,' shouted Francis.

'Please, Mother! Remember Father was at fault as well,' said Helene.

The *Hollander* was at the mercy of the storm and was being driven ashore.

The lifeboat was in trouble; the sea was too rough for it to make progress. Tom Simmons could see the *Hollander*, but had his own problems. This was one of the worst storms he could remember, having been a member of the lifeboat crew for fifteen years. The boat was being lifted up and down like a cork on water. The crew were pulling hard. They were tired and hungry, having been out fishing all day. Then disaster struck. A huge wave caught the boat broadside, and it capsized.

The crowd had dispersed from the harbour wall. The only ones remaining were the constabulary officers, Captain Baines, and shore workers in the lifeboat house. Inspector Longfield saw movement along the harbour wall and went to investigate. Nathan Cartwright's son, Billy, appeared.

'Billy Cartwright, what are you doing out here in this weather?' asked Longfield.

'I've something to tell you,' replied Billy.

'Not now. Go home,' said Longfield.

Out at sea, disaster had certainly struck. The lifeboat was upside down, with no sign of life from the crew. A strong swimmer would have had difficulty surviving in that sea.

The *Hollander* had run aground on the Eastsea foreshore. Francis van Rowhe, Helene and Jonas de Smits were in the aft cabin. They had managed to get Hugo's body into the wheelhouse.

'We must get help,' said Francis.

'Nothing can be done until the storm abates,' insisted Jonas.

'He's right, Mother. Just settle down,' said Helene.

'Where have you been, Billy?' asked Amelia as he entered the cottage. 'I was out of my mind with worry and with this storm. Haven't seen you all day and I have some bad news for you,' she continued.

'I know what it is. Father has been lost at sea,' replied Billy.

'You've heard then?' asked Amelia.

'Better than that,' replied Billy.

There was a knock at the door, which Amelia answered. Inspector Longfield stood there.

'Hello, Mrs Cartwright. How are you?' he asked.

'Bearing up. Reverend and Mrs Ives have been very kind looking after me and Mary,' she replied.

'It's Billy I've come to see. Saw him earlier on the harbour wall. Said he had something to tell me,' said Longfield.

Billy reappeared, having changed into dry clothing.

'Billy, too stormy to talk down the harbour,' said Longfield. 'What have you got to tell me?' he asked.

'Think I know how my father fell overboard,' said Billy.

'That's enough for now, Billy. Say no more of this to anyone. An inquest will be held in due course and sadly, were his body to be discovered, that would be helpful. Good night then,' said Longfield as he took his leave.

Amelia wondered, as did the others, what it was Billy had to tell the police.

Back at the lifeboat house, Inspector Longfield was getting anxious, as everyone was.

'Lifeboat has been gone two hours. However, expect them to be a while. Battling around in this storm is gruelling and it is showing no signs of abating,' he said.

'Archie, is there any need for all of us to be here on watch?' asked Baines.

Longfield thought for a while. 'You're right, Percy. You, Dawlish and Palmer, go home and return when refreshed. Please let our wives know what's happening,' he said. 'Hope you don't mind staying, George?'

'Of course not, Sir,' replied Alexander.

The customs officer and the two constables departed, wanting no second telling.

About one and a half hours had passed since the lifeboat capsized, and there was no sign of life.

The *Hollander* lay stranded on the foreshore, Francis van Rowhe and the de Smits still sheltering in the aft cabin.

'You know, I'm sure I saw a boat out there earlier, but I've not seen it since,' said Jonas.

The storm showed no sign of abating.

'By the way, what is the cargo?' asked Francis. 'I asked earlier but got no reply.'

There was still no reply on this occasion. Jonas had fallen asleep.

'Don't know how he can sleep with the noise of that storm,' said Francis.

'We should try to sleep as well, Mother,' said Helene.

Inspector Archie Longfield and Constable George Alexander felt exposed to the elements.

'Let's go over to the lifeboat house and get some vittles, George,' suggested Longfield.

'Good idea,' replied Alexander.

It was quite crowded. Alec Morse and Henry Matthews were trying to keep morale high.

'Come on in. Help yourselves to vittles. Wondered how long before you both came and joined us,' said Alec Morse.

'Thank you. It's quite worrying, but it'll be a bit longer before we shall get really concerned,' said Longfield.

As time went by the mood grew more sombre.

The trio on the *Hollander* had not been asleep for long when there was an almighty banging and cracking noise.

'What on earth was that?' asked Francis van Rowhe.

Jonas went outside to check.

'Be careful,' shouted Helene.

Jonas guessed his worst fears had manifested.

He returned to the cabin.

'What was it?' asked Francis.

'The hull has broke in two,' Jonas replied.

'What are we going to do,' asked Helene.

The storm was still raging.

'Can't do anything until the storm dies down,' he replied.

At the lifeboat house, concern was written on the face of every man.

'Gentlemen, as all this time has gone by, we have to assume the worst,' said Longfield.

'Keep hoping and praying until the storm finishes,' said Alec Morse.

CHAPTER TWO
1895

Sixteenth of October – towards dawn
THE STORM was starting to abate.

Inspector Longfield and Constable Alexander were either dozing or asleep, as were most of the others.

The door opened and Captain Baines entered.

This disturbance roused them.

'Archie, it's time you, George and the rest went home to freshen up. I assume from your demeanour there is no sign of the lifeboat, and the storm seems to be dying down,' said Baines.

Constables Palmer and Dawlish returned.

'Thanks, Percy. We'll do as you say and plan the next move when I return later; or if there are any earlier developments, let me know,' said Longfield.

Longfield, Alexander and the rest departed.

There was a knock at the door of the Cartwrights' cottage.

Dick Matthews and Mary Cartwright were sitting on the sofa, Dick comforting Mary. Their relationship was the focal point of the argument between Nathan Cartwright and Henry Matthews.

Billy opened the door.

'What do you want?' he asked Henry Matthews.

'I saw there were lights, and wanted to tell you all of my sorrow and give my condolences for what has happened,' replied Henry.

'Who is it?' asked Amelia.

'Henry. I'd have thought he's the last person you would want to see,' replied Billy.

At this, Dick jumped up.

'Go home, Father. I'll be along later,' he said.

'Suppose I should. Been at the lifeboat house all night. Still no sign of the boat returning,' said Henry, and he then departed.

Francis, Helene and Jonas had managed to get some sleep in the aft cabin. Hugo's body was in the wheelhouse.

Jonas awoke first.

'Wake up, you two. Can you hear it?' His voice was excited.

'I can't hear anything,' replied Helene.

Francis then roused up.

'Exactly! The storm has abated,' said Jonas.

Francis was now fully awake.

'Thank God,' she said.

Jonas looked thoughtful and expected to be questioned.

'What happens now?' asked Helene.

'The cargo?' requested Francis forcibly.

'Helene, we wait until daylight and then make for that port at the end of the channel. Francis, I do not know. Hugo never mentioned it,' replied Jonas.

'A likely story,' said Francis, voice full of disbelief.

'Rest a while longer; it won't be long before daylight,' said Jonas.

Later, darkness did give way to daylight.

As Inspector Longfield walked towards the lifeboat house he was joined by Constable Alexander.

'Morning, George,' said Longfield.

'Morning, Sir,' replied Alexander.

There were wagons and a pony and trap outside.

'Looks like His Lordship is here,' said Longfield.

They entered. Lord Courtenay was talking to the assembled shore workers, anxiety etched in faces, wondering the fate of their colleagues.

'Good morning, Inspector. Appears we could have a tragedy on our hands,' said Lord Courtenay.

'Good morning, My Lord. You've obviously come to the conclusion we have: to assume something terrible has happened. But still we must hold onto hope,' said Longfield.

The shore workers were getting restless to find out the fate of the lifeboat.

'Constable Palmer, please go and man the police station,' requested Longfield.

'My Lord, Inspector, can we go to the foreshore?' said Henry Matthews. 'I believe we will find answers there.'

Jonas de Smits awoke to a sound and quietly went out onto the deck. Close by was a boat stranded on the foreshore. It was most likely the one he had seen. In the distance was a group of people with horses and wagons – the sound he had heard – heading towards the *Hollander*.

Inspector Longfield and the rest of the group realised their worst fears had manifested. Before them was a scene of carnage. Strewn about were six bodies, a vessel with a split hull, and the lifeboat.

'My Lord, gentlemen, we have an horrendous task,' said Longfield.

Constables Alexander and Dawlish were sent onto the *Hollander* to look for survivors.

'Inspector, please, come here,' called Alexander.

Longfield clambered onto the deck.

'What is it?' asked Longfield.

'There are two women alive in the aft cabin, and the body of a man in the wheelhouse,' replied Alexander.

They went to investigate.

The demeanour of both women indicated to Longfield that they were traumatised, tired and hungry.

'Good morning, ladies. I'm Inspector Archie Longfield of the Eastsea Constabulary,' he said with a welcoming smile.

'Eastsea?' questioned a weakened Francis van Rowhe.

'Yes, on the east coast of England,' replied Longfield. Then turning to Alexander, he said, 'Alexander, have a look around. See if you can find a rope ladder to hang over the side to help these ladies down.'

Alexander had success.

'Either of you feel like answering a few questions?' asked Longfield.

'I will,' replied one of the ladies.

'Your names, please?' requested Longfield.

'I'm Helene de Smits, and this is Francis van Rowhe, my mother,' she replied.

'The man in the wheelhouse?' asked Longfield.

Helene looked sorrowful.

'Hugo van Rowhe, my father, the skipper,' Helene replied.

'Can you tell me how he died?' asked Longfield.

'A mast is down, as you would have seen. It fell on my father. He went outside to see if there was any response to the rocket,' replied Helene.

'There was a response. There is a small boat outside, wrecked, the lifeboat, all hands lost,' said Longfield.

'So sorry that has happened,' said Helene.

She looked questioningly at Longfield.

'Have you seen another man: my husband Jonas?' she asked.

'No sign of anyone else,' replied Longfield.

'Inspector, Captain Baines would like to see you,' called Constable Dawlish.

Longfield made his way to fulfil this request.

'You wanted to see me, Captain Baines,' asked Longfield.
'Yes, Inspector. Look – an interesting cargo,' replied Baines.

Dick Matthews arrived back at the Cartwrights' cottage.

'Let's go for a walk,' he said.

'Yes, I would like to,' Mary replied.

The foreshore was a hive of activity. As the gathering of the bodies, proving to be some of the lifeboat crew, began, Herbert Noakes, one of the helpers, made a startling discovery. Fingers had been bitten off, and rings and jewellery removed.

'Inspector Longfield,' he called.

Longfield was in discussion with Captain Baines as to what was the best course of action regarding the cargo.

Longfield reacted to Noakes' hailing.

'Coming,' he replied.

'Look at this, Inspector,' Noakes said.

Longfield was not totally surprised.

'Constables, Captain Baines, we've more of this activity,' he said.

The inspector then stood a few minutes, deep in thought.

'Lord Courtenay, please use your wagons to take the bodies to the mortuary.'

His Lordship agreed.

'Captain Baines, constables, stay here with the cargo for the time being. I will go ahead to take the two ladies to the hospital and make Dr Moore aware of the bodies,' said Longfield.

Someone was watching all this activity from the cover of the sandhills.

Mid-morning

Longfield entered the hall of the hospital and rang the bell.

'Good morning, Sister Banner,' said Longfield.

'To you also, Inspector,' she replied.

The sister looked at the two women questioningly.

'These ladies are Francis van Rowhe and Helene de Smits, her daughter. They were on board a vessel that ran aground on the foreshore. I would like Doctor Moore to check them over. Sadly, Mrs van Rowhe's husband was killed when a mast fell on him, and Mrs de Smits' husband is missing,' said Longfield.

A side door opened and Doctor Moore appeared.

'Good morning, Doctor,' said Longfield.

'Good morning to you, Inspector,' replied the doctor.

'Sister Banner will explain regarding the ladies. There are bodies on the way that will require attention from you and Lancelot Dunton,' said Longfield.

Lancelot Dunton was the district coroner.

'Expected as much,' said Doctor Moore.

Rotterdam Harbour – late morning

The administration office displayed the following notice:

A vessel has run aground and broken in two on Eastsea foreshore, east coast of England. Believed to be the *Hollander*. Please contact within for further details.

Two men were reading this with great interest.

In the harbour a boat was being made ready to leave.

Eastsea – afternoon

Inspector Longfield, accompanied by Reverend Ives, went about informing the relatives of the lifeboat crew that had perished – firstly, Anne, wife of Tom Simmons. Longfield knocked on the door of the cottage. Anne responded.

'Hello, Anne. May we come in?' said Longfield.

'I've been praying for this moment to be good news but I guess you have bad, after all this time,' said Anne.

'Afraid so. I'm so sorry. All hands lost,' replied Longfield.

'I will give you solace should you so desire,' said Reverend Ives.

'Mr Ives, I'm sorry, but it's times such as this, that I wonder if there is a god. All those brave and wonderful men gone,' said a distressed Anne Simmons.

'God moves in mysterious ways his wonders to perform. I understand how you feel, and sympathise,' said Reverend Ives.

As was pretty much the reaction and sentiments of the other families as Inspector Longfield and Reverend Ives visited each one.

Captain Baines and constables Alexander and Dawlish were sat talking by the wreck of the *Hollander*. Heading towards them was a crowd of people consisting of infantrymen, Lord Courtenay and Inspector Longfield; and some wagons.

'Looks like we are being relieved at long last. I shall be glad to get this cargo secured,' said Captain Baines.

'Hello, gentlemen. Everything all right?' asked Longfield.

'Are we glad to see you lot,' said Captain Baines.

The Queen's Infantrymen were based at Looseley Barracks, a few miles along the coast, and from time to time assisted the constabulary.

'Sergeant Hart with his men will be keeping a 24-hour watch over the cargo while it is secured at Eastsea Hall. Whoever owns this will most probably come looking for it,' said Longfield.

Captain Baines then organised the loading of the crates onto the wagons.

The party then set off just as someone, after doing some shopping in Eastsea and booking in at the Cockleshell Inn, arrived back on the sandhills in time to see them leaving.

'Mother,' shouted Mary, in tears, as she entered the Cartwrights' cottage with Dick Matthews.

'Whatever is the matter?' asked Amelia.

Mary was sobbing so much that she could not speak.

Dick Matthews spoke. 'We discovered Nathan's body on the foreshore; and worse, his fingers were bitten off,' he said.

Amelia sat down and cuddled a distraught Mary, and burst into tears herself.

'Were his rings still there? I'd like to have them,' asked Amelia.

'Sorry, no sign of any jewellery,' said Dick.

Billy entered the room.

'What's wrong?' he asked.

'We found your father's body,' replied Dick.

At this Billy got upset and further learnt: no rings.

Surely no one local would have taken the rings. Must be strangers, Billy thought.

Inspector Longfield arrived back at the police station. Constable Palmer was inside, talking to Dick Matthews.

'They've found Nathan Cartwright's body,' said Palmer.

Longfield looked at Dick.

'You found it? Take me to where it is, and we'll take it to the mortuary,' said Longfield.

'Mary and me discovered the body whilst out walking. It has really upset her and Amelia,' said Dick.

The party arrived at Eastsea Hall. The wagons were unloaded and the cargo secured.

'Marcia, do not be alarmed by the presence of the infantrymen, and please inform the staff,' said Lord Courtenay.

That was good enough for Lady Courtenay, and she knew better than to ask the reason why.

Cargo secured, Captain Baines and Constables Dawlish and Alexander then set off back to Eastsea.

A figure had been watching all this activity from the woods.

Baines and the constables met Longfield on his way to the mortuary, and were told of the discovery of Nathan Cartwright's body.

Evening

On arrival at the mortuary, Longfield was advised by Doctor Moore that Nathan Cartwright's body would be ready as soon as possible, and then the formal identification of him, Hugo van Rowhe and lifeboat crew could be held. Inquests and funerals would come later.

Both Mary and Amelia, though with difficulty, had accepted what had happened. Mary looked indecisive.

'Mary, you look pensive. Is there something to tell me?' asked Amelia.

'Yes, but I'm not sure this is the time,' replied Mary.

Amelia looked quizzical.

'Now you've said as much as that, tell me. I shall worry otherwise,' said Amelia.

'While we were out today, Dick asked me to marry him,' replied Mary.

Amelia was shaken and taken aback.

'No! You mustn't wed Dick. You're too young and he is your first boyfriend. You need to experience life and meet others,' Amelia more or less demanded.

Mary gathered her thoughts.

At this juncture Billy entered.

'Billy, Dick has asked Mary to marry him,' said Amelia.

At this, Billy looked apprehensive.

'Neither of you know my answer,' said Mary.

'Well, what was it?' asked Billy.

'As a matter of fact, yes,' replied Mary.

Amelia sat, looking thoughtful.

'I expect there will be inquests and then the funerals. Get them over and then we can consider you and Dick,' said Amelia, thinking hopefully that that would stall them for a while.

Seventeenth of October – morning

Constables Alexander and Dawlish were walking the town.

'That person over there looks lost,' said Alexander.

Dawlish looked to where Alexander had pointed.

'He's a stranger to me, George,' said Dawlish.

'Me as well,' replied Alexander.

The stranger looked startled to see the constables approaching.

'Good morning, Sir. Can we help you?' asked Dawlish.

'Maybe you can,' replied the stranger with a foreign accent.

'Not seen you around here before,' said Alexander.

"No, you will not have done. I arrived this morning. I am Hans Lundjen, a naturalist from Copenhagen, gathering material for a book about this coast,' he replied.

'Where are you staying?' asked Dawlish.

'The Cockleshell Inn,' Lundjen replied, adding, 'Please, I am looking for a bookshop.'

Directions were given to him.

The Matthews family were having vittles.

'I have something to tell you both,' said Dick.

'What might that be?' asked Henry.

'I've asked Mary to marry me and she said yes,' replied Dick excitedly.

'You what?' shouted Henry.

'Now calm down, Henry,' said Susie.

'After all that has gone on between me and Nathan Cartwright, you now want to connect the families. I bet he would be against it were he around now. I strongly believe he thought you were not good enough for Mary. Got above his station when he was made skipper of the *Canute*,' ranted Henry.

'What does Amelia think about it?' asked Susie.

'I don't know. Mary hasn't told her yet as far as I know. I do love her,' replied Dick.

'That's as maybe. Your mother and me will have to think about this,' said Henry.

'Give us time, Dick; it's come as rather a shock,' said Susie.

Dick walked out of the room with the last word.

'Mary and me will be together, whatever happens,' he said.

Constables Dawlish and Alexander returned to the police station and told Longfield of the encounter with Lundjen.

'We've checked. He is staying at the Cockleshell,' said Alexander.

'Now, Alexander, collect Mrs van Rowhe and Mrs de Smits from the hospital, first getting them to do the formal identification of Hugo van Rowhe. I've arranged for them to stay at the Cockleshell,' said Longfield.

Afternoon

Captain Baines and Inspector Longfield returned to Eastsea Hall to check everything was in order. The infantrymen were on their guarding duties.

'Vigilance at all times. As I said before, someone is going to be looking for that cargo,' said Longfield.

'It would be a valuable cargo to lose,' said Captain Baines.

'We'll look after it,' replied Sergeant Hart.

Longfield and Baines departed, satisfied with the arrangements.

Constable Alexander arrived at the hospital and was greeted by Sister Melrose.

I've to collect Mrs van Rowhe and Mrs de Smits,' he said.

The Sister then led Alexander to the day room, where the two ladies were.

'Doctor Moore has given them both a thorough examination and declared them both physically fit, but they still need time to get over what has happened,' said Sister Melrose.

'I'm Constable Alexander and will be taking you both to stay at the Cockleshell Inn in Eastsea, but first would like the body of Hugo van Rowhe to be formally identified,' he said.

'Are you feeling able to do this?' asked Alexander.

Mrs van Rowhe and Mrs de Smits conversed quietly.

'We will together,' said Helene de Smits.

Doctor Moore was in the mortuary with Lancelot Dunton when they arrived.

'Please come in, ladies,' said Doctor Moore.

'Mrs van Rowhe and Mrs de Smits to identify the body of Hugo van Rowhe,' said Constable Alexander.

'I shall lift the sheet,' said Doctor Moore.

Both ladies nodded in agreement to confirm the body as that of Hugo van Rowhe.

'Thank you. Please sign this confirmation form,' said Lancelot Dunton.

'The ladies then departed from the hospital with Constable Alexander. Nobody spoke on the way to Eastsea.

Evening

Toby Hughes was behind the bar of the Cockleshell. Miranda, his wife, was in the kitchen preparing supper for three guests. The place was quite full – of seafaring folk discussing the storm and the aftermath.

'Shall have to see Lord Courtenay about the manning of the *Canute*. Nobody appointed skipper. We're just a crew of three at present. That makes it hard work,' said Henry Matthews.

'I'd like to join the crew instead of doing shore work,' said Billy Cartwright.

'It will be dealt with after the inquests and funerals,' said Henry.

Peter Smith and Isaac Morris nodded in agreement.

Henry then departed.

In the dining room, Miranda had begun serving supper. Francis van Rowhe and Helene de Smits were at a table when the third guest entered and sat opposite them.

'Good evening, ladies,' he said.

Francis and Helene returned the salutation.

Longfield was just settling down in his chair after supper, when there was a knock at the door.

'Goodness! Who is that, when I thought this would be a restful night?' he said.

His wife Margery went to see who was there.

'It's Henry Matthews. Wants to speak to you,' she said.

Henry was taken to the office.

'Well, what is it, Henry?' asked Longfield.

'I did go down to the foreshore early hours to see if I could bite a few fingers. But I swear to you they were already bitten off by the time I arrived,' said Henry.

Longfield looked at Henry thoughtfully.

'That's as maybe. Any sign of jewellery or rings?' he asked.

'Nothing,' replied Henry.

'I assume that had there been, you would have taken them to Captain Baines or to me, for these would be folk you know – lifeboat colleagues,' said Longfield.

'Of course I would have done,' said Henry.

'Mind you, the only other dead body was on board the wrecked cargo vessel, out of your sight,' said Longfield.

'Are you saying I would have abused that one, had I known of its existence?' said an agitated Henry.

'I've had my suspicions of who the "bitefingers" characters were. Hearing of Billy Cartwright's ranting in the Cockleshell from a reputable source, then telling me evidence maybe on the foreshore. This "bitefingers" activity has got to stop, Henry. It's despicable,' said Longfield.

'It's tradition, Inspector. Fishermen's fathers' and their fathers before them did the activity. The reputable source is Toby Hughes,

I suppose. Never could keep his mouth shut, but I promise to stop,' replied Henry.

'You had better,' said Longfield authoritatively.

At the Cockleshell, after the three guests had finished supper they left the dining room and returned to the bar. Francis van Rowhe and Helene de Smits were sitting down sipping wine and the third guest, drinking a glass of ale, bid them goodnight.

'Mr Hughes,' Francis addressed the Landlord.

'Yes, Ma'am? Is everything all right – the accommodation, the supper?' asked Toby.

That's fine. No, your other guest. Can you tell me who he is?' asked Francis.

Helene joined her mother at the bar.

'Hans Lundjen from Copenhagen: a naturalist, studying nature on this coast,' Toby informed them.

'Thank you,' said Helene.

The ladies left the bar and went to their room.

'Lundjen unnerves me. I caught him staring at us once or twice,' said Helene.

'Yes, I did feel uncomfortable with his presence,' replied Francis.

Billy Cartwright was also taken with Helene.

Night

Secreted in the woods of Eastsea Hall Estate, a figure was observing the activities of the infantrymen.

'Good evening, Sir. Jack. Over here,' said an infantryman.

The stranger turned around, surprised, as a second infantryman appeared.

'What's up, Stan?' he asked.

'This gentleman, lurking here,' replied Stan.

'I'll have you know I was doing no such thing,' said the stranger.

'Better let Sergeant Hart deal with this,' said Jack.

Sergeant Hart listened to the stranger's explanation.

'I'm Hans Lundjen, a naturalist from Copenhagen, interested in the nature of this coast, seeing if there was anything of interest in the woods. I'm staying at the Cockleshell in Eastsea.'

'Take him back to Eastsea,' said Hart.

At the Cockleshell, Billy Cartwright was asking Toby Hughes about Helene de Smits.

'I'm taken with her,' said Billy.

'She's married. Her husband is missing at present,' said Toby.

'Yes I know,' replied Billy.

A wagon with two infantrymen and Hans Lundjen on board drew up outside the Cockleshell. Lundjen alighted and entered the inn. The wagon then departed with the two infantrymen still on board.

At Eastsea Hall Estate, for such a late hour, there was activity being carried out in a clandestine manner.

Sergeant Hart was deep in thought.

'You know, chaps, I'm concerned about that Lundjen fellow and you are wondering why I did not ask to see his papers. Well, I don't want to alert him. He may have seen something of interest to him. We'll have to keep an eye on him. Shall discuss this matter with Inspector Longfield,' he said.

CHAPTER THREE
1895

Eighteenth of October
INSPECTOR LONGFIELD, Constable Alexander and Captain Baines arrived at Eastsea Hall Estate as Lord Courtenay and Sergeant Hart were concluding their business.

'Good morning, My Lord, Sergeant,' said Longfield.

Both Lord Courtenay and Sergeant Hart looked pleased.

They both returned the salutation.

'Judging by the look on your faces, everything went to plan,' said Captain Baines.

'To the letter, though there is a matter I was just discussing with His Lordship. We caught a Hans Lundjen lurking in the woods last night as we were loading up. I did not ask for his papers so as not to alert him. Could be something or nothing,' said Hart.

Hart then told them Lundjen's excuse for being there.

'That was wise. We'd better keep vigilant where he's concerned. You know, I cannot figure out Jonas de Smits' disappearance. Apparently there one minute, gone the next. Suppose we shall have to wait and see what occurs,' said Longfield.

'I now await to hear of a successful delivery,' said Baines.

'Thank you all for your help,' said Longfield.

They then all went their separate ways.

On arrival back at the police station, Constable Palmer conveyed a message to Inspector Longfield from Doctor Moore.

'The bodies of Nathan Cartwright and the lifeboatmen are ready for formal identification.'

Longfield then went to Eastsea Hall to organise transport for the wives to make the identifications at the mortuary.

'Come in, Inspector. What can I do for you?' asked Lord Courtenay as Longfield was shown into the drawing room.

'I'd like to have the use of one of your large carriages to convey the wives to the mortuary for the formal identifications of the bodies. Our pony and trap is too small and would have to make two journeys,' said Longfield.

'Of course you can. I'll send Herbert Noakes with one to the police station at thirty minutes after one o'clock,' said Lord Courtenay.

'Thank you very much,' said Longfield, and he then departed.

All the ladies concerned: Amelia Cartwright, Anne Simmons, Phoebe Stewart, Joan Saunders, Susan Mistley, Molly Brandon and Sarah Evans were contacted and asked to be ready when the transport arrived.

As good as His Lordship's word, Herbert Noakes was at the police station at the allotted time.

Constable Dawlish then had the task of collecting Amelia Cartwright and the other widows of the stricken lifeboat crew. First call was Amelia Cartwright.

Amelia saw the constable arrive, and let him in her cottage.

'Come on in, Constable. I did not realise we were to be taken in such fine style,' said Amelia.

'Our pony and trap would not have been big enough to take you all in one go, so Lord Courtenay has let the constabulary use that fine carriage,' said Dawlish.

'I've seen the Courtenays in such carriages and wished I could take a ride in one, but not in these unfortunate circumstances,' said Amelia.

Then on to collect the other widows, who held the same sentiments as Amelia Cartwright regarding the transport.

All of them were apprehensive, but identification was something that had to be done.

Sister Banner greeted Constable Dawlish and the widows at the hospital door and took them to the mortuary, where Doctor Moore was waiting with Lancelot Dunton.

'Ladies, I will take you through to the autopsy room one by one. When I lift the sheet please confirm that the body shown is that of your husband. On confirmation, Mr Dunton will then ask each of you to sign a confirmation paper. Thank you for coming. I realise this is distressing for you, but the procedure needs to be carried out,' said Doctor Moore. 'Would you like to be first, Mrs Cartwright?' he asked.

Amelia looked pale, and accompanied Doctor Moore to the autopsy room. The doctor then exposed Nathan Cartwright's body.

'Yes, that is Nathan Cartwright,' said Amelia.

This same procedure was then followed by the rest of the widows.

'That is Thomas Simmons, my husband,' said Anne.

Phoebe Stewart was inconsolable but managed, 'Yes. Lawrence Stewart.'

Joan Saunders: 'Yes, my loving husband, Donald Saunders.'

'My dearest, Eric Mistley,' said Susan Mistley.

'Yes. My treasure, Alan Brandon,' said Molly Brandon, in tears.

'Why? Why? My darling Silas Evans,' Sarah Evans exclaimed.

The widows were all now in a distressed state and taken to the hospital day room for a cup of strong tea each.

Afterwards they were returned to their respective abodes.

'I will let Reverend Ives know you are all back home,' said Dawlish.

In due course, Reverend Ives visited the widows.

Coming to terms with the tragedy proved difficult.

CHAPTER FOUR
1895

Twenty-fourth of October – morning
THE INQUESTS were held at Eastsea Town Hall, presided over by the coroner, Lancelot Dunton. On official attendance were officers of Eastsea Constabulary, namely Inspector Longfield and constables Alexander and Dawlish. Amongst the large assemblage were Lord Courtenay and Captain Baines, along with members of the stricken families. Constable Palmer was manning the police station.

Lancelot Dunton opened the proceedings.

'Good morning, My Lord, ladies and gentlemen. Today we shall try to ascertain the cause of the deaths of Nathan Cartwright, Thomas Simmons, Lawrence Stewart, Donald Saunders, Eric Mistley, Alan Brandon, Silas Evans and Hugo van Rowhe through eye witnesses. One by one they will be brought to the stand to give their accounts under oath. Henry Matthews, Isaac Morris, Peter Smith, William Cartwright, Francis van Rowhe and Helene de Smits: when I call your name please leave the main hall with the usher,' he said.

The coroner ended his opening remarks.

'What's this about William Cartwright?' asked Henry Matthews. 'I didn't know he was on the *Canute*.'

'Please, Mr Matthews, go with the usher,' said Dunton.

The witnesses and the constables departed to the side room. The constables were present to ensure there was no collusion between the witnesses.

'When the proceedings commence, the assemblage must remain silent. Anyone interfering will be asked to leave. Beginning with the case of Nathan Cartwright, skipper of the *Canute*. Please call Henry Matthews to the stand,' said Dunton.

The usher brought in Henry Matthews and asked him to take the oath, which he did.

'You are Henry Matthews, deck hand on the *Canute*?' asked Dunton.

'Yes, Sir,' replied Henry Matthews.

'Mr Matthews, please describe the events as you saw them on the *Canute* on the fifteenth of October, eighteen ninety-five,' requested Dunton.

'I was helping to prepare the *Canute* to return to Eastsea. A storm was blowing up. During the trip back the sail ripped. There was strong wind and heavy rain. I called Nathan Cartwright to help me. He came onto the foredeck. Trying to contain the sail, I turned my back and next thing I heard a shout. I turned around. Nathan Cartwright had disappeared overboard. I believe the boom had swung around and hit him. With the help of the other deck hands – Isaac Morris and Peter Smith – we did a rescue attempt, sadly to no avail,' said Henry Matthews. 'If William Cartwright was aboard, why didn't he try to help us?' he asked.

'Being on the foredeck in that weather, Mr Matthews – wasn't that rather a dangerous place to be?' asked Dunton.

'Yes, Sir, but we had to try to repair the sail,' replied Henry Matthews.

'Thank you, Mr Matthews. You may stand down,' said Dunton.

Henry Matthews returned to the side room.

'Please call Isaac Morris to the stand,' said Dunton.

The usher brought Isaac Morris to the stand. Isaac then took the oath.

'You are Isaac Morris, deck hand on the *Canute*?' asked Dunton.

'Yes, Sir' replied Isaac Morris.

'Mr Morris, please describe the events as you saw them on the *Canute* on the fifteenth of October, eighteen ninety-five,' requested Dunton.

'I was aft collecting up nets and cleaning the deck. There was wind and rain. Nathan Cartwright and Henry Matthews were on the foredeck, apparently trying to repair a ripped sail. I carried on working. Suddenly Henry Matthews called me and Peter Smith, the other deck hand, to help him; Nathan Cartwright had fallen overboard. We tried to rescue him but, sadly, were unsuccessful,' said Isaac Morris.

'Thank you, Mr Morris. You may stand down,' said Dunton.

Isaac Morris returned to the side room.

'Please call Peter Smith to the stand,' said Dunton.

The usher brought Peter Smith to the stand and took the oath.

'You are Peter Smith, deck hand on the *Canute*?' asked Dunton.

'Yes, Sir,' replied Peter Smith.

'Mr Smith, please describe the events on the *Canute* as you saw them on the fifteenth of October, eighteen ninety-five,' said Dunton.

'A heavy storm blew up as I was clearing the decks to head back to port. Henry Matthews and Nathan Cartwright were on the foredeck repairing a sail that had ripped. I heard shouting, and turned around to see Henry Matthews beckoning me to go forward. He wanted help to rescue Nathan Cartwright, who had fallen overboard. Unfortunately we were unable to save Nathan,' said Peter Smith.

'Thank you, Mr Smith. You may stand down,' said Dunton.

Peter Smith returned to the side room.

'Call William Cartwright to the stand,' requested Dunton.

The usher brought William Cartwright to the stand. William then took the oath.

'You are William Cartwright, son of the deceased, Nathan Cartwright?' asked Dunton.

'Yes, Sir,' replied William Cartwright.

'Although not a member of the crew of the *Canute*, you were on board on that fateful day?' asked Dunton.

'Yes, Sir,' replied William Cartwright.

'Mr Cartwright, please describe the events on the *Canute* as you saw them on the fifteenth of October eighteen ninety-five, but firstly, your reason for being there,' said Dunton.

'I had learnt that the working relationship between my father, Nathan Cartwright, and Henry Matthews had changed. This matter was, apparently, affecting the working of the *Canute*, and I wanted to see for myself,' said William Cartwright.

'How did you learn of this?' asked Dunton.

'From Isaac Morris and Peter Smith. They were concerned that if this feud between my father and Henry Matthews continued, something awful would happen. Sadly, this point has been proven,' said William Cartwright.

'Now the events of the day, please, Mr Cartwright,' said Dunton.

'I quietly left home that morning ahead of my father, and hid under the foredeck. Later in the day there was activity on the foredeck and raised voices. Due to the wind and rain I could hardly hear, so I sneaked a look. My father and Henry Matthews were arguing,' said William Cartwright.

'Why were they on the foredeck, and what was the argument about?' asked Dunton.

'Trying to repair a ripped sail, and most likely arguing over the relationship of my sister Mary and Henry's son Dick, and how my father had altered since becoming skipper of the *Canute*,' said William Cartwright.

'Why would the issues of the relationship and your father being skipper cause arguments?' asked Dunton.

'Henry Matthews always said that my father thought Dick was not good enough for Mary. As for being skipper, my father had got to thinking he was better than the deck hands,' replied

William Cartwright.

'So, Mr Cartwright, how do you think your father fell overboard?' asked Dunton.

'That Henry Matthews pushed him overboard. Henry wanted to be skipper,' replied William Cartwright.

'That is a serious allegation, Mr Cartwright. Did you actually see Henry Matthews push Nathan Cartwright overboard? And remember, you are under oath to tell the truth,' said Dunton.

William Cartwright thought for a moment.

'No, I didn't see how my father fell overboard,' replied William Cartwright.

'As you were present, why did you not try to help to rescue Nathan Cartwright?' asked Dunton.

'I was afraid of Henry Matthews, not sure of his reactions when he knew I was on board,' replied William Cartwright.

'How did you expect Henry Matthews to react?' asked Dunton.

'That he would probably be angry,' replied William Cartwright.

'Why would you think that?' asked Dunton.

'Me being on board and not helping would put him in a bad mood. I'm quite worried now when he finds out what I've been saying,' said William Cartwright.

'If you had helped, do you think Nathan Cartwright could have been saved?' asked Dunton.

'I'm not sure. The sea was very rough,' replied William Cartwright.

'Thank you, Mr Cartwright. You may stand down,' said Dunton.

William Cartwright returned to the side room.

'Call Francis van Rowhe to the stand,' said Dunton.

Francis van Rowhe came from the side room, and although in a distressed state, took the oath.

'You are Francis van Rowhe off the *Hollander*?' asked Dunton.

'Yes, Sir,' replied Francis van Rowhe quietly.

'Mrs van Rowhe, I appreciate these are difficult times for you,' said Dunton. 'Do you feel able to give an account of the events on the *Hollander* on the fifteenth of October eighteen ninety-five?' asked Dunton.

'I think so. I'll try,' replied Francis van Rowhe, faintly.

'Please speak louder, Mrs van Rowhe,' requested Dunton.

'Sorry, Sir. The *Hollander* was caught in a storm. On board were my husband Hugo van Rowhe…' At this Francis van Rowhe drifted off and fainted.

'Doctor Moore, pleased attend to Mrs van Rowhe and get her back to the side room.

On seeing the state of her mother, Helene de Smits protested.

'Mother cannot go on,' she said.

'I'll look after her,' said Doctor Moore.

The usher came into the side room.

'Helene de Smits, please come and take the stand,' he said.

By this time Francis van Rowhe was conscious, although in shock.

'I must go to the stand. Doctor Moore will see to you,' said Helene de Smits.

Helene de Smits took the stand and the oath.

'You are Helene de Smits off the *Hollander*?' asked Dunton.

'Yes, Sir,' she replied.

'Do you feel able to give an account of the events on the *Hollander* on the fifteenth of October eighteen ninety-five?' asked Dunton.

'I'll be all right, but my mother has been terribly shaken by all of this,' said Helene de Smits.

'I realise it will be difficult for you. Please continue,' said Dunton.

'We were caught in a terrible storm: rain, wind, thundering and lightning. My father, Hugo van Rowhe, had taken the *Hollander* illegally. Hence there was no crew: just me, my mother and my husband, Jonas de Smits, who at present is missing. We were the only ones on board. In the storm, with no crew, the ship was difficult to handle. The sails began to rip and the steerage broke. The *Hollander* was drifting towards the shore. My father went outside to launch a maroon rocket. An hour or so later he went outside to see if there was any response. It was then that the mast broke and fell on him, causing his death. We have since learnt that there was a response. Sadly, that ended in tragedy and we are devastated it was our actions that caused the loss of the lifeboat and crew,' said Helene de Smits.

'Thank you, Mrs de Smits. You may stand down,' said Dunton.

Helene de Smits returned to the side room.

'Doctor Moore, how is my mother?' she asked.

'She is recovering satisfactorily. The inquests have brought the events on the *Hollander*, which were in the back of her mind, to the forefront. Peace and quiet in comfort and she'll be fine, but it will take time,' replied Doctor Moore.

'Then Mother will not be able to take the stand again?' asked Helene.

'No. I will explain to the coroner,' replied Doctor Moore.

The usher came into the side room.

'Doctor Moore, the coroner would like a word with you,' he said.

The doctor went into the main hall.

'Doctor Moore, Mrs van Rowhe – is she well enough now to continue?' asked Dunton.

'I'm afraid not. She is not able to take the stand again. If it is in order to do so, I shall take Mrs van Rowhe and Mrs de Smits back to their accommodation,' replied the doctor.

'Certainly you can. Thank you, Doctor Moore,' said Dunton.

'Moving onto the deaths of the lifeboatmen, namely Thomas Simmons, Lawrence Stewart, Donald Saunders, Eric Mistley, Alan Brandon and Silas Evans; then there is the case of the lifeboatmen whose bodies have not been given up by the sea, namely

Derek Mistley, Martin Carter, Marcus Thorpe, Thomas Jackson, Harry Lightman, George Moody and Rodney Lucas. As there are no witnesses to this tragedy we must assume the lifeboat was capsized by the rough sea whilst attempting to go to the aid of the *Hollander*,' Dunton added.

He then stood up. 'I would like to give my sincere and heartfelt condolences to all the families involved and, taking into consideration the accounts of the witnesses, I can only record a verdict of accidental death in all the cases. These inquests are now concluded. The case of Jonas de Smits cannot be discussed at present as his fate is unknown,' said Dunton.

Throughout the inquests Inspector Longfield had taken notes.

'Only verdict you could have reached, Mr Dunton. No proven criminal activity, apart from the *Hollander*, which will be dealt with by the Dutch authorities,' said Longfield.

'Open-and-shut cases in the end. There were accounts from people present at the times. The only eye witnesses were those on the *Hollander* to a degree. Apart from that, not much to go on,' replied Dunton.

'Hans Lundjen was in the hall. Wouldn't have thought the inquests were of interest to him,' said Longfield.

Inspector Longfield, Lancelot Dunton, Captain Baines and the constables then departed the now empty Town Hall.

Outside, people were milling around, standing in groups, most likely discussing the outcome of the inquests, and the forthcoming funerals.

CHAPTER FIVE
1895

Twenty-sixth of October

EIGHT HORSE drawn hearses stood serenely on Eastsea harbour wall, each containing a coffin. The local undertaker had provided two, and three undertakers from the outlying district two each.

The Reverend Paul Ives officiated at the funeral service, which was attended by a large assemblage.

'All the families concerned have agreed that this should be a mass burial at sea. The souls to be offered to God were born by the sea, lived by the sea and died by the sea, namely Nathan Cartwright, Thomas Simmons, Lawrence Stewart, Donald Saunders, Eric Mistley, Alan Brandon, Silas Evans and Hugo van Rowhe. Let us also remember those souls not given up by the sea: Derek Mistley, Martin Carter, Marcus Thorpe, Thomas Jackson, Harry Lightman, George Moody and Rodney Lucas. All were members of the lifeboat crew apart from Nathan Cartwright and Hugo van Rowhe,' said Reverend Ives.

The coffins were then placed on boats for the passage to open waters.

"Eternal Father, Strong to Save" was sung, and followed by prayers of offering, the Lord's Prayer, and "The Lord Is My Shepherd".

The grieving families then boarded boats to follow those carrying the coffins.

Out in open waters, the souls were offered up to Heaven as each coffin was dropped in the water.

'Lord God, we commend these souls to your keeping,' said Reverend Ives.

The offering service completed, the flotilla returned to Eastsea.

Inspector Longfield, Captain Baines, the three constables, along with a crowd, were still assembled on the harbour wall, awaiting the return of the boats.

'Hello, Mrs de Smits. How is your mother?' asked Longfield as Helene stepped off one of the boats.

'She is recovering well, but felt it best not to attend the funeral,' replied Helene.

'Hans Lundjen is standing over there, Archie,' said Baines.

'That chap intrigues me,' replied Longfield.

Reverend Ives then gave his blessing to the grieving families of Cartwright, Simmons, Stewart, Saunders, Mistley, Brandon, Evans and van Rowhe.

'Let us also remember those families whose souls are unaccounted for. Another Mistley, Carter, Thorpe, Jackson, Lightman, Moody and Lucas,' he said.

Helene de Smits then headed for the Cockleshell, entered, and went up to the room shared with her mother.

'Hello, Mother. How are you?' asked Helene.

'Feeling much better now, thank you, Darling. The stark truth of events on the *Hollander* being brought to light again at the inquest upset me,' replied Francis. 'How was the service?' she asked.

'Very poignant and moving. Had Father and Jonas not been so foolish… Sadly, nothing can bring Father back,' said Helene.

'There is the worry of what has happened to Jonas,' said Francis.

'He must have drowned or he would be looking for us, and it is hard to bear,' said Helene, in tears.

'Every day that passes without them both does not help,' said Francis.

'Hans Lundjen was out there on the harbour wall. Caught him staring at me again,' said Helene.

'You are an attractive young woman. Come. Let us go have some food,' said her mother.

'When we are settled again after these upsets, I must talk to you,' said Amelia Cartwright to Henry and Susie Matthews.

They then departed company.

'Wonder what that's all about. Probably something to do with Dick and Mary's big ideas,' said Henry.

'You could well be right,' replied Susie.

Later, under the cover of darkness, a small vessel was secreting itself into a cove in hills to the north of Eastsea harbour, under the watchful eyes of infantrymen.

CHAPTER SIX
1895

Twenty-eighth of October – morning
AMELIA, BILLY and Mary Cartwright were at their cottage, along with Henry, Susie and Dick Matthews.

'I've asked you here as there is something you all need to know. It's been a difficult decision and the hardest thing I've ever had to do,' said Amelia.

The others all looked on in wonder.

'The marriage of Dick and Mary is out of the question,' said Amelia.

'Why? What's the problem?' asked Henry. 'Same attitude that Nathan had, I guess,' he said.

Amelia was very uncomfortable at the confidence she was about to break.

'They cannot marry as Mary is Henry's daughter,' Amelia declared.

There was a stony silence.

'What? Amelia Cartwright, how can you make such an allegation?' shouted Susie Matthews.

'It's true. I once heard Mother and Father discussing the matter,' said Billy Cartwright.

'Mary and Dick were struck dumb by the news.

'Henry Matthews, is this true?' asked Susie angrily.

Henry was speechless.

'I'm sorry you had to find out, Susie,' said Amelia.

Susie Matthews was now in a real temper.

'Henry, is this true?' Susie shouted again.

Henry recovered as from a knockout blow. 'I don't know. Just a ruse to prevent Mary and Dick marrying,' he replied.

Mary and Dick had left in utter disbelief.

'I'm afraid it's true. It was at a time when me and Nathan were going through a difficult patch,' said Amelia.

Henry regained his composure. 'It's not true, Susie. Please believe me, I beg of you,' he pleaded.

'I'm so sorry, Susie, that I have to tell you. Henry has always been after my affections. He comforted me when I was vulnerable,' said Amelia.

'Is that what you call it?' replied an angry Susie, who then departed.

Inspector Longfield entered the Cockleshell Inn and looked around the bar and dining room.

'Good afternoon, Inspector,' said Toby Hughes. 'Can I get you a drink?' he asked.

'No thank you, Toby. I'll be back later,' replied Longfield.

Captain Baines entered the Eastsea Police Station.

Inspector Longfield was in his office.

Constable Palmer was at the duty desk.

'Hello, Constable,' said Baines.

'Good afternoon, Captain Baines,' replied Palmer.

Longfield came out of his office.

'Thought I heard you, Percy. Come into the office,' he said.

'Good news, Archie. The cargo is now secured at Woolwich Arsenal,' said Baines happily.

Longfield looked relieved.

'Excellent! We didn't want that falling into the wrong hands,' he said.

Henry Matthews was trying to persuade Susie to let him into their cottage.

'Please let me in to explain,' pleaded Henry.

I'll let him sweat it out for a while, she thought, smiling.

'Come on in, you blaggard, and start explaining,' she said.

'As Amelia says, Mary could be my daughter,' said Henry.

Susie thought for a moment.

'Henry, give me time to think about our situation. Come back later,' she said.

Mary and Dick had been walking since leaving the cottage after Amelia's revelation. After careful consideration they had decided upon a course of action.

Previous to the confrontation with the infantrymen, Hans Lundjen had kept a low profile. Further, he had attended the inquests and funerals, which made Inspector Longfield wonder why a visitor new to the area had taken such an interest.

Henry returned to learn Susie's decision.

'I've given it a lot of thought. Nathan must have calculated years ago that when Mary was born there was infidelity. Rather than have a scandal he took her as his daughter, hoping the situation would never be exposed. He would not have reckoned with a relationship between Dick and Mary,' said Susie.

Henry looked thoughtful.

'Do you forgive me?' he asked.

Susie gathered herself to continue.

'I believe Amelia is telling the truth. Don't think she would make up a story such as this. We can continue to live together but our marriage will never be the same. If you go astray again, no more chances – out of my life you'll be,' warned Susie.

Henry looked relieved.

'I still love you, Susie, and promise to do as you ask. Thank you,' he said.

The Cockleshell Inn was quite full. Inspector Longfield entered with Constable Alexander. Susie and Henry Matthews along with Amelia Cartwright were sitting in the bar. Longfield headed towards the dining room.

'Well, what do you want us for, Amelia?' asked Henry.

'I was about to ask you the same thing,' replied Amelia.

At that precise moment three minds were as one.

'Dick told Susie and me you wanted to meet us here,' said Henry.

'Mary told me you'd like to meet me at the Cockleshell,' said Amelia.

The three of them then hurried out.

Longfield stood in the entrance to the dining room.

Good, he thought. The Dutch ladies and Hans Lundjen are having supper.

'Jonas de Smits,' he called.

Whether it was a lack of concentration, but in that split second Hans Lundjen responded to the call.

'Take off that wig and those false whiskers,' requested Longfield.

Hans Lundjen did so.

'Jonas,' shouted Helene de Smits with surprise.

'Sorry for that, Mrs de Smits. I will now have to take your husband to the police station for a chat,' said Longfield.

Inspector Longfield, Constable Alexander and de Smits left the inn, inquisitive eyes following them.

At the Cartwright cottage, Amelia, along with Henry and Susie, found their worst fears were confirmed. The note read:

Dear Mother,
Sorry to cause you further upset, but Dick and me love each other and want to be together. Don't worry. We'll get by. Once we are settled somewhere will contact you.
Give my love to Billy.
Your loving daughter, Mary.

'Amelia, Henry, now look at what has happened due to selfishness,' said an angry Susie.

Henry and Susie would find a note in similar vein when they arrived home.

As the police left the Cockleshell Inn, two men were alighting from a vessel onto the harbour wall.

Inspector Longfield and Constable Alexander were about to commence the interview with de Smits when two men entered.

'Good evening,' said Alexander. 'Can I help you?' he asked.

'We are from the Rotterdam Constabulary. I am Inspector Vendren and this is my colleague Constable Metzer, here to collect Jonas de Smits and Hugo van Rowhe,' he said.

Longfield checked their credentials.

'Been expecting you,' said Longfield.

Leaving Constable Alexander with de Smits in the interview room, Longfield and the two Dutch officers went into his office.

'Gentlemen, first of all I will explain,' said Longfield. 'The *Hollander* was shipwrecked on our foreshore due to a terrific storm. When we finally reached the wreck we found two females alive and one male dead, and discovered they were Dutch nationals. The dead man was Hugo van Rowhe, the skipper, killed when a mast fell on him. The two females were his wife Francis and daughter Helene de Smits. We then got told one male was missing – Jonas de Smits, husband of Helene, who disappeared before we reached the scene.'

'You obviously found him,' said Inspector Vendren.

'I will tell you how later. As regards Hugo van Rowhe, after an inquest, he was buried at sea at the request of his widow and daughter. You will be shown a record of the inquest,' said Longfield.

The three officers then went to the interview room.

'Mr de Smits, please tell us what were yours and Hugo van Rowhe's intentions?' asked Inspector Vendren.

De Smits then proceeded to explain how they felt at being cheated by Hogmyre and van der Lugen. He continued, 'We were to deliver the cargo to London. Where it would be taken after that, I do not know. We hoped to sell it, pocket the money, take on a crew and head for South America.'

'Constable Alexander, take Mr de Smits to the cells,' requested Longfield.

'Gentlemen, you may wish to know how I found Mr de Smits. He suddenly disappears without trace and, behold, a stranger is in town, just as sudden. I had a hunch, went to see George Wilson, who runs a haberdashery, and he confirmed a blonde wig and false whiskers had been purchased recently. Then I called out Jonas de Smits' name in the Cockleshell and Hans Lundjen responded. I would have looked a fool had he not,' said Longfield.

'Where do the two ladies fit in this charade?' asked Inspector Vendren.

'Have talked to them, and they appear to be unwilling collaborators, but of course make your own mind up after talking to them,' said Longfield.

Longfield and Vendren left the interview room.

'Alexander, please fetch Mr de Smits back from the cells,' requested Longfield.

Ten minutes later Longfield and Vendren returned.

'You are free to go at the moment, Mr de Smits,' said Vendren.

De Smits started to speak.

'Go, but keep yourself available, as we are to make further investigation,' said Longfield.

'If you do leave the area it will make us suspicious and make matters worse for yourself,' said Vendren.

'By the way, Mrs van Rowhe and my wife Helene are not involved in any way. They are innocent,' said de Smits.

Jonas de Smits then departed and immediately went to the dining room in the Cockleshell.

'Hughes, have you seen a small bag? I left it under the table in the dining room,' he said forcibly to the landlord.

'No, Mr de Smits, we've not seen the bag,' replied Toby Hughes.

There was a stranger sitting in the corner of the bar.

'Hello, de Smits,' said the stranger.

Turning around, de Smits saw who it was and panicked. He ran to the rear entrance, only to run into a second stranger.

Both strangers to Eastsea but not to de Smits.

'How nice to bump into you again, de Smits,' he said.

This latest episode and the earlier arrest of de Smits had set the Cockleshell buzzing.

'So that young Dutch woman had found her husband. I was taken with her,' said Billy Cartwright to Toby Hughes.

Toby Hughes grinned.

'Could be in with a chance. He's in trouble with the police, and just who those two are, I don't know. Been hanging around here for a while. De Smits obviously knows them,' said Hughes.

Twenty-ninth of October – morning

Helene de Smits responded to a knock on the door of the room she shared with her mother.

Inspector Longfield stood there.

'Hello, Mrs de Smits. May we come in? These gentlemen

are Inspector Vendren and Constable Metzer of the Rotterdam Constabulary,' he said.

'Yes, of course. Come in,' said Helene.

'How can we help?' asked Francis van Rowhe.

'Do not be alarmed. First of all, our condolences. We are here to investigate the theft of the *Hollander* from Rotterdam harbour. We have spoken to Mr de Smits and he has pleaded guilty to the theft of the *Hollander* in league with Mr van Rowhe, and points out neither of you were party to the offence in any way. This is also endorsed by Inspector Longfield. Whilst further investigations are carried out Mr de Smits is free for the time being, with conditions. When investigations are concluded Mr de Smits will be taken to Rotterdam, along with you, Mrs van Rowhe, and Mrs de Smits. Neither of you are under arrest, but I am sure you both need to get home to sort things out. If other plans come to fruition there could be further people to accompany us,' said Vendren.

'What were my husband and father planning to do?' asked Helene de Smits.

'As you and your mother are innocent parties, better you didn't know the details,' replied Vendren.

'Have you seen Mr de Smits?' asked Longfield.

'No, we haven't,' replied Helene de Smits.

'Thank you, ladies,' said Longfield.

The officers then departed.

Outside the Cockleshell the three officers were chatting.

'That is strange, de Smits not going to see them. Wonder where he is. Must have been distracted in some way,' said Longfield.

The three of them then grinned knowingly.

CHAPTER SEVEN
1895

Twenty-ninth of October – afternoon
THREE FIGURES were moving stealthily through the trees on Eastsea Hall Estate.

'That's the buildings where the cargo was stored,' said one.

They studied the area carefully.

'You told us there were guards,' said a second.

Figures two and three looked at each other.

'Are you sure? It will do no good to patronise or lie,' said the third.

The first figure looked shaken.

'No guards. It's probably been moved,' he said.

They swung around when a voice boomed out.

'You're right, Mr de Smits,' said Inspector Longfield.

With Longfield were Constables Dawlish and Alexander, Captain Baines, the two Dutch policemen, Sergeant Hart and some infantrymen.

'You are being arrested, Mr de Smits, on suspicion of felony; Mr Hogmyre and Mr van der Lugen on suspicion of illicit trafficking,' said Inspector Vendren.

'Take them to Eastsea Police Station,' said Longfield.

A flotilla of six fishing boats led by the *Canute* headed out of Eastsea harbour into the North Sea. Lord Courtenay had appointed Henry Matthews as skipper and Billy Cartwright a deck hand.

The party arrived back at Eastsea Police Station from Eastsea Hall Estate woods.

'I was told I was free to go,' protested de Smits.

'You did not really think yourself not guilty of any misdemeanour such as stealing a boat and its cargo?' asked Longfield.

'Our expectations were that Mr Hogmyre and Mr van der Lugen would be coming to find the *Hollander*,' said Vendren.

De Smits was placed in a cell whilst the interviews of Hogmyre and van der Lugen were conducted by inspectors Longfield and Vendren.

"Mr Hogmyre, would you like to explain?' asked Longfield.

'You've no right to arrest me and van der Lugen. We were merely looking for the cargo stolen from us by van Rowhe and de Smits,' said Hogmyre.

'Steal from you they certainly did. They found out you were paying them less than you could have in the past. This wasn't a normal cargo. No papers for it. To get back at you they carried out this plan. Most likely would have got away with it had it not been for the storm,' said Longfield.

'Why did you come into Eastsea in such a clandestine manner?' asked Vendren.

'Didn't want van Rowhe and de Smits to know we were here. We then learnt van Rowhe wasn't around. Poetic justice, that!' replied Hogmyre.

'Have you anything else to say?' asked Vendren.

'Nothing,' replied Hogmyre.

Hogmyre was placed in a cell whilst the inspectors spoke to van der Lugen.

'Mr van der Lugen, please tell us why you are here in Eastsea.' said Longfield.

'Hogmyre and I came to get our property back, and end up getting arrested. I don't know why; we've done nothing wrong,' said van der Lugen.

'Then why enter Eastsea in such a secretive way?' asked Longfield.

'So that van Rowhe and de Smits would not see us. Poor old van Rowhe got his comeuppance though,' replied van der Lugen.

'We'll be the judges of right and wrong, later on,' said Vendren.

'Carry on,' said Longfield to the two men.

'Nothing else to say,' replied van der Lugen.

Van der Lugen was put in a cell.

The inspectors then retired to correlate their findings.

Out at the fishing grounds the crew of the *Canute* were going about their tasks, as were the crews of the rest of the fleet. Another boat approached the *Canute*.

Henry Matthews hailed the visitors.

'Hello, Anton,' he shouted. 'How are you?' he asked.

Anton Besten, a fishing boat skipper from Rotterdam, returned the salutation.

'I have nothing for you,' said Henry.

Anton looked disappointed.

'I'm sorry, Anton. Nothing. Our ventures have to cease; the authorities are taking interest,' said Henry.

Over the years Henry Matthews and Nathan Cartwright had built up a lucrative dealing situation with Anton Besten.

'Will this do?' asked Billy Cartwright.

Billy handed Henry a package.

'Who is he and where is Nathan?' asked Anton.

Henry explained the circumstances surrounding Nathan and that Billy was Nathan's son and now a member of the *Canute* crew.

Henry then handed the package to Anton Besten, who then checked the contents.

'These are good,' said Anton.

He then hesitated.

'Where did you get these?' he asked. 'Some of this stuff belonged to me, and other bits to fishermen in Rotterdam,' he said.

'What do you mean?' asked Henry.

'We lost these gambling. They were won by a Jonas de Smits.'

Henry Matthews then explained how he and Billy had met Jonas de Smits.

'Yes, Rotterdam is buzzing with the news of the *Hollander*. Didn't realise de Smits and van Rowhe were involved. Hogmyre and van der Lugen were the owners. They won't be very happy,' said Besten.

He then handed Henry Matthews a package.

'Thank you, thought there would be nothing for me after getting your own stuff returned,' said Henry.

'You're welcome, Henry. Really glad to have got the stuff back, as the others will be, although it's a pity we have to stop,' replied Besten.

'Don't think you'll get any bother from de Smits. Him and the other two are in trouble with the authorities,' said Henry.

'Sorry to hear about your father, Billy. Bye, Henry; see you around,' said Anton.

'So long, Anton,' replied Henry.

Henry looked at Billy.

'The stuff was in that bag de Smits was looking for in the Cockleshell, wasn't it? So it was you that took it, Billy?' asked Henry.

'Not only that; there was other stuff in there as well – my father's jewellery and some belonging to the lifeboat crew. I've given Mother my father's stuff, and Mrs Simmons the rest to sort out for the widows of the lifeboat crew. Told them I had managed to recover it and say no more,' said Billy.

'You've done well. Your father would be proud of you. De Smits must have collected that up soon after the storm finished before the authorities arrived. The activity must stop though, with Longfield and Baines nosing around,' said Henry.

'But it's a tradition,' said Billy.

'Tell you what: leave it for a while till things quieten down. Not as if it's a regular thing; that storm was the most violent I have experienced,' said Henry.

'Yes, that sounds good,' replied Billy.

'Right, let's get cleared up. We've had a good catch,' said Henry.

The *Canute* then headed for Eastsea.

Inspectors Longfield and Vendren emerged from their deliberations regarding de Smits, Hogmyre and van der Lugen.

'Palmer, Alexander, please bring the prisoners from the cells,' requested Longfield.

The two inspectors faced the three prisoners across a table in the interview room. The two constables were in attendance.

Longfield then spoke to de Smits.

'Mr de Smits, you have admitted being party to the theft of the *Hollander* belonging to the Rotterdam Shipping Company, and consequently an illicit cargo. Hugo van Rowhe's action contributed to his death. You are not without blame and changing your appearance did not help. These matters will be dealt with on your return to Rotterdam,' said Longfield.

Vendren then spoke to Hogmyre and van der Lugen.

'Mr Hogmyre, Mr van der Lugen, you are both involved in illicit trafficking of guns and ammunition, proven by the lack of papers. The shipping company is a legitimate front to your activities. Charges will be made in Rotterdam,' said Vendren.

Longfield gave further evidence.

'When we realised both of you could be involved, we took action. You were observed concealing your boat and going over to the *Hollander*, when Mr de Smits was intercepted and then followed to Eastsea Hall Estate,' said Longfield.

Constable Metzer, assisted by Constables Dawlish and Alexander, took the three suspects to the Dutch police vessel in the harbour. Unknown to the suspects, Mrs van Rowhe and Mrs de Smits were already on board.

'Thank you for your help, Longfield. We've been aware of Hogmyre and van der Lugen for a while, but by laundering through the shipping company there was always an explanation. On this occasion the storm helped and we should get a result, although at a terrific cost to your community,' said Vendren.

The two inspectors then took their leave of each other.

CHAPTER EIGHT
1895

Thirtieth of October – morning
AMELIA CARTWRIGHT was in her cottage when there was a knock at the door. Upon opening it she found a handsome young man standing there.

'Mrs Cartwright?' he asked.

Amelia was in awe of him, not really concentrating on what was being said.

'Oh, yes,' she replied.

'I'm Daniel Courtenay from Eastsea Hall,' he said.

'The son and heir,' said Amelia, remembering.

'I suppose I am. Been away at agricultural college learning estate management,' he replied.

Amelia bid Daniel to enter, wondering why he was there.

'I can see you are surprised to see me,' he said.

'I am rather,' she replied.

They both sat down.

'Bearer of good news, I'm pleased to say. Your daughter and her man are staying with my sister Jessica and her husband Cedric, a doctor, at our town house in London,' said Daniel.

'I knew they were acquainted; Mary often spoke of Jessica,' said Amelia.

'Apparently they were friends due to the fishing boats business. Jessica would often go with my father to the harbour to see your husband, and Mary would be there. By the way, my condolences on the loss of him,' said Daniel.

'Thank you,' said Amelia, looking puzzled.

'Mary contacted Jessica, and the rest is history,' said Daniel.

Amelia was taken with Daniel.

'Would you like tea and scones?' she asked.

Amelia went into the scullery. Daniel followed.

'Another reason for my visit: Mother would like you to take tea with her at the Hall this afternoon,' said Daniel.

This set Amelia's mind racing, thinking why would a lady of standing such as Lady Courtenay wish the likes of Amelia to have tea with her.

On the way to Eastsea Hall, they called at the Matthews' cottage to give the news regarding Dick and Mary. Susie was delighted and relieved.

The rest of the journey to the Hall, Amelia was deep in thought.

'Why are you so quiet?' asked Daniel.

'I'm still wondering why your mother would want to see me,' replied Amelia.

'I honestly don't know. You'll soon find out though,' said Daniel as the carriage arrived at the Hall.

'Come in, Mrs Cartwright. Good news from London,' said Lady Courtenay as Amelia was shown into the drawing room by Daniel.

'Now be off with you, Daniel. Leave us in private and when we are finished I'll call you to take Mrs Cartwright home,' said Lady Courtenay.

Amelia appeared overawed.

Lady Courtenay rang a bell and within a few moments a maid was bringing in afternoon tea.

'This is Jane. You probably know her,' said Lady Marcia.

Amelia looked at Jane, who was from Eastsea and a schoolfriend of Mary's.

'Yes I do. Hello, Jane,' said Amelia.

'Good afternoon, Mrs Cartwright,' replied Jane.

With the formalities over Lady Courtenay began.

'I've asked you here, Amelia; and Jane will stay as this somewhat involves her,' she said.

In her mind Amelia was confused.

Lady Courtenay continued. 'Jane is going to London to keep house for Jessica, who has just qualified as a doctor, and that would leave a vacancy here at the Hall. Amelia, would you like to work here?' she asked.

Amelia was flattered but stunned by the offer.

The fishing boat flotilla was heading back down the channel to Eastsea harbour, all boats having had a successful trip with their catches. As soon as the *Canute* catch had been unloaded onto wagons to be taken to Eastsea Hall ice houses, Billy Cartwright went to the Cockleshell Inn and Henry Matthews' home, where he would receive unexpected good news.

'Hello, Toby,' said Billy on entering the inn.

After looking around the bar, Billy looked disappointed.

'They've gone back to Holland, those two ladies. The Dutch police have de Smits and those other two chaps who were about here, under arrest. Must be some connection between them,' said Toby.

Billy had a pint of ale and then went home.

Henry Matthews was delighted with news of the whereabouts of his son and, as a matter of fact, his daughter.

'Well, are they returning to Eastsea?' asked Henry.

'There was no mention of it at present,' replied Susie.

She then disappeared into the scullery to prepare supper.

Inspector Longfield and Captain Baines were hoping their evenings would not be disturbed after the previous hectic days. Thankfully this proved to be the case.

Billy Cartwright received the good news on his arrival home. Amelia then set about getting supper.

After supper Amelia then told Billy the other news.

'Lady Courtenay wants you working at the Hall?' asked Billy, surprised.

'I was just as surprised,' replied Amelia.

Billy looked thoughtful.

'Mother, I can see by your manner, you have agreed,' he said.

'Wages will be helpful, but I have to live in,' said Amelia. 'You'll be all right, won't you, on your own here?' she asked.

'Of course I will,' replied Billy.

Thirty-first of October – *morning*

The Dutch contingent were back in Rotterdam. De Smits, Hogmyre and van der Lugen were in custody, awaiting trial.

Helene de Smits was visiting her husband.

'What on earth were you and Father thinking about?' she asked angrily.

De Smits sat shamefully.

'We believed the cargo could be sold easily; there are usually buyers around. Then we could head for South America and a new life,' he said.

'You must have both been mad to think the two of you could do what usually requires at least eight crew,' said Helene.

De Smits began to apologise. 'The storm – '

'Save your apologies. Neither of you should have put Mother and me in such a situation. We had a happy life. Goodbye Jonas,' she said, and departed.

At Eastsea Hall, Lady Courtenay had assembled the staff in the kitchen.

'In a few weeks the annual estate ball will be held. It is a busy time. You've all worked hard at these in the past, and His Lordship and I very much appreciate it,' she said.

They were then dismissed and went about their work.

Two of the other maids, Annie and Ruth, both of whom had been there a few years, warned Amelia of the antics that could go on at the ball.

'A time of eating and drinking. Need I say more?' said Annie.

CHAPTER NINE
1895

Twenty-second of November
ARCHIE LONGFIELD woke up with a start. This disturbed Margery.

'Goodness, it's another of those violent storms. Better get out there and see what's happening,' he said.

A quick breakfast.

'Be careful,' said Margery as he departed.

The storm was just as strong as the previous one a month or so earlier. Thunder and lightning. Rough seas in the harbour, whipped up by the strong winds.

To assess the situation, Longfield went to the lifeboat house.

Captain Baines, Henry Matthews and Billy Cartwright were already there, with several others.

A few minutes later Lord Courtenay arrived.

Salutations were exchanged.

'Thank God you people weren't out fishing in this. These storms are blowing up more or less without warning and fortunately this one is in the early hours,' His Lordship said.

'I'm tempting providence, but I hope a lifeboat is not needed,' said Henry Matthews.

As time went by the storm continued. After they had been at the lifeboat house about two hours they had the sight and sound they had all dreaded – a maroon rocket. Several of them had been on watch out of habit. No lifeboat; how could they help?

'Henry,' shouted Billy Cartwright.

Words were exchanged and they both disappeared.

Some time later the *Canute* was battling through the heavy seas, thunder and lightning showing the way at times to the direction of where the maroon rocket had been sighted.

'Billy, we'll never make it to that vessel,' said Henry Matthews. Torrential rain was making it difficult to see.

'We've come this far; let's carry on,' replied Billy.

The *Canute* got as close to the cargo vessel as possible in the heavy seas. Eight men were going to try to leap from the cargo vessel across at least a six-foot gap onto the *Canute* – a dangerous manoeuvre at the best of times, but in heavy seas a death-defying feat. One by one they managed to jump to safety, judging skilfully as the waves lifted the *Canute* and the ship level for a split second. As the last two leapt over a high wave hit them, throwing them into the water with Billy Cartwright, who was trying to grab at them. In those seas no man would survive. Henry Matthews settled the survivors, all devastated at the loss of life, but with their help he managed to keep the *Canute* afloat, and they headed for Eastsea harbour.

Those in the lifeboat house saw a boat, which proved to be the *Canute*, battling its way back down the channel, confirming what they had suspected earlier – Henry Matthews and Billy Cartwright were doing a rescue act with the *Canute*.

At her cottage, Susie Matthews was concerned with the length of time Henry had been away from home, which at present was several hours. With living in at Eastsea Hall, Amelia Cartwright was unaware of Billy's absence and was soon to be the recipient of a further tragedy in her family.

The mood in the lifeboat house was sombre after the explanation by Henry Matthews of the loss of Billy Cartwright and the crewmen of the stricken vessel, although there were six survivors. Captain Douglas Andrews, the skipper of the cargo vessel, the *Tynesider*, then spoke:

'We had left Newcastle in fine weather with a cargo of coal bound for London. The storm hit us as a southwards passage was being made. Off Eastsea the ship had collided with an object in the water, which put a hole in the hull. However, we are eternally grateful for the efforts of those two men with a fishing boat, which sadly, cost three lives, though six of us are thankful for being spared.'

Lord Courtenay then spoke:

'Although it was foolhardy but also brave action on the parts of Henry Matthews and Billy Cartwright, the cost of it in lives was high, though not all in vain for, as Captain Andrews says, there are six thankful mariners. The last thing on Henry's and Billy's minds, as seafarers, although likely mindful of it, was their own safety. As Billy's mother, Amelia, now works and lives in at the Hall, I now have the unenviable task of giving her further bad news.'

Lord Courtenay then departed.

The six survivors were taken to the Seamen's Mission.

The storm continued.

Inspector Longfield looked deep in thought.

'When the storm abates the foreshore will have to be checked as usual,' he said.

'Can't reclaim coal if it's all in the water, as it most likely is. Any washed ashore will be gathered by the townspeople,' said Captain Baines.

'I don't envy Lord Courtenay having to tell Amelia Cartwright the news. However, Billy is missing at present and I shall have to give her the confirmation should we find his body,' said Longfield.

Amelia Cartwright was in the drawing room at the Hall with Lord and Lady Courtenay, and was inconsolable after hearing of the fate of Billy.

By mid-afternoon the storm had abated.

Inspector Longfield, Captain Baines and Lord Courtenay, with estate workers and wagons, and Henry Matthews and others who had been at the lifeboat house, arrived at the foreshore and found a scene of devastation there. Washed up on the shore were five bodies: Billy Cartwright, two more of the lifeboat crew and two that nobody recognised but assumed were off the *Tynesider*, which would have sunk.

'Captain Baines, please have a look at these bodies,' said Longfield.

Baines looked. 'Longfield, the point I believe you are putting across is that the fingers are bitten off but the jewellery and rings are intact,' he said.

Longfield looked questioningly at Henry Matthews, who returned a knowing look.

'That's exactly it, Baines,' said Longfield.

Estate workers were asked to walk the foreshore. Around the bend there was an amazing discovery. Longfield, Baines and the rest followed to where they had been hailed. As they approached, the first party were standing around a huge black inanimate creature.

'What on earth is that?' asked Longfield.

There wasn't an answer forthcoming, for all that everybody could see resembled a large shark, all of sixty feet long and weighing several tons.

Longfield looked thoughtfully at the creature.

'What are we going to do with it?' he asked.

Lord Courtenay put forward a solution.

'In a couple of days' time it's the estate ball. Quite by chance one of the guests is a school chum, Guy Bartholomew, now a professor of Nature at the British Museum. He should be able to help,' he said.

'That sounds fine. I'll get the infantry to keep an eye on it,' said Longfield.

They all then departed, leaving the foreshore deserted apart from the creature.

There was a knock on the door of the Matthews' cottage. Henry opened the door.

'Come in, Amelia. I was coming to see you somehow at the Hall,' he said.

'Hello, Henry. I want to put the record straight,' said Amelia.

'How did you get to the town from the Hall?' asked Henry.

'Daniel Courtenay gave me a lift. He was going into town,' replied Amelia.

Henry and Amelia went into the parlour.

'What do you want?' asked Susie sarcastically.

'Give Amelia a chance to explain,' said Henry.

Amelia sat thoughtfully before beginning.

'I felt that Henry was having a devastating effect on my family. Neither me nor Henry were blameless for the relationship. He was present on both occasions when Nathan and Billy died. Thank you for trying to save them. Billy suggested using the *Canute* to help the stricken vessel and Henry agreed to do so. Henry, resentment of you is no more,' said Amelia.

'Thank you, Amelia. That means a lot to me,' said Henry.

'I'm glad that is all sorted out. I'll go and do some vittles,' said Susie.

Later, Daniel Courtenay collected Amelia from the Matthews' cottage.

'You seem more relaxed than you were before that visit,' said Daniel.

'Yes I am, thanks to your family and a much better understanding of how I lost my husband and son,' said Amelia.

They then headed back to Eastsea Hall.

As predicted by Captain Baines, the townspeople had the good fortune to be able to collect coal from the foreshore from time to time.

Twenty-third of November – *morning*

Amelia Cartwright knocked on the door of the drawing room at Eastsea Hall and entered when summoned.

'Come in, Amelia,' said Lady Courtenay.

Also in the room were Lord Courtenay and Inspector Longfield.

'Good morning, Mrs Cartwright. I am here to confirm the tragic news Lord Courtenay conveyed to you. Billy's body has been discovered and is now at the mortuary. Regretfully, I have to ask you to formally identify. I will be in touch as to when,' said Longfield.

Although news to be expected, this was still a shock to Amelia.

'I am so sorry to be the bearer of bad news again and in such a short time,' said Longfield.

As Longfield departed Amelia was being comforted by Lady Courtenay.

After leaving Eastsea Hall, Inspector Longfield visited the Seamen's Mission to let Douglas Andrews know five bodies had been recovered, two of which were thought to be crew of the *Tynesider*.

'If that is the case, they will be Joshua Monroe and Charlie Baldwin,' said Douglas Andrews on hearing the news.

'The bodies are at the mortuary. I shall need you to make a formal identification some time,' said Longfield.

'I have let the shipping agents in Newcastle know of our plight, and they are sending someone to Eastsea,' said Andrews.

'One more thing: you need to find out whether the bodies should be buried here at Eastsea in the sea, or returned to Newcastle for the families. Mind you, best done here, taking into consideration the time the bodies have been exposed,' said Longfield.

'I'll ask, but will recommend your suggestion,' said Andrews.

Longfield then left the Mission.

Amelia Cartwright was now settled comfortably into her work at Eastsea Hall and had overcome the recent upheavals in her life, although she still had the painful task of having to identify Billy. However, her demeanour was further enhanced by people around her being kind and helpful, especially Annie and Sarah, the other two maids. Further, Lady Marcia had informed Mary in London of Billy's death.

Longfield arrived at the mortuary for Doctor Moore's advice.

'Two of those bodies recovered are most likely lifeboat crew. When the rest of the widows hear of the recovery they will want to know who they are. Being in the water for a while, they are unrecognisable. I cannot ask the ladies to identify them in that state,' said Longfield.

'Don't worry, I realised there would be a problem and contacted Jacob Woods, the dentist, and from his records he had identified them as Martin Carter and Thomas Jackson. Fortunately, they were patients,' said Doctor Moore.

'Thank you so much for that, Doctor; that's a great help,' said Longfield.

Mary and Dick returned to Eastsea after receiving the news of Billy and her mother. They would live in the Cartwright cottage. They had married in London and Mary was with child. Amelia, Henry and Susie were happy to accept the situation, just to have the pair back home. Dick became a member of the crew of the *Canute*.

Longfield knocked at the door of Kate Carter's cottage, and got a reply.

'Good afternoon, Mrs Carter,' he said.

'Hello, Inspector. I've heard two more bodies from the lifeboat have been found. You being here tells me one is Martin,' she said.

'I'm afraid so,' he replied.

'You'll want me to make a formal identification?' asked Kate.

'There is no need. Let's just say Martin had to be identified by his dental records,' said Longfield.

'May I know who else?' she asked.

'Tom Jackson,' replied Longfield.

'Poor Maria as well now has to cope,' said Kate.

'Will you be all right?' asked Longfield.

'Thank you, yes. I've got the family. I knew there was a chance it was Martin, but still it comes as a shock,' said Kate.

'You will be informed later as to arrangements for inquests and funerals,' said Longfield.

He gave his condolences and departed to see Maria Jackson, thinking to himself, what a thankless task!

Maria Jackson opened the door to Inspector Longfield.

'Come in, Inspector,' she said, in a manner as if he was expected.

'You're not surprised I'm here?' he asked.

Longfield realised no explanation was required for his visit.

'Not really; I felt that one of those bodies was Tom's,' Maria replied.

'Would you like me to get Reverend Ives to come and see you?' asked Longfield.

'No, thank you. I'll go to my daughter's and let her know the news,' said Maria.

'You will be made aware later of the times for the inquests and funerals,' said Longfield.

Again he gave his condolences and left.

She was a restrained woman. Had it all worked out before I arrived. No questions about who was the other member of the lifeboat found. Thankfully did not raise identifying. Rather a private woman with her grief, thought Longfield.

Captain Douglas Andrews and Amelia Cartwright were at the mortuary with Inspector Longfield.

Doctor Moore came into the waiting room.

'Hello, Mrs Cartwright. Sadly, due to recent events, you are familiar with procedure here,' he said.

Amelia Cartwright and Doctor Moore then entered the autopsy room where the coroner, Lancelot Dunton was waiting.

On the sheet being lifted, 'Yes, that is Billy,' said Amelia tearfully.

'Mrs Cartwright, please sign this confirmation sheet,' asked the coroner.

This done, Amelia returned to the waiting room.

'Mr Andrews, are you aware of the procedures here?' asked the doctor.

'Yes Sir, I am. The sea occasionally produces bodies for me to identify,' he replied.

Douglas Andrews, on each sheet being lifted, confirmed the other bodies as Joshua Monroe and Charlie Baldwin.

'Please sign this confirmation sheet, Mr Andrews,' requested the coroner.

Douglas Andrews then returned to the waiting room.

The confirmation sheets for Martin Carter and Thomas Jackson had been endorsed by Jacob Woods, the dentist.

'Inspector Longfield, I have to tell you that the Baldwin and Monroe families would like the burials to be carried out here at Eastsea and will be attending when arranged,' said Douglas Andrews.

Twenty-fourth of November – morning

Although the estate ball had been cancelled for the time being due to the recent disasters, Professor Guy Bartholomew had come to Eastsea posthaste on receiving the message from Lord Courtenay.

Professor Bartholomew was now on the foreshore standing beside the creature, carefully analysing. After a while, came his decision.

'Courtenay, this is extraordinary. What you have here is a mammal, a male *Basilosaurus* of the Eocene period. Extinct for thirty-six million years. Native to the coastal fringe of the warm and shallow Tethys Sea of the Egyptian Sahara. They will dismember bodies – something of which I understand has been happening here,' he said.

Longfield stepped forward.

'Recent years have seen the activity of bitefingers, whereby after disasters such as occurred here of late, disreputable characters will strip the victims' bodies of jewellery and, if the need arises, bite off fingers for the rings,' said Longfield, giving long hard looks at Henry Matthews.

CHAPTER TEN
1895

Twenty-seventh of November – evening
TOBY HUGHES was busy in the bar of the Cockleshell. Miranda Hughes was just as busy in the dining room. Apart from the regulars, Douglas Andrews with the other survivors of the *Tynesider* were in the dining room together with Carrie Moore and Josie Baldwin – the widows of Joshua and Charlie – and members of their families, having arrived earlier from Newcastle with shipping agents Leonard Holliday and Stephen Mallory, who were also present. Miranda was busy preparing meals. Her children Michael and Doreen were waiting at tables along with two other general workers called upon from time to time when business was hectic.

The mood of the Newcastle visitors was sombre, as was only to be expected, considering the circumstances.

'Douglas, you haven't told us what happened,' said Carrie Moore.
'You'll hear it all tomorrow at the inquest,' he replied.

They all then ate their meals. Later, Andrews and the other survivors returned to the Mission. A few of the visitors were accommodated at the Cockleshell, and the rest at boarding houses in the area.

Twenty-ninth of November – morning
The Town Hall was full, with notably Lord Courtenay, Professor Bartholomew, the respective directly affected families, shipping

agents, and townsfolk also eager to hear any news of the creature on the foreshore.

'The townspeople of Eastsea are marvellously resilient to cope with inquests again in such a short time, as the numbers gathered here show,' said Lancelot Dunton, the coroner opening the proceedings.

Inspector Longfield was overseeing the lawful connotations of the events from the witnesses' statements. Constable Dawlish was in a side room ensuring there was no collusion between the witnesses: Henry Matthews and Douglas Andrews.

'Although still tragic, fortunately, the fatalities are low on this occasion. The cause of the deaths of William Cartwright, Joshua Monroe and Charles Baldwin will now be ascertained,' said Dunton.

The assemblage settled down.

'Please do not interrupt proceedings. Anyone doing so will be asked to leave. Usher, please bring Henry Matthews to the stand,' requested Dunton.

Henry Matthews took the stand and the oath.

'Mr Matthews, it is unfortunate that, due to your bravery, you have to be a witness at an inquest again. However, please tell in your own words the events surrounding the deaths of William Cartwright, Joshua Monroe and Charles Baldwin on November the twenty-second, eighteen ninety-five,' said Dunton.

'Yes, Sir, I will. As you are aware, there isn't a lifeboat available here at present. During that second storm we were hoping and praying that a lifeboat won't be needed. This wasn't to be the case. A maroon rocket alerted us, which proved to be from the *Tynesider*. The feeling in the lifeboat house was one of utter disbelief; someone needed us and we couldn't respond. Billy, sorry, William, Cartwright suggested we took our fishing boat the *Canute*. This I agreed to. It was rather a perilous trip. We reached the *Tynesider*. The sea was heavy, but we managed to get Douglas Andrews and five others onto the *Canute*. As the last two, Joshua Monroe and Charles Baldwin, jumped, sadly, a huge wave hit them. William Cartwright, in trying to save them, was also swept overboard. The three of them in a merciless sea,' said Henry.

'Thank you, Mr Matthews. You may stand down. That was an excellent account of which, fortunately, you have a strong will to cope,' said Dunton.

Henry Matthews returned to the anteroom.

'Usher, please bring Douglas Andrews to the stand,' requested Dunton.

Douglas Andrews came to the stand and took the oath.

'Mr Andrews, please in your own words recollect the events of November the twenty-second, eighteen ninety-five, concerning the *Tynesider* and your rescue by the *Canute*,' said Dunton.

'We were making good passage south from Newcastle when this extraordinary violent storm blew up. It made very heavy going in those seas. A while later there was a terrific bang on the hull, which caused a large hole and the *Tynesider* to take in water. That was when I activated the maroon rocket. About an hour later this boat was battling through the rough water towards us. We thought a lifeboat was approaching. As it closed in we realised it was a fishing boat manned by two men. My immediate thought was that this will surely not be able to rescue us. However, this boat managed to get alongside the *Tynesider*. Those two brave men, who proved to be Henry Matthews and William Cartwright, beckoned at the precise moment for us to jump onto the *Canute*. Myself, Paul Appleton, John Stone, Stanley Downs, David O'Hara and Gordon Montgomery were successful. The last two to jump, Joshua Monroe and Charles Baldwin, were not so lucky. As they leapt a huge wave hit them, throwing them into the water. William Cartwright tried in vain to save them and was, sadly, swept overboard. Never saw any of them again until the bodies were washed ashore,' said Andrews.

'Thank you, Mr Andrews. We appreciate this was an ordeal and thank you for your frankness. You may stand down,' said Dunton.

Douglas Andrews returned to the anteroom.

'It is my belief that those two accounts are sufficient, not wanting the other survivors remembering a night they would rather forget. As regards the lifeboatmen, Martin Carter and Thomas Jackson, we will take as read the findings of the previous inquest. Therefore, the verdict on all five men is death by misadventure. I offer my condolences to all those concerned. Before I declare these inquests closed, most of you would like to hear the comments of an eminent authority on nature from the British Museum, and he will explain,' said Dunton.

Professor Bartholomew began, 'The creature is a mammal, known as a *Basilosaurus*; extinct for thirty-six million years; native to seas of the Middle East. They dismember bodies — something of which has been occurring here, apparently. I can only assume how the *Basilosaurus* reached here, possibly by the currents of the tides from the Mediterranean Sea through the Straits of Gibraltar, the Atlantic Ocean, and finally the North Sea. How long it took to reach this far is open to conjecture: a million years, centuries, decades or weeks. I understand the storms were violent — nothing like it in living memory, as Captain Andrews described. The lightning would be highly charged with electricity, water being a conductor carrying it down below the surface, and by chance it hit the creature with enough power to start the heart, and it became alive. The *Basilosaurus*, I have been told, has been credited with an attack on the Eastsea foreshore a month or so ago, when fingers were bitten off bodies, and then it was able to return to the sea. My reasoning for it being beached: Captain Andrews described how the *Tynesider* was hit below the waterline and holed. I believe the *Basilosaurus* collided with the ship, resulting in it being killed instantly and washed ashore. Its reputation leads me to calling the creature "Basilbitefingers", he said.

The audience applauded, and Inspector Longfield thanked the professor.

Captain Andrews then stood up. 'Thank you all for your hospitality, on behalf of all of us from the north-east. I am devastated that it was not in happier circumstances. Our thanks to a brave man, Henry Matthews, and our condolences to the family of Billy Cartwright, whose bravery cost him his life. We shall always be eternally grateful and will return home after the funerals,' he said.

Henry Matthews then shook Douglas Andrews' hand.

'A fair verdict, once again, and the only one that was feasible, Lancelot,' said Inspector Longfield.

'I now declare these inquests closed,' said Dunton.

The assemblage departed from the hall.

Folk stood around outside in groups, no doubt discussing the findings of the inquests, and the forthcoming funerals.

Inspector Longfield and Captain Baines were having a conversation. Longfield speaking: 'Percy, recall the time the *Basilosaurus* was discovered dead on the foreshore? Ever since I've had misgivings with the situation. Professor Bartholomew said that it would have been killed instantly when the collision with the *Tynesider* occurred. If that is the case, how did those fingers get bitten off and rings strewn around? However, it may be that the Basilosaurus was initially only injured, got swept ashore, did the dastardly act and later died from his injuries. If Professor Bartholomew's assumption is correct, a further scenario, did someone, not mentioning any names, succumb to temptation, afterwards seeing the error of their ways?' he said.

'Must admit, I've been thinking of that situation and you have given a feasible explanation. Thank you,' said Baines.

CHAPTER ELEVEN
1895

First of December – afternoon
ONCE AGAIN a large crowd had assembled on the harbour wall at Eastsea for the funerals.

Five hearses stood on the harbour wall, each containing a coffin.

The Reverend Paul Ives spoke. 'Once again, in such a short time, we are gathered here to offer souls to God, namely William Cartwright, Martin Carter, Thomas Jackson, Charles Baldwin and Joshua Monroe. The recent tragedies have touched almost every family in Eastsea and beyond, as proved of late, and there are still souls unaccounted for, namely Derek Mistley, Marcus Thorpe, Harry Lightman, George Moody and Rodney Lucas. Our thoughts and prayers are with these families,' he said.

On this occasion "Abide with Me" was sung, followed by prayers of offering and the Lord's Prayer. "Eternal Father, Strong to Save" was then sung.

The coffins were then lifted onto the boats taking them out to open water, and followed by those carrying the mourners.

'Lord God, we commend these souls to your keeping,' said Reverend Ives as each coffin was dropped into the water.

The flotilla then returned to Eastsea.

The crowd was still assembled on the harbour wall, awaiting their return.

Inspector Longfield greeted the mourners as they disembarked. To Amelia Cartwright and the other widows, he offered his condolences. Then to Douglas Andrews and his Newcastle party, the same.

'We shall now go aboard our vessel, after eating, and make way for Newcastle,' said Andrews.

The Reverend Ives stood by the gangplank giving his blessing to each person as they passed by.

'Have a safe journey,' said Longfield as he shook Douglas Andrews' hand.

Henry Matthews and Captain Baines also gave their salutations.

Later, the ship departed for Newcastle.

The huge crowd, still assembled, waved their goodbyes.

Afterwards, Longfield took Henry Matthews aside.

'Henry, you heard Professor Bartholomew mention the *Basilosaurus* had been on the foreshore twice: once to do the evil act and secondly, washed ashore?' he asked.

Henry Matthews looked as though this was a conversation expected.

'Yes I did,' replied Henry.

Longfield continued. 'On the first occasion, fingers were bitten off and the rings taken, with the rest of the jewellery,' he said.

Henry Matthews explained. 'When I told you it had nothing to do with me, it was the truth,' he said.

He was ready for the next question from Longfield.

'Do you know what happened to the jewellery?' asked Longfield.

Henry thought for a moment. 'Yes I do. That fellow de Smits had taken it. Billy Cartwright managed to get it back and return it to the rightful families,' he said.

'I suppose you can't tell me the whereabouts of the other bounty over the years?' asked Longfield.

'If I told you that I would be speaking ill of the dead and besmirching the name of a hero,' replied Henry.

Longfield realised what Henry meant. 'Your gallant efforts recently, Henry, lead me to believe you've mended your ways, and after the *Basilosaurus* was beached, the rings and jewellery were intact on the bodies,' he said.

Henry looked aggrieved. 'I told you I had,' he said.

Evening

Longfield, Baines, Lord Courtenay and Professor Bartholomew sat down to decide the fate of the *Basilosaurus*.

Longfield took control of the discussion.

'Your feelings, Professor,' he requested.

The professor thought for a moment.

'Being a naturalist, my role, I feel, is to promote the preservation of nature's creatures. It was a quirk of nature that gave us the Basilosurus, a mammal of terror. Were it to be revived in the future, it would harm other creatures of the ocean. Dispose of by burning,' he said.

Lord Courtenay then gave his decision.

'I see myself as a guardian of nature. Bearing in mind the animals on the estate, from domestic to wild, I am therefore are of the same mind as the professor. Dispose with,' he said.

Captain Baines gave his opinion.

'My job as a customs officer is to ensure all dealings are above the law. The presence of the *Basilosaurus* has curtailed a despicable act which has gone on over the years. However, my feelings are as of His Lordship and the professor,' he said.

Longfield put forward his feelings.

'Professor, is there a chance that the *Basilosaurus* are evolving again? If so, by returning the dead body to the sea it could then be resurrected by a quirk of nature, that is, struck by lightning,' he said

The professor replied, 'One *Basilosaurus* does not signify another Eocene age. There is not enough evidence. For some inexplicable reason this particular one, on extinction, has lain dormant for millions of years, then to be resurrected by nature. However, those storms as described are a feature of the Eocene period.'

Longfield thought for a while.

'We could burn it on a pyre and release it into the ocean,' he said.

'I shall have my craftsmen build one,' said His Lordship.

The four of them agreed this should happen.

Second of December – morning

Meanwhile, at Eastsea Hall, preparations were being made for the estate ball to be held in a few days' time. Lily Doughty, the housekeeper, controlled the catering. She had been in service there nigh on forty years, having served Lord St John's parents prior to St John's inheritance. Lily had met her husband Timothy whilst there. Timothy had been an estate worker who had worked his way up to become estate manager for the last twenty years.

'Now then, you girls, gather round. You're aware that Mr Doughty and me are retiring in a few weeks, so take note of the running of the house and particularly these busy times preparing for an estate ball,' said Lily.

Inspector Longfield, Captain Baines, Lord Courtenay and Professor Bartholomew were greeted by Sergeant Hart, who, with the infantrymen, had been watching over the *Basilosaurus*.

'Thank you, Sergeant Hart. Later we are to burn it on a pyre and put it back into the ocean,' said Longfield.

He explained the earlier discussion between the four to Sergeant Hart.

'Sounds a reasonable conclusion,' said Hart.

'We will return with more help and equipment,' said Longfield.

The kitchen at the Hall was still a hive of activity, although everyone was having a break, drinking tea and eating scones.

'Mrs Doughty, you spoke earlier of us taking note on preparation. It makes sense, but another housekeeper will guide us,' said Amelia.

Lily Doughty looked thoughtful, and told them of her life at the Hall and the circumstances arising out of her meeting Timothy Doughty.

'So think on; it could happen to one of you. At the moment Lord and Lady Courtenay are busy. After then they will be talking to you all,' she said.

Afternoon

There was plenty of activity on the foreshore. Ropes were being lashed around the *Basilosaurus*. The idea was to put it back in the water on a pyre the moment the tide, which at present was high, began to ebb. Three horses, Longfield, Baines, Professor Bartholomew, Lord Courtenay, infantrymen and estate workers should be able to drag the *Basilosaurus* to the waterline. After a while the tide began to ebb.

'Right,' shouted Longfield.

The heaving and pushing began to get the pyre into the ebbing tide. Dry straw had been laid around the body. As the pyre floated away the straw was set alight.

'Well done and thank you all for your efforts. I feel the correct decision has been made,' said Longfield.

Sergeant Hart approached Longfield.

'Inspector, look at this,' he said.

Hart was showing Longfield a gold cup.

'Goodness! Where did you get that? asked Longfield.

'Along the foreshore. I was just wandering around, awaiting your return. There's more,' replied Hart, showing Longfield a bag of assorted jewellery, chalices and cups.

'Professor, Your Lordship, Captain Baines,' shouted Longfield.

The three hurried to the spot where Longfield and Hart were.

'Goodness gracious! I shall have to take this to London, to analyse with colleagues. If it's what I think it is… I'll say no more for now,' said the professor, who was looking at the haul admiringly.

'Where did you find it?' he asked Hart.

'Sir, my guess is, washed up during the storm, then the wind covered it with sand and it's now exposed again,' said Hart.

Captain Baines was in agreement to have the haul analysed.

CHAPTER TWELVE
1895

Fifth of December – evening
THE ESTATE BALL was in full swing. Guests included local dignitaries and landowners, the Longfields, the Bartholomews, the Matthewses, estate workers, and crews of the fishing fleet. The fare was venison, duck, roast pork, cakes, scones and other festivity foods. Wine flowed like water. There was music, singing, dancing and laughter.

During the evening the festivities were halted and Lord and Lady Courtenay took centre stage.

'Lords, ladies and gentlemen, may I have your attention for a while,' said His Lordship.

Everyone stopped the chatter and laughter, and looked at him intensely.

He continued. 'Firstly, I am pleased to see you all enjoying yourselves, after the events of recent weeks. Secondly, Timothy and Lily Doughty have decided to retire, and deserve to do so. They have served this family well over the years and it is much appreciated. Lily and Timothy, please join us,' he said.

Lady Courtenay then presented Lily with a necklace and Timothy with a tankard that had a small package inside.

'Timothy, Lily, inside the package is something further as a token of our esteem for you both. Spend it wisely,' said Lord Courtenay.

The couple gave their thanks, and told everyone how much

they had enjoyed working at the Hall and how love had blossomed. They were going to live in Eastsea when they retired in a few weeks' time.

Lord Courtenay then spoke further.

'What I am about to announce is tinged with a certain amount of sadness. However, recently, myself and fellow landowners have decided to purchase another lifeboat. It will be named the *William Cartwright*. The reason will be obvious. Henry Matthews, you will be the coxswain. You've earned it. The vessel is to be powered by an engine, invented by a German engineer named Diesel,' he said.

Lord Courtenay looked towards Amelia Cartwright, who was crying.

'Thank you, My Lord. That is a wonderful gesture. My tears are of joy and sadness,' she said.

Mary Matthews, with the same feelings, comforted her mother. Then everyone cheered and applauded.

The music and entertainment resumed.

Later on this was interrupted.

Lord Courtenay took the floor.

'The announcement about to be made, I was unable to do so earlier, as the person concerned has only just arrived from Yorkshire,' he said.

There were mumblings of expectation from the assembled company.

Lord Courtenay continued.

'Myself and Lady Courtenay have much pleasure in welcoming back to Eastsea Hall, Mr Max Hunworth as the new estate manager,' he said.

Amelia Cartwright was startled and her heart missed a beat.

Lord Courtenay carried on speaking. 'A new housekeeper will be appointed. Now let us carry on with the festivities.'

Lord Courtenay approached Longfield and Baines.

'Can you both be back here at midday tomorrow?' he asked.

'The professor has news for us,' he said.

They both confirmed that they could.

Later, in her room, Amelia gathered her thoughts. Max Hunworth: she had put him at the back of her mind for years. A sudden thought sent a chill down her spine. All those years ago, about the same time as the affair with Henry Matthews, there was a relationship with Max Hunworth. Was Max the father of Mary? Had Henry Matthews been wrongly accused?

Max Hunworth had been an estate worker in his early working life for a few years at Eastsea Hall. He had a chance to become an estate manager in Yorkshire and both he and his wife, Rosemary, had moved there.

A knock on the door brought Amelia out of her thoughts. It was Mary.

'Mother, are you all right?' she asked. 'Dick and me are going home. You looked rather pale and shocked earlier,' she said.

Hopefully you'll never know why, Amelia thought.

'Yes, Darling, I'm fine, just tired. Been hectic here lately. You and Dick be gone,' replied Amelia.

As Dick and Mary left, the festivities were still going on.

Sixth of December – morning

Lord Courtenay, Professor Bartholomew, Inspector Longfield and Captain Baines sat around a table in the drawing room.

'Thank you for coming, gentlemen' said the professor.

'No sacrifice on our part, Professor; we want to hear your news,' said Longfield.

'The gold cup and other treasures have been analysed. These are some of King John's treasure lost in The Wash around the year thirteen hundred,' said the professor.

The other three were dumbfounded.

'These can be claimed as treasure trove, I believe, and returned to this area,' said Captain Baines.

'There has been an inquest. Government officials and senior customs officials officiating. Captain Baines, you are correct in your assumption,' replied the professor.

Lord Courtenay looked thoughtful.

'Maybe it could be housed here at the Hall and put on show. I'm thinking of opening up to the public to assist with running costs,' he said.

Longfield looked concerned.

'Don't worry, Longfield; the treasure won't be here. I'm sorry, Your Lordship, but it was decided to have it at Bishops Lynne, a town closer to where it was lost,' said Baines.

Lord Courtenay looked disappointed.

'My Lord, let me explain further. It was felt that it is public property and should be housed in a town facility, for all to see. It is not a private family heirloom and it would be unfair to other local estates,' said Baines.

'I understand,' said Lord Courtenay, although he did not look convinced.

'This still creates problems for us, Captain Baines, I wonder how much more is out there, and I don't suppose we are the only ones who know of its existence now,' said Longfield.

Midday

During a short break from their service workload, Amelia was walking in the rose garden with Annie and Sarah.

'Hello, Amelia,' said a voice behind her.

Turning around, she was facing Max Hunworth.

'Oh hello, Max,' she replied.

They both looked longingly at each other.

'Would you please excuse us?' Max asked Annie and Sarah.

Annie and Sarah then departed, giggling.

'I saw you last night. Thought it was you and made discreet enquiries,' he said.

'Why did you leave so quickly, Max, all those years ago? And what of Rosemary?' asked Amelia.

He took her hand as they walked. Amelia pulled it away.

'Max, remember your position. I am a serving wench,' said Amelia.

'As regards leaving, I had just married Rosemary, but had fallen in love with you. Fortuitously that job in Yorkshire came up at the right time. Rosemary died of consumption six months ago. Sadly, she never did really enjoy good health, and as a consequence there were no children. Lord Courtenay contacted me a few weeks ago, telling me Timothy Doughty was retiring and would I like to become estate manager at Eastsea Hall… and here I am,' he said.

'I must get back. We shall soon have to be preparing supper,' said Amelia.

She departed, her feelings in turmoil. An old flame had been rekindled and she remembered what Lily Bates had said.

Maybe, just maybe, Amelia thought.

'You two can stop giggling,' Amelia said to Annie and Sarah as she entered the kitchen.

The others in the kitchen were aware of what had happened in the garden as they were amused.

'Get on with your work,' said Amelia.

'Listen to her; getting in practice for when she is housekeeper,' said Annie.

'Remember what I said,' added Lily Doughty.

Amelia ignored the remarks and set about her duties.

During the serving of supper, Lady Marcia requested Amelia to attend in the drawing room at ten o'clock next day.

Amelia retired for the night, full of excitement. Lady Marcia wanted to see her; there was Max Hunworth. Mary looked well forward with child and would soon give birth. However, the great concern was the inter-relationship of Mary and Dick. Another thought entered her head. Mary and Dick were away less than a month. Could they have left quickly as she was already in that condition. Hopefully Henry and Susie won't work it out. She tossed and turned most of the night, but managed to get some sleep, though not for long. She was woken by Sarah knocking on the door. Time for work.

Seventh of December
Amelia knocked on the door of the drawing room.

'Enter,' called Lady Marcia.

Amelia entered with apprehension.

'Sit down, Amelia. Don't look so worried. Over the past few weeks you have been here, there is a noticeable change in your demeanour. Before the tragedies that befell you, your life was full and exciting. Quite understandably, you became withdrawn. You've come through that and with maturity you became more thoughtful and responsible,' said Lady Marcia.

Amelia was looking contented with what had been said.

'Thank you, Your Ladyship,' said Amelia.

Lady Marcia continued. 'His Lordship and I have discussed the matter, and we have no hesitation in offering you the post of housekeeper. Would you like to accept?' she asked.

'I am honoured to be offered the post, Your Ladyship. Please give me time to think about it,' replied Amelia.

Amelia told Mary of this opportunity.

'How marvellous! You must accept it, Mother,' advised Mary.

Eighth of December – morning
Lord and Lady Courtenay were both delighted that Amelia had decided to become the housekeeper.

'It is a particularly busy time with Christmas just a few weeks away but I am sure you will cope very well, as you have proved with your earlier work,' said Lady Marcia.

Year end of eighteen ninety-five

As Lady Marcia predicted, Christmas was a busy period. A vast amount of fine fare had to be prepared, with family and friends coming and going. The festivities were enjoyable, and times happy.

The flame rekindled between Amelia and Max Hunworth was burning bright.

The fishing fleet was having a successful time with the catches.

As Amelia had feared, Henry and Susie remarked of how forward with child Mary was. They had obviously worked it out.

However, for the time being life at Eastsea was normal after the events of the previous few months, and remained so for the several months following.

CHAPTER THIRTEEN
1896

January
MARY MATTHEWS had given birth recently to a boy, Cedric, who was a normal healthy child, dispelling any fears of Amelia's, although she could never be sure of one particular point: Mary's biological father.

Henry and Susie Matthews were reconciled and living happily together, often looking after their grandson.

March
There was a surprise return to Eastsea of Francis and Helene van Rowhe. Helene had reverted to her maiden name, having divorced Jonas de Smits, who was serving a prison sentence in Rotterdam along with Hogmyre and van der Lugen.

The area that fate had brought them to was pleasant. Life in Rotterdam had been unbearable thanks to the actions of Hugo van Rowhe and Jonas de Smits.

They had a cottage in Eastsea. Francis made a living by book-keeping, and Helene as a seamstress. During their previous stay Helene had made the acquaintance of Billy Cartwright and was quite upset on learning of his death. She was now in a relationship with Daniel Courtenay.

The estate manager and housekeeper at Eastsea Hall, Max and Amelia Hunworth, were looking forward to becoming parents. Although in her mid-forties, Amelia hoped she would be able to cope. The day Max and Amelia married, Lily Doughty quipped to her, 'I told you so.'

Fourth of June – morning
Today, walking along the foreshore were Inspector Longfield and Captain Baines.

'Thank goodness the wreck of the *Hollander* has been cleared away,' said Longfield.

'It was a blot on the landscape and we had better be getting back to town. Looks like there's a storm brewing,' said Baines.

The new lifeboat, *William Cartwright*, was in place. It had had a few calls out, such as to a fishing boat with broken steerage, and an injured seaman off a coaster to be brought to Eastsea hospital. Fortunately there was nothing of the magnitude of some months ago.

A storm manifested, as Baines had predicated, of such magnitude it was likened to the two violent ones of recent months.

Fifth of June – afternoon
Longfield and Baines were back on the foreshore after the storm had abated, checking for any damage or occurrences.

'Some storm again. It's weird. It was almost as those two we had in quick succession some months ago. How fortunate there weren't any ships requiring assistance,' said Longfield.

They walked on. Suddenly Longfield stopped in his tracks.

'Percy, look,' he said.

'My goodness!' replied Baines.

Ahead of them the foreshore was glittering in the sun.

'Looks like gold,' said Longfield.

They hurried from the foreshore to inform Lord Courtenay, who in turn would contact Professor Bartholomew.

Sixth of June – afternoon

The professor came from London as soon as he received the news, and left just as quickly to analyse the nuggets, as he described them, not wanting to commit himself.

Eighth of June – afternoon

The professor returned. Longfield, Baines and Lord Courtenay were again in the drawing room at Eastsea Hall for the second time within a few months, awaiting the professor's analysis.

The professor gave his findings.

'Gentlemen, these nuggets are pure gold, as I thought,' he said.

Longfield interrupted. 'Apologies, Professor; as you speak, infantrymen are in place on the foreshore,' he said.

'Thank you, Longfield; that is a comfort,' the professor replied. 'Another of those terrible storms was endured recently. Third one in about six months, I understand. What it has done this time is disturbed the seabed and uncovered a vein of gold and not evolved any *Basilosaurus*, thank goodness! I have been in touch with acquaintances around the world and there is no evidence of *Basilosaurus* activity. As I have said before, it is inexplicable as to why this phenomenon has occurred.'

The three of them sat silently diagnosing the professor's findings.

'Even this business will need policing, Percy. This is your domain as well,' said Longfield.

Baines was deep in thought.

'We could have a gold rush,' he said.

Lord Courtenay spoke up.

'That means we shall have to stake claims,' he said.

'Not at the moment, My Lord. At present it belongs to the Government and is my responsibility,' said Baines.

'I hope these storms cease. Each time, they cause problems,' said Longfield.

'The size of the vein, of course, we cannot tell. Now it is uncovered, each time the tide flows, more will be washed up,' said the professor.

Longfield and Baines looked at each other with disbelief.

'Cheer up, chaps; Eastsea could become a boom town,' said the professor.

'I'm beginning to wish the *Basilosaurus* was our problem and not this,' said Longfield.

Lord Courtenay went over to the wine cabinet.

'Brandy, everyone?' he asked.

'Yes please,' the other three chorused.

'We certainly need it,' said Longfield.

All four then sat pondering what the future held.

Tenth of June – *morning*

The *Canute* was heading out down the channel with Henry Matthews as skipper, the usual two deck hands, and Dick, who had joined the crew. The fleet had managed to get good catches recently, pleasing everyone, including Lord Courtenay.

'Don't wish anyone bad luck but would like to do another mission with that new lifeboat. That engine is something,' said Henry. 'What's it called?' he asked.

'It's a diesel engine, and a godsend,' replied Dick.

'Quite enjoyed those test runs down the channel,' said Henry.

Henry was a happy man. Skipper of the *Canute*, coxswain of the lifeboat. Life was good. He enjoyed doing his hobby.

Captain Baines entered the police station.

'I've to go down to London, Archie. The authorities want explanations as to what's going on here. Please will you help with details,' he said.

'Of course,' replied Archie.

Afternoon

'Mother, you are looking pale,' said Mary Matthews.

Amelia Hunworth, if she was to admit it, was worn out.

Mary came to see her mother and stepfather quite often.

'Cedric has grown more each time I see him,' said Amelia.

Max Hunworth entered the cottage.

'Hello, Mary. Dick not with you?' he asked.

'Out fishing today,' she replied.

CHAPTER FOURTEEN
1896

Thirteenth of June – early evening

INSPECTOR ARCHIE LONGFIELD was waiting at the railway station at Eastsea for the return from London of Captain Percy Baines, Customs and Excise officer. When the train arrived Baines alighted, followed by two other men.

'Welcome back, Captain Baines,' said Longfield formally, not certain who the other two were.

Introductions followed. Lewis Stanley and Ronald Burton were government inspectors sent to oversee the gold field on Eastsea foreshore.

'We'll take the gentlemen to stay at the Cockleshell Inn,' said Longfield.

No other conversation was made during the short journey to the Cockleshell.

Stanley and Burton were booked in. Longfield and Baines made arrangements to meet them later.

When they were alone, Longfield began questioning Baines.

'Why didn't you let me know they were coming?' he asked. 'I could have got them booked in earlier,' he said.

'Didn't know until the last minute, when they joined me at the railway station just before the train departed. I'd been in a meeting with them earlier as well,' replied Baines.

Longfield thought for a moment.

'That's strange. It's as if they didn't want us forewarned,' he said.

Fourteenth of June – midday

Lord Courtenay and Professor Bartholomew were chatting in the drawing room at Eastsea Hall.

'My colleagues are looking forward to visiting and will arrive later today, and thank you for accommodating them here at the Hall. Michael Stewart and Austin Turner, as well as being naturalists, are taxidermists,' said the professor.

'You're all most welcome,' replied Lord Courtenay.

Mary Matthews was again showing concern for her mother's health.

'Max, I think Mother should take things easy and go into confinement. She's at the age when being with child can be difficult,' she said.

'I agree. Mrs Doughty has offered to come out of retirement to help for the duration. Helene, who is walking out with Daniel, says she would like to help,' said Max Hunworth.

Mary thought for a moment.

'Suppose I could also help from time to time,' she said.

'That would be helpful. Thank you. The Courtenays are doing a lot of entertaining at present,' said Max.

Afternoon

Longfield, Baines and the two government inspectors were on the foreshore surveying the scene.

There were crowds collecting the nuggets.

Sergeant Hart approached.

'I am sorry, but there were so many people, my men were unable to stop them,' he said.

The Inspectors moved out of earshot to have a discussion.

'Not to worry, Sergeant. This activity is of an unexpected magnitude. Let the nuggets be freely picked,' said Lewis Stanley, one of the inspectors.

Amelia Hunworth escorted three men to the drawing room at Eastsea Hall, knocked, and on the command to enter, announced, 'Your Grace: the professor, Mr Michael Stewart and Mr Austin Turner.'

'Thank you, Amelia. You may go,' said His Lordship.

Formal introductions were made and salutations exchanged. Lord Courtenay, Professor Bartholomew, Michael Stewart and Austin Turner then sat and relaxed, each with a brandy, and discussed the occurrences at Eastsea.

'Two more for dinner,' said Amelia as she entered the kitchen on her return from the drawing room.

Fifteenth of June – morning
Lord Courtenay, Bartholomew, Stewart and Turner were on the foreshore.

'What an amazing sight,' said Michael Stewart.

Before their eyes, people were shovelling the nuggets into bags and putting them onto small handcarts. Fortunately the amounts were low due to the weight. The carts would sink in the sand otherwise.

Austin Turner was deep in thought.

'I regret not being here when the *Basilosaurus* was in residence,' he said.

The four of them wandered around.

'Help yourself to nuggets,' said Lord Courtenay.

Sergeant Hart approached.

'Good Morning, Your Grace, gentlemen,' he said.

'Everything all right?' asked Lord Courtenay.

'Yes, Sir. The government inspectors gave permission that the nuggets could be collected by folk, and they will change them for cash at the bank,' he replied.

'Government inspectors?' queried Lord Courtenay.

'Yes, Sir. Those two gentlemen walking this way with Inspector Longfield and Captain Baines,' Sergeant Hart replied.

The eight men exchanged salutations and introductions were made.

'Longfield, Baines and your companions will join us for dinner at the Hall tonight, I hope,' said Lord Courtenay.

'Thank you, Your Grace; I'm sure we all would,' replied Longfield.

'Four more for dinner,' said Amelia in the kitchen, sounding rather exasperated, after receiving the order from Lady Courtenay.

Lord and Lady Courtenay entertained to dinner those same men who had all been introduced to each other on the foreshore earlier.

'Your Ladyship, may I say thank you for an excellent meal,' said Ronald Burton.

The rest of the visitors echoed these sentiments.

'How long will you stay?' Lord Courtenay asked the inspectors.

'We'll stay a few more days. Depends how long this gold vein lasts,' replied Lewis Stanley.

Lady Courtenay pondered for a moment.

'Were it proved to be a rich vein…?' she asked.

'Then we would return to London and send replacements,' replied Stanley.

'There's King John's treasure to go to Bishops Lynne,' said Baines.

'We'll see it gets there,' said Ronald Burton.

Later Lord Courtenay took Captain Baines to one side.

'Baines, how did the inspectors get involved?' he asked.

'I had to report what was happening here and they decided they would come and see for themselves. No doubt, with the professor being involved, the museum had mentioned it as well,' he replied.

Sixteenth of June – morning

There were long queues at the bank. Burton and Stanley were overseeing the cash-for-nuggets procedure. Fishing communities such as Eastsea relied on good catches. Seaman's wages were most likely the only source of income. The nuggets had rendered prosperity, causing an increase in drunkenness. Toby Hughes at the Cockleshell wasn't complaining, although Inspector Longfield was.

Evening

Daniel Courtenay and Helene van Rowhe were relaxing in the Cockleshell.

'Time to take you home,' said Daniel.

'Yes, all right. I am rather tired. The ladies of Eastsea are keeping me busier than usual, with their new-found wealth,' said Helene.

Daniel drew the pony and trap to a halt outside the van Rowhe cottage.

'Before you go in, I want to give you something,' said Daniel.

He took a small box out of his pocket and gave it to Helene, which she then opened.

'It's beautiful, Daniel,' she said. 'Why have you given it to me?'

'That is an engagement ring. Passed down the Courtenay family for many years. Great-grandfather had it made. He declared, after his wife died, that this ring should be handed down to the next-in-line Courtenay male for when he is betrothed. That's me. Father and Mother have seen us together and believe it should now be given to me for my betrothal. I love you, Helene,' he said.

Helene was thoughtful.

'I am touched by this gesture and I do love you, Daniel. Having been hurt by Jonas has made me cautious. However, engagement is a basic commitment. Yes, I will be engaged,' she said.

Daniel helped her down from the pony and trap.

'Let's keep this a secret for a while. Jessica and Cedric are coming to stay shortly. We'll announce it then,' said Daniel.

Helene laughed and skipped up the garden path.

'That way I cannot wear the ring. I shall have to tell my mother but tell her not to say anything. I am in her company a lot and so happy I need to tell someone. One other thing – Mary and Dick Matthews' son has the same Christian name as Jessica's husband,' she said.

'There's an easy answer to that. When Mary and Dick ran away, they stayed in London with them. So grateful were they, Jessica and Cedric were made their son's godparents, and he was named after Doctor Cedric,' said Daniel.

Helene and Daniel exchanged goodnights and kissed.

Francis van Rowhe was delighted at the news, and promised to keep quiet.

CHAPTER FIFTEEN
1896

Seventeenth of June – evening
'HENRY, ARE YOU coming in for supper?' shouted Susie.

Henry came as soon as he was called.

'What are you doing out there?' Susie asked. 'Spend most of your spare time in that outhouse at present,' she remarked.

'It's matters to do with the *Canute*. Being the skipper, have to see to things,' he replied.

Susie looked doubtful.

'Never heard Amelia complaining of Nathan busying himself at home. Here's your supper.'

Eighteenth of June – morning
Amelia Hunworth answered the knock on the main door of Eastsea Hall. Standing there was someone who she felt was familiar.

'I've come to see Lord Courtenay,' he said.

Amelia took a long hard look.

'I know you. The Dutchman off the *Hollander*. I thought you – '

The visitor cut her short.

'Were in prison; out because of good behaviour,' he replied.

'Have you an appointment?' Amelia asked.

'No, but he'll see me, I'm sure,' de Smits replied.

'Please wait outside. I'll see if Lord Courtenay will see you,' said Amelia.

Amelia explained to Lord Courtenay, who, she felt, was rather shaken by her news.

'Bring him in,' said Lord Courtenay, sharply.

Whilst Amelia fetched de Smits, Lord Courtenay recalled that at the time the Dutch party were shipwrecked, the name was familiar and back now to haunt him.

Amelia returned with de Smits to the drawing room, and left the two men together.

'Well, what a turn up for the book! Thought we'd seen the last of you,' said Lord Courtenay. 'What do you want?'

'Can we sit down?' asked de Smits.

As they sat down, Lord Courtenay realised his past could be about to catch up with him.

'Father, stop playing games. I've come to claim my inheritance,' said de Smits.

Lord Courtenay took his mind back twenty-five years or more ago when he'd spent a month or so in Rotterdam at a conference on containing sea erosion and building dykes. He was totally shaken by this man claiming to be his son.

'So the storm had a silver lining for you, enabling you to find me,' said Lord Courtenay.

'Certainly did,' replied de Smits.

Lord Courtenay was really on his back foot now.

Lady Courtenay entered.

Hoped you would not appear, thought Lord Courtenay.

'What's going on, St John? Who is this man?' she asked.

Lord Courtenay was uncomfortable.

'Alexandra de Smits' son, Jonas,' he replied.

'Oh, is it?' she said in a cursory manner.

Lady Courtenay looked suspicious.

'Am I supposed to know the name?' she asked.

Lord Courtenay took his time to answer.

'You were told I stayed at a guesthouse owned by Alexandra de Smits when I attended a conference in Rotterdam,' he said.

Lady Courtenay thought carefully to remember.

'Yes, I do recall. Must be twenty-five years since,' she replied.

Lord Courtenay paced up and down the room.

Lady Courtenay, aware of the consequence about to be revealed, allowed Lord Courtenay to ponder.

'One night, Alexandra and me were both feeling lonely, so we drank and drank,' he said.

'What you're saying, St John, is that she accommodated you above the call of duty?' asked Lady Courtenay.

She looked at de Smits.

'Have you any proof to your claim?' she asked.

De Smits took a sheet of paper from his pocket and gave it to Lady Courtenay.

'As far as I can see, it's legitimate, which is more than can be said for you, de Smits,' said Her Ladyship sarcastically.

Lord Courtenay flopped down in a chair.

'What is that?' he asked.

Lady Courtenay handed the sheet of paper to him.

'I would say it's some sort of birth certificate, naming you as the father. Stupid man, St John! You could have used any name,' she said.

'Yes, I suppose it is, but I shall let Gilbert Harrison check it out. I was already signed in under my real name at the guesthouse and the conference anyway. I didn't think,' said Lord Courtenay.

'You certainly didn't think, in more ways than one,' said Lady Courtenay.

Gilbert Harrison was the family solicitor.

'Where did you get this certificate?' Lord Courtenay asked de Smits.

'Mother died of a heart attack six months ago. I was told by a doctor that it was caused by shock. I blame myself for her death, hearing of all I had been involved with,' said de Smits remorsefully.

Lord and Lady Courtenay looked at each other for inspiration.

De Smits continued. 'We were quite poor. She needed the certificate to get help from the town trust fund for the needy. I found it sorting out her papers. During the recent time I was in Eastsea, I heard the name Courtenay being mentioned. That name is on the birth certificate as the father, St John Courtenay, address, the guest house, to indicate Mother and His Lordship were living together,' he said.

'If I remember correctly, St John, you were there about a month – a month that has changed part of your life drastically,' said Lady Courtenay.

Lord Courtenay began to destroy the certificate.

'Don't bother; I have other copies,' said de Smits.

'These are words on paper,' said Lord Courtenay. 'Can you prove I am your father?'

De Smits looked thoughtful and smiled.

'You've admitted to knowing my mother and staying at the guest house, and I would think your names are unique,' he replied.

Lady Courtenay was getting agitated.

'What do you want from us?' she asked.

'My inheritance – next in line to become Lord of the Manor,' replied de Smits.

'We have a son, Daniel,' said Lord Courtenay.

'Compare both certificates to see who is the elder. If it is proven Daniel is the elder, then I will leave, maybe with a sum of cash to compensate,' said de Smits.

'Don't know about compensation,' said Lady Courtenay.

The Courtenays were deeply concerned. They knew the date of Daniel's birth, and the date of birth on Jonas de Smits' certificate.

'If I am the elder, I shall take my rightful place as Lord of the Manor,' said de Smits.

CHAPTER SIXTEEN
1896

Nineteenth of June – morning
TWO LOCAL MEN who had been collecting the gold nuggets on the foreshore came to the police station in anxious moods.

'Inspector Longfield, on the foreshore is a body of one of those creatures,' said Andy Dixon hurriedly.

Longfield sat down and bid the two men do the same.

'Now, calm down, Andy,' said Longfield. 'What do you mean by one of those creatures?' he asked.

Philip Murphy, rather calmer, interjected. 'He means, Inspector, one of those creatures like a few months ago,' he said

Longfield's heart sank.

My god! Not another *Basilosaurus*, he thought.

Afternoon
Gilbert Harrison was looking at the birth certificates.

'I'm sorry, St John. De Smits' birth certificate is legitimate,' he said.

Lord Courtenay looked downhearted.

'What can be done?' he asked.

Harrison thought for a moment.

'Contest it through the courts,' he replied.

'Too public. Want to keep this quiet. I've yet to tell Jessica and Daniel,' said His Lordship.

'Let's hope de Smits keeps his mouth shut,' said Lady Courtenay.

'That, unfortunately, is a hold he has over you,' said Harrison.

Professor Bartholomew was studying the small creature as Longfield and Baines approached.

'Good morning, Professor. Fortunate you were still at the Hall whilst this has happened,' said Longfield.

The professor looked at them with a smirk.

'It's a hoax – a clever one, mind. A baby, as there was some urgency, I suspect. Whoever has done this wants the foreshore empty, and it has worked,' he said.

'From what you are saying, I gather that whoever the perpetrator is wants the nuggets for themselves,' said Longfield.

Longfield and Baines looked thoughtfully at each other.

'Somehow it's been placed here, even with the infantry around,' said Baines.

'You obviously heard nothing, Sergeant Hart?' asked Longfield.

'No, Sir,' replied Hart.

'Professor, how did you happen to be on the foreshore?' asked Longfield.

'Inspector, that question gives the impression you think I'm involved,' replied the professor.

'My apologies, Professor; you've misinterpreted the question,' said Longfield.

'I know, Inspector. Just joking. Quite simple, really. Lord Courtenay had business to deal with, so I decided to come down here. It was me who sent those two chaps,' said the professor.

'I wondered where His Lordship was,' said Baines.

Longfield thoughtfully weighed up the situation.

'Whoever has done this has not given much thought to the infantry being present. Probably thinks if a creature can be put here, collecting gold nuggets is possible,' he said.

'I'll get Lord Courtenay to organise the removal of this thing,' said the professor.

Jessica and Cedric Lewis arrived later that evening at Eastsea Hall from London after being summoned to come posthaste.

'What's this all about?' asked Jessica on being greeted by her parents.

'Later you will learn,' replied her mother.

———————

The next outgoing tide took the gold nuggets away as quickly as they had arrived.

Twentieth of June – afternoon

Inspector Longfield, accompanied by Constable Dawlish, had been summoned to Eastsea Hall. The men were waiting in the library.

'Wonder what this is about,' said Dawlish.

'Not a clue, just had a request that we attend,' replied Longfield.

The door opened and Amelia Hunworth entered.

'I've to take you two gentlemen to the drawing room,' she said.

Upon entering they saw Lord and Lady Courtenay, Gilbert Harrison, Jessica, Daniel and, to their surprise, Jonas de Smits, all seated around a table. They were bid to do the same.

Gilbert Harrison opened the proceedings.

'Gentlemen, thank you for attending, and I understand your surprise at seeing Mr de Smits in our midst. What I am about to divulge will need the utmost discretion. Mr de Smits has returned here after leaving prison for good behaviour. The reason he is here is to claim he is the son of Lord Courtenay,' he said.

Gilbert Harrison then outlined how this had occurred.

'Lord Courtenay spent a month or so in Rotterdam at a conference twenty-five or more years ago. To cut a long story short, he had a meaningful liaison with the landlady of a guest house. Jonas de Smits is the outcome, for want of a better word. There are papers to consolidate this claim,' he said.

Longfield and Dawlish were aghast at this disclosure.

Daniel and Jessica attempted to interrupt.

'Please, let me continue. This does create an issue as to who is the son and heir to the Courtenay estate. This birth certificate of Jonas de Smits is legitimate and proves him to be the elder of Daniel Courtenay,' said Gilbert Harrison.

Daniel jumped up.

'This is preposterous,' he said. 'Is this true, Father?' he asked.

Jessica was just as angry.

Harrison continued. 'In your presence, to confirm this, Inspector Longfield and Constable Dawlish have been asked here to endorse the legitimacy of the Jonas de Smits birth certificate and compare it with Daniel Courtenay's,' he said.

Longfield and Dawlish confirmed positive in favour of Jonas de Smits.

'Cedric Lewis, Helene and Francis van Rowhe need to be made aware of this situation. Apart from to them, nothing must be spoken of this outside these four walls,' said Harrison. 'That will be in order, I hope, Your Graces?' he asked.

Lord and Lady Courtenay both nodded in agreement.

Daniel and Jessica walked out in disgust.

'Mr de Smits, how long have you been back in Eastsea?' asked Longfield.

'Two days. Staying at the Cockleshell,' replied de Smits.

'I've not seen you about,' said Longfield.

'Keeping a low profile,' said de Smits.

Must have made it worthwhile for Toby Hughes to keep his mouth shut, thought Longfield.

Evening

Later on, Longfield was in Henry Matthews' living room admiring the cases of stuffed animals.

'What do you want, Inspector?' asked Henry.

Longfield was captivated by the display.

'To congratulate you on being appointed coxswain of the lifeboat,' replied Longfield.

'Thank you,' said Henry with disbelief.

'On occasions when I've been here I've not really studied these. They are very good,' said Longfield.

'My father was skilful at the art,' said Henry.

Susie Matthews entered.

'Admiring their work, Inspector? Father-in-law Fred's and Henry's. Henry is good at it,' she said.

'I thought some were dated after Fred's death,' said Longfield.

Henry gave Susie a black look.

'Yes, you are very good, aren't you Henry?' said Longfield knowingly.

Longfield wondered if Henry would make any comment about the taxidermists from London.

Daniel was fuming on his arrival at the van Rowhe's cottage.

'Daniel, whatever is the matter?' asked Helene.

'Both of you, be prepared for some startling news,' he replied.

Francis and Helene both appeared apprehensive and tense.

He then told them of Jonas de Smits return to Eastsea and his claim.

'My goodness! Surely that cannot be!' said Helene.

'Thought we'd seen the last of him,' said Francis.

There was a knock at the door, which Helene answered. Inspector Longfield stood there.

'Hello, Miss van Rowhe,' he said. 'May I come in?'

'Of course,' replied Helene.

They went into the parlour, where Francis and Daniel were.

'Good evening, Mrs van Rowhe, Daniel. I have just received shocking news from Inspector Vendren of the Rotterdam Constabulary. He thought I would be interested to know that Jonas de Smits was dead. There were no details,' said Longfield.

All there were visibly shaken and lost for words.

Longfield continued. 'I was just as surprised as you all are. The question now is, who could that person at Eastsea Hall be, if it's not Jonas de Smits? I recognise him as Jonas, as Constable Dawlish does.'

Francis and Helene looked at each other.

'Are you thinking the same as me, Mother?' asked Helene.

'I probably am,' replied Francis.

'That man is most likely to be Herman de Smits, Jonas' half-brother. You can be forgiven for believing him to be Jonas; they are so much alike, having the same mother. Alexandra was married to Peter de Smits. He died soon after Herman was born,' said Helene.

'Whatever revelation shall we hear next?' asked Daniel.

'I would like you all to come with me. When you see him, treat him as though he really is Jonas,' said Longfield.

'Why would we want to do that?' asked Daniel.

'To make him think his charade is working and hopefully keep him around until an arrest can be made,' replied Longfield.

It was a surprised and disappointed Henry Matthews walking on the foreshore, thinking of all the time and effort he had put in.

As Longfield, Daniel, Helene and Francis headed along the harbour wall, de Smits was entering the Cockleshell, something which did not go unnoticed by them.

'Daniel, ladies, go in there. Hopefully he will be in the bar. Remember to treat him as if he is Jonas,' said Longfield.

Henry Matthews appeared on the scene.

'Hello, Henry, you don't look very happy,' said Longfield.

'I'm all right,' replied Henry, which was clearly untrue, and he then went into the Cockleshell.

Longfield went into the backyard of the Cockleshell, to the kitchen.

'Miranda,' he called.

She came to the door. He handed her money.

'Please give this to Toby. Ask him to keep Henry and de Smits supplied if their money runs out,' said Longfield.

Captain Baines was at the police station when Longfield returned.

'How did things go with Henry?' he asked.

'I think he realises we're onto him, although he expected those two taxidermists from London to get the blame. Likely he used one of those smugglers' tunnels to get the stuffed mammal there without anyone knowing,' replied Longfield.

'Are you going to bring any charges?' asked Baines.

'I could for wasting constabulary time, but poetic justice has probably been done. I've just seen him, not a happy man, gone in the Cockleshell to drown his sorrows,' said Longfield.

The door opened and Inspector Vendren and Constable Metzer entered.

'Welcome back, gentlemen. I'd think he is now ready to be detained,' said Longfield.

'Good! We are not staying too long; don't want to get caught in one of your infamous storms,' said Vendren mockingly.

'Alexander, Dawlish, come with us,' said Longfield.

The sight of five law enforcement officers entering the Cockleshell almost sobered up Henry Matthews and de Smits.

Daniel, Helene and Francis were at a table and gave Longfield the nod that Herman de Smits was standing at the bar.

'Take Henry home, please, Alexander,' said Longfield.

Least that can be done. Likely partly my fault Henry's in that condition, Longfield thought.

'De Smits, I'm arresting you for being drunk and disorderly,' said Longfield.

Longfield went over to Daniel and the two ladies.

'Thank you for your help and please, all of you, don't speak of these matters to anyone,' he said.

On arrival at the police station Herman de Smits was put in a cell to sober up.

'Vendren, you arrived sooner than expected,' said Longfield.

'Yes. Metzer and I were in London when we received your message, at Woolwich Arsenal, sorting out the guns and ammunition that were on the *Hollander*. It was contraband, owners unknown, so will be shipped back to Rotterdam for the Dutch government. There is a theory that the British government may purchase if a deal can be made. We'll leave that to the politicians,' he said.

Longfield thought for a moment.

'Best leave de Smits alone tonight, then tomorrow we can talk to him,' he said.

'We'll be here at nine o'clock,' said Vendren.

Twenty-first of June – morning

The *Canute* headed out down the channel. Henry Matthews was deep in thought after his encounter with Longfield. Thoughts that he kept to himself.

'Father, will you daydream for the rest of the day or, from what I have heard, could it be a hangover?' said Dick.

Henry glared at Dick.

'Watch your tongue, boy. I've a lot on my mind,' replied Henry.

'Mother said you'd been in a bad mood with her ever since Inspector Longfield was at the cottage recently,' said Dick.

Isaac Morris and Peter Smith stood watching.

'Get on with what you should be doing,' said Henry angrily.

Meanwhile, Herman de Smits sat facing inspectors Longfield and Vendren across a table.

'De Smits, the charade is over. We know who you are – Herman, not Jonas – and have for a while,' said Longfield.

Longfield looked at Vendren and nodded.

'Herman, time to confess. What possessed you to do this,' said Vendren.

Herman de Smits looked thoughtful and prepared himself.

'While Jonas was in prison in Rotterdam he had appendicitis. Sadly, it burst before they could get him to hospital, and he died. Inspector Vendren will confirm this as the verdict of the inquest. I collected his belongings from the prison and found, among some papers, the birth certificate. He had earlier told me that while he was in Eastsea he had heard the name St John Courtenay, Lord of the Manor. As Jonas and I looked alike, I thought a claim that I was Courtenay's son would work and give my wife and child a better life. So I arrived in Eastsea and put the plan to the test. At first, I thought it was going to be successful. I had not seen Helene and Francis for a while. Imagine my surprise when they walked in the Cockleshell yesterday, and I realised the game was most likely up,' he said.

'Herman de Smits, you have committed a crime in England. Therefore your trial will be here. You are accused of impersonating a person to achieve financial and social standing, and harassing the Courtenay family. Anything you may say now will be used as evidence at your trial,' said Longfield.

'I have pleaded guilty,' said de Smits. 'Does there need to be a trial?'

'We shall have to think about that, and for the time being you remain in police custody,' replied Longfield.

De Smits was then returned to the cells.

Afternoon

Longfield was in the drawing room of Eastsea Hall with Lord and Lady Courtenay and Gilbert Harrison the solicitor.

'Herman de Smits has pleaded guilty to the charges against him, which are attempting to defraud and harass Lord and Lady Courtenay. By virtue of this, a trial can be averted were Their Graces not to proceed with the matter,' said Longfield.

'Are Your Graces prepared to meet the proposal of Inspector

Longfield and drop the charges?' asked Harrison.

The Courtenays looked at each other for inspiration.

'What are your feelings, Marcia?' asked Lord Courtenay.

'Whilst your disgraceful behaviour all those years ago has brought this into our lives, I forgive you; and the same attitude should be yours, St John, towards Herman de Smits, for you are partly to blame,' said Her Ladyship.

Lord Courtenay pondered a while.

'Yes, you are right, Marcia. I am deeply ashamed, and relieved that the matter can be forgotten. My appreciation to you, Longfield, and the Dutch officers for all your efforts. Drop the charges,' he said.

'I'll prepare a document to this effect, for you to sign, Your Grace, and then myself and Longfield will countersign it as true and legal,' said Harrison.

As Longfield left, estate workers were erecting the model of the baby *Basilosaurus* among the other statues on the lawn. He was smiling and thinking to himself, how very fitting, as the species had been of help in a way, although he didn't think Henry Matthews would agree.

At the police station, Inspector Vendren and Harold Shelly, a solicitor for Herman de Smits, were advising de Smits.

'Sign a legal document, that I shall prepare, declaring yourself guilty of harassing and attempting to defraud Lord and Lady Courtenay,' said Shelly.

'Thank you; I will do as you suggest,' said Herman de Smits.

'I will countersign, and I'm sure that Inspector Vendren will endorse the document,' said Shelly.

Vendren nodded in agreement.

The documents were drawn up, Gilbert Harrison overseeing his side with the Courtenays, and Harold Shelly dealing with Herman de Smits. All the signing and countersigning was duly completed.

Twenty-first of June – morning

All the relevant parties were now assembled in the office of the town magistrate, Stacey Oldman, who was carefully studying the documents.

For a good thirty minutes Oldman scrutinised them.

'Having taken into consideration both parties' attitudes, I have come to the conclusion that the forthcoming verdict will be accepted by the victims, Their Graces Lord and Lady Courtenay, and by the perpetrator, Herman de Smits. The gracious submission by Their Graces Lord and Lady Courtenay leads me to believe they would like leniency shown towards Herman de Smits. Although an erroneous plot of his, no real harm occurred. You are free to go, Mr de Smits. A warrant will be drawn up declaring that you will not be allowed to visit or reside in England ever again, and you will report to the Rotterdam Constabulary twice a week,' he said.

The two solicitors were satisfied with the verdict and advised acceptance by their clients, who did so.

Later, the Dutch Constabulary boat departed Eastsea with Inspector Vendren, Constable Metzer and Herman de Smits aboard.

CHAPTER SEVENTEEN
1896

WITH THE MATTER of the Herman de Smits claim put to rest, Lord and Lady Courtenay felt they needed to relax and socialise.

Twenty-fifth of June – evening
A celebration ball was proceeding. As usual, guests were from the Courtenays' social circle, plus estate workers and certain townsfolk.

During the evening Daniel Courtenay took centre stage with Helene.

'At this joyous time I am delighted to announce that Helene and I are to marry,' he said.

Everyone cheered and champagne bottle corks popped.

After the party, in the early hours of the next morning, a violent storm manifested once again.

Twenty-seventh of June – morning
Max Hunworth was at his desk in the estate office. Herbert Noakes and Sam Morgan entered.

'Mr Hunworth, please come with us to the marshes. Something we would like you to see,' said Herbert Noakes.

Hunworth, Noakes and Morgan arrived at an area on the marshes. Hunworth had a great surprise and heart-stopping moment. Before them was a large area of black liquid. Hunworth dipped his finger in the liquid and smelt it.

'If I'm not mistaken, this is crude oil,' he said.

Noakes and Morgan were taken aback.

'Goodness gracious! Where's that come from?' asked Morgan. 'Didn't know of any oilfields around here.'

'Would be useful on the estate,' said Noakes.

Hunworth studied the liquid carefully.

'Being crude, it will need processing. Shall have to get experts to check,' he said.

Amelia Hunworth was now well forward with child.

'Considering work and your age, you must take things easy,' Max insisted.

Amelia took confinement time off and Lily Doughty covered the work.

'I'll soon be back, and then you can get back to your retirement,' Amelia would say.

'Take your time, Amelia,' Lily would reply.

Discreetly she was enjoying being back in the throng.

Twenty-ninth of June – morning

Max Hunworth had moved quickly to get expert advice about the finding on the marshes. Lord Courtenay had informed Professor Bartholomew, who was now back at Eastsea with a colleague, Hardy Dawson, an American geologist. The three of them were at the scene of the oil slick with Hunworth.

'You were correct, Mr Hunworth. Crude oil it is,' said Dawson.

'Amazing! This is the third time I've been to Eastsea. First a *Basilosaurus*, secondly gold nuggets, both on the foreshore; and now this, all occurring after those violent storms. Truly phenomenal,' said Bartholomew.

Dawson looked quizzically at Bartholomew.

'Forgive me, Hardy. You've been at the museum only a short while. I'll explain later,' said Bartholomew.

Lord Courtenay gave his consent to proceed with the testing.
'I'd better get some equipment organised,' said Dawson.
'Thank you for coming so quickly,' said Hunworth.
'Our pleasure! Love it here. Place is full of surprises,' said Bartholomew.
Inspector Longfield and Captain Baines then arrived at the scene.
'Thank you for letting us know of this oil,' said Longfield.
They were introduced to Hardy Dawson.
'Leave it to me to see what can be achieved,' said Dawson.
They all then parted company to do various tasks.

'Well, Percy, what do you make of that oil business?' Longfield asked Baines on their arrival at the police station.
'With the other occurrences, I find it all a bit weird. To be honest, Archie, I don't know what to think,' said Baines.
'You and me too. Shall just have to wait and see,' replied Longfield.

Sixth of July – morning

A wagon train, resembling a western scene, was rolling through Eastsea, much to the amusement of residents. This was the equipment and workers for the oilfield on the marshes. Inspector Longfield and Captain Baines then led the way. Awaiting its arrival were Lord Courtenay, Professor Bartholomew, Hardy Dawson and Max Hunworth and other interested townsfolk. On the convoy's arrival, a well-built man jumped down from the first wagon. Hardy Dawson went forward to greet him.
'Jason, pleased to see you again. Gentlemen, may I introduce an acquaintance of mine, Jason O'Keefe. He will be in charge of the operation to exploit the oilfield and he will, if at all possible, with many previous successes under his belt. If it can be done, he will do it,' he said.

'Thanks, Hardy, I will do my best. With that introduction, you've certainly given me a lot to live up to. Pleased to meet you all,' O'Keefe replied.

They all then gathered to get acquainted.

'Right, lads, let's get camp set up,' shouted O'Keefe.

There was plenty of activity. The kitchen wagon was set up, whilst the other wagons were prepared for living in.

Longfield approached O'Keefe.

'Mr O'Keefe, I appreciate that these men work hard and play hard, but please try to steer them clear of trouble, and no doubt the local innkeepers are rubbing their hands, especially Toby Hughes at the Cockleshell,' he said.

'Take your point, Inspector, and I'll try to keep them in order, though they are grown men and need to let their hair down from time to time, as I do,' he said.

Longfield, as he left O'Keefe, thought, not too much to bother about, I hope.

Longfield was correct in one of his assumptions. Toby Hughes had ordered in extra ale and spirits, and food as well, in case the oilfield workers got fed up with the provisions provided in camp. Other innkeepers were also living in hope.

Tenth of July

Amelia Hunworth gave birth to a son. Mother and child were in good health; Max and the rest of the family and friends were absolutely delighted. The boy would be named David.

Lily Doughty was enjoying housekeeping duties at the Hall again whilst Amelia attended to her new son. With Professor Bartholomew and Hardy Dawson still staying there while the oilfield business proceeded, domestic staff were extra busy.

Activity on the oilfield had resulted in the erection of six sets of drilling apparatus, working in various areas. This had been the procedure for a fortnight, with gangs working around the clock.

There were some boisterous nights at the inns, fortunately trouble free, although there were one or two heated moments between locals and oil workers over a game of cards or some lass.

Twentieth of July – morning
The oil slick still lay on the surface of the marsh, though no amount of drilling produced further oil. Lord Courtenay, Hardy Dawson and Max Hunworth were observing the scene.

'Good morning, gentlemen,' said Jason O'Keefe as he approached them.

They returned the salutation.

'We've moved around this area for a fortnight or more, and still no positive outcome – only the original slick,' said O'Keefe.

'Please, My Lord, give them a few more days,' requested Hunworth.

'It's a costly exercise, you must realise,' replied Dawson.

Hunworth looked at Lord Courtenay for counsel.

'Mr Dawson is right, Max; we could be putting good money into a bad investment. One more week,' said Lord Courtenay.

'Thank you, Your Grace,' said Hunworth.

Twenty-first of July – morning
The *Canute* was heading out down the channel, followed by the rest of the fishing fleet, for a day's work fishing.

On the *Canute*, Henry Matthews was complaining about how the oilfield workers were being given preference over the locals by Toby Hughes in the Cockleshell.

'Keeps them well served with ale and us locals have to wait. He gets our custom all the time and then treats us like that. Be glad when they've gone. Shouldn't think they'll be here much longer; apparently can't find any oil. I'll probably boycott him and go to the Tankard,' he said.

'Don't think so, Father. Toby's the only one will let you run a slate for your ale.' said Dick.

'Mind your own business and get on with your work,' replied Henry.

Isaac Morris and Peter Smith grinned at this exchange between father and son.

'That goes for you two as well,' said Henry angrily.

At the marshes, Jason O'Keefe, mindful of his reputation, was feeling embarrassed and annoyed that oil had not been struck. This was also the feeling of the crew.

'Jason, I hope we strike oil soon. We're getting snide remarks from the locals about our inability to discover oil,' said Ben Innes, a leading hand of the crew.

'I know it's frustrating, Ben. We're experienced; tried everything that me, you and the crew know. Just keep going a few more days,' said O'Keefe.

Evening

The *Canute* and the rest of the fishing fleet returned, all with good catches. After unloading was completed some of the fishing crew, including Henry Matthews, went to the Cockleshell. The place was busy, mainly with oilfield workers.

'Come on, Toby, let us have ale. We've had a hard day at sea. I'm thirsty and tired, as the rest of the fishermen are,' said Henry.

'Have you got money?' asked Toby.

'Now look here, Toby, as matter of fact, yes I have,' replied Henry.

There were oilfield workers standing at the bar.

'He's serving us. Wait your turn,' said a voice.

'Who do you think you are?' asked Henry. 'We keep this place going all year. Toby seems to forget that,' he said.

'I'm Ben Innes,' the voice replied. 'You say you're tired after fishing? Oilfield work is a lot harder, and you smell of fish,' he said.

Henry glared back at him.

'I smell of fish because I caught some. You don't smell of oil because you've not discovered any,' he said.

At this Ben Innes squared up to Henry Matthews.

'Now, you two, stop it. Don't want any trouble,' said Toby.

The door opened and Constables Dawlish and Alexander entered whilst doing a town patrol.

'Trouble, Mr Hughes?' asked Alexander, knowing full well some was brewing.

'It's all right,' replied Toby.

'Mr Matthews, get home to your wife,' said Dawlish.

'Wife? This scruffy sod hasn't got a wife, surely,' said Innes.

'You, Sir,' said Alexander, looking at Innes, 'go and settle yourself down.'

Jason O'Keefe came over.

'Come on, Ben, we don't want any trouble,' he said.

'Get yourself home, Mr Matthews,' said Dawlish, who then turned to O'Keefe and said, 'Try and keep your men under control.'

Henry Matthews and the constables departed.

With Ben Innes now in a happier mood, the evening continued with the men playing cards and singing.

'We'd better keep an eye on the Cockleshell tonight in case of any more bother,' said Alexander to Dawlish.

Twenty-sixth of July – morning

Lord Courtenay, Professor Bartholomew, Hardy Dawson and Max Hunworth were surveying the scene on the marshes with Jason O'Keefe.

'Well, that's about it, Your Grace, Mr Hunworth. The week is about up and still no sign of any other oil; just the original slick,' said Dawson.

'We've tried everything we know to get oil out of the ground.

My reputation is tarnished. I shall be a laughing stock in the industry,' said O' Keefe.

'It's not your fault, O' Keefe. There have been some phenomenal things occurring around here of late. I'm sorry that you and your crew have been put in this position and been caused embarrassment. I won't think this matter would get beyond our community. Shut the operation down,' said Lord Courtenay.

'What does His Lordship mean, phenomenal?' asked O' Keefe.

Professor Bartholomew then explained the occurrences to O' Keefe.

'Those occurrences. They were reported in the London papers, well they would be, extraordinary things like that. I wouldn't have even considered coming here, had I known. Papers just said east coast of England. They'll have a field day when it's known I got involved,' said O' Keefe. 'Why didn't you tell me, Hardy?' he asked.

'Didn't know myself until it was too late, and I hoped this would be a positive outcome,' replied Hardy.

Max Hunworth's stare was fixed across the marshes.

'Look at that,' he called with excitement.

Everyone looked in amazement.

The oil slick was slowly absorbing into the marsh.

'What is going on here? Prehistoric mammals, gold nuggets and an oil slick that both suddenly appear and just as quickly disappear, for no apparent reason,' said Lord Courtenay.

Hardy Dawson was lost for words.

The drilling crew were clearing up.

'I've never seen them move so quick before. Probably think the marsh will swallow them,' said O' Keefe cheerfully.

'Thank you for your efforts, O' Keefe, and sorry it proved to be a wild goose chase. Hunworth, give him an extra hundred guineas on top of his payment,' said Lord Courtenay.

'Thank you, Your Lordship, that's big of you,' said O' Keefe.

'Small compensation for the embarrassment it has caused and

will cause in due time, I expect,' said Lord Courtenay.

'I just cannot explain it,' said Hardy Dawson.

'Me neither,' replied Professor Bartholomew.

Twenty-eighth of July – afternoon
The wagon train rolled out of Eastsea to a few jeers and snide remarks from certain townsfolk as it made its way through the town.

Inspector Longfield and Captain Baines were watching.

'That's unfair of the townsfolk, Percy. Those oil workers would have been heroes, had they found oil,' he said.

Evening
Henry Matthews entered the Cockleshell.

'Bit quiet in here today, Toby,' he said.

'All right, Henry, I know what you mean. I was rather blinded by their business. I do appreciate you locals who keep me going all the time. Let's forget what happened and have some ale on the house,' said Toby.

'Thanks, Toby, I shall have to complain more often,' said Henry.

Toby gave Henry a tankard of ale.

'Don't bother; it won't happen again,' said Toby.

'What about the others in here?' asked Henry.

'Don't push your luck,' replied Toby.

Thirtieth of July – afternoon
Professor Guy Bartholomew and Hardy Dawson arrived back in London.

Dawson bought a newspaper.

'Oh no!' he exclaimed.

'What's wrong?' asked the professor.

Dawson gave him the paper.

The professor winced.

"Oilfield Expert Defeated", read the headline, and the paper went on to report Jason O' Keefe's failure to find oil on the east coast.

'I'd like to see him, for it's me got him into this mess. Think I know where he'll be,' said Dawson.

They found him in a club for oil workers – "The Slick".

'I've seen it,' O' Keefe said, on seeing the paper in Dawson's hand.

'Took some guts to come in here after that,' said Dawson.

'You need guts to do the work. Got ribbed for a while, ignored it, then, and it stopped,' replied O' Keefe.

Another person arrived on the scene.

'Excuse me, gentlemen. Good to see you, Jason. What a shame; no success at Eastsea. Higher you are, harder you fall,' he said and then departed.

Who's that?' asked Dawson.

'Jeremy Philpot, the reporter that wrote that piece. We go back a long way. He's an old adversary, always looking for a chance to decry me, fortunately not very often. One or two disasters though. The woman he was to marry met me, so she married me instead. Ever since, he's carried on this kind of vendetta. Need I say more?' replied O' Keefe.

'Thought I recognised him. Saw him skulking around Eastsea, didn't we, Professor? He looked quite suspicious, so I made the local constabulary aware,' said Dawson.

'Yes, he certainly looks like that fellow,' replied the professor.

'Most likely loosening a few tongues in the Cockleshell,' said O'Keefe.

'Once again, Jason, deeply sorry that you got into this debacle,' said Dawson.

'Think no more of it, Hardy; not really your fault. Blame quirks of nature. Have some ale with me,' said O' Keefe.

To be sociable, they did. After a few ales, they parted company.

CHAPTER EIGHTEEN
1896

Twenty-fifth of August
THE WEATHER was kind – a beautiful hot sunny day. There were sounds of merriment and music in the grounds of Eastsea Hall.

It was the occasion of Daniel Courtenay being made Lord of the Manor, and of his marriage to Helene van Rowhe.

Lord and Lady Courtenay had retired and would now be in the background to groom the new incumbents of the estate.

Francis van Rowhe, Max and Amelia Hunworth, the Matthewses, and Jessica and Cedric Lewis were in attendance, and as it had been a strange previous few months, to lift up the hearts of townsfolk, some were invited, including the Mayor and Mayoress of Eastsea. Professor Bartholomew and his wife Louise were also there for a more joyous visit.

'This makes a nice change and I hope all we'll have to do in future is chase drunks and felons, and none of this phenomenal business,' said Inspector Longfield as he walked around with Captain Baines.

'I hope so too,' replied Baines.

Just then Doris Perkins, the organist, struck up the "Wedding March".

Out of the main door of the Hall and down the steps came Helene, looking radiant in a pink wedding dress, on the arm of a very pleased Max Hunworth, who had jumped at the chance when asked if he would give her away. Following Helene and Max were the bridesmaids, Amelia Hunworth and Jessica Lewis, their attire colour co-ordinated with the bride's. Ahead of them on the lawn standing in front of a rose covered arch, the bridegroom, Daniel Courtenay, and the best man, Cedric Lewis. Facing the wedding party and guests was the Reverend Paul Ives.

The parson allowed everyone to settle down after the complimentary remarks towards the wedding party.

'Welcome to you all on this joyous occasion. The first hymn will be "All Things Bright and Beautiful",' he announced.

When the hymn was completed the Reverend Ives said, 'Please be seated. We are gathered here today in the sight of God to witness the coming together of Daniel and Helene. Before the ceremony can begin, I ask that if there is any person here present that can give any reason or impediment that this couple should not be married, to declare now, or forever hold their peace.'

A tense moment followed, with Helene thinking, please, nobody spoil my happiness. There was silence.

'I shall now commence with the ceremony,' said Reverend Ives. 'Do you, Daniel Frederick St John Courtenay, take Helene Marguerite van Rowhe to be your lawful wedded wife, to have and to hold, for richer, for poorer, in sickness and in health?' he asked.

'I do,' replied Daniel.

'Do you, Helene Marguerite van Rowhe, take Daniel Frederick St John Courtenay to be your lawful wedded husband, to have and to hold, for richer, for poorer, in sickness and in health?' asked Reverend Ives.

'I do,' replied Helene.

'The ring for the bride, please,' said Reverend Ives.

Cedric Lewis handed the ring to Daniel.

Reverend Ives then spoke to Daniel. 'Repeat after me: with this ring I thee wed and declare undying love.'

Daniel repeated those words, and placed the ring on Helene's finger.

'The ring for the groom, please,' said Reverend Ives.

Cedric Lewis handed the ring to Helene.

Reverend Ives then spoke to Helene. 'Repeat after me: with this ring I thee wed and declare undying love.'

Helene repeated the words, and placed the ring on Daniel's finger.

'I now declare the couple as husband and wife,' said Reverend Ives.

Prayers and the blessing were followed by the hymn, "Love Divine, All Loves Excelling".

'Daniel and Helene will now accompany me to the library to sign the register,' said Reverend Ives. 'Would the witnesses please join us?' he requested.

'Would the rest of you go to the Great Hall?' requested Cedric Lewis. 'A wedding feast is laid out. We'll join you in a few minutes,' he said.

They found a feast fit for a king. The wedding party returned from the signing. Grace was said by the Reverend Ives and then everyone began eating the fare. After the meal, toasts and speeches were made, followed by the evening entertainment, music and merriment.

With it being dusk, the dark clouds on the horizon went unnoticed.

Twenty-sixth of August

The storm broke in the early hours of the morning, more intense than anything experienced in the past. Everyone at Eastsea Hall was awake.

'What was the terrific bang?' asked Lady Courtenay.

'I'll go and see,' replied Lord Courtenay.

Donning his greatcoat at the main door, Lord Courtenay went out into the maelstrom. He looked up and saw lightning had struck the west wing of the Hall, causing fire.

'No, no, no,' he cried.

A large piece of masonry loosened by the strike and blown off by the wind, crashed down on him, killing him instantly

Lady Courtenay, who was concerned that her husband had been gone a long while, went downstairs and found him. Daniel and Helene were close behind. Lady Courtenay was kneeling, sobbing, beside Lord Courtenay's body.

'Come, Mother. He must have been killed in an instant. It's too dangerous for us out here as well,' said Daniel.

The estate workers had formed a bucket chain trying to contain fire at a lower level. Fire, though, raged at the top of the building.

'I'm riding into Eastsea, to raise the alarm for the fire brigade,' said Max Hunworth.

'No, you can't, Max; it's too dangerous in this weather,' said Daniel.

Then, fortunately, they heard a bell – the fire brigade.

'Well, they've made it,' said Max Hunworth.

'Yes, they have done well,' replied Daniel.

'That is one of the most difficult journeys I have ever made in all my ten or more years as a fireman, and the same applies to the fire just as much. Someone in Eastsea spotted the fire and raised the alarm,' said Martin Gibbs, the leading fireman.

The fire brigade worked hard, but to no avail. The water tank volume on the engine was no match for the flames, and although the heavy rain was helping to douse them to a degree, the high wind was fanning them.

Then other bells were heard and four other units arrived. Apparently the fire could be seen five miles away, and had alerted these other brigades.

Inspector Longfield arrived with his three constables: Dawlish, Alexander and Palmer, followed by two ambulances, with Doctor Moore and Lancelot Dunton the coroner on board one of them.

'Inspector, Father has been killed, we think, by falling masonry. Amelia has taken Mother, Jessica, Helene and her mother to her cottage,' said Daniel.

'You could well be right. Appears that a lump of masonry by his body hit him on the head, causing the wound, but I'll let Doctor Moore and Mr Dunton carry out their work before making any further judgement,' said Longfield.

As hard as the firemen worked, they were fighting a losing battle. The Hall was now a burning inferno.

'Inspector Longfield, Daniel, it's a hopeless task and a dangerous one. I've spoken to the other leading firemen and have decided that we let the fire burn itself out. It's a difficult decision, but sadly, it has to be made,' said Martin Gibbs.

'Unfortunately, although devastated, as we all shall be, I have to agree with you. We have lost priceless paintings, tapestries, furniture and, above all, our ancestral home,' said Daniel.

'Let's get out of this weather. Doctor Moore, you and Mr Dunton use the summerhouse on the lawn to do what you have to. I need to talk to Lady Courtenay,' said Longfield.

Two of the estate workers carried the body of Lord Courtenay to the summerhouse. Constables Palmer and Dawlish accompanied them.

'This is not the time to be jocular, but I have just had a thought. With the untimely death of my father, although he had already handed the title to me, Helene is Lady Courtenay as well,' said Daniel.

'Your mother is the person who I have to speak to; she was almost certainly the last one to see your father alive,' said Longfield.

They both entered the Hunworth cottage, accompanied by Constable Alexander.

'Mother, Inspector Longfield needs to talk to you,' said Daniel.

'Your Grace, I am sorry, so soon after, but I need you to give a few details regarding His Grace's death while still fresh in your memory,' said Longfield.

'I understand, Inspector,' said Lady Courtenay.

She then recounted how a bang had been heard and her husband had gone to check outside. When he did not return as quickly as expected, she went to investigate and found him.

'Was he dead when you found him?' asked Longfield.

'Yes,' she replied, and then broke down sobbing.

'I think that will be enough, Inspector,' said Jessica.

'Thank you, Your Grace; I realise that was difficult. We'll leave you now to grieve in peace,' said Longfield.

Longfield and Alexander then left the cottage and met Max Hunworth on his way in.

'What do you make of all this, Inspector?' asked Hunworth.

'With due respect, Mr Hunworth, we'll leave explanations for later. There are folk in your cottage that need comforting,' replied Longfield.

Longfield and Alexander then made their way to the summerhouse.

'How's it going, Doctor?' asked Longfield.

'The body was soaking wet. It is now cleaned sufficiently to be taken to the mortuary for a thorough examination,' replied Doctor Moore.

Lord Courtenay's body was then stretchered into an ambulance.

'I'll let you have the results as soon as possible,' said Doctor Moore as the ambulance left with the coroner on board as well.

The fire crews were still busying themselves as best they could. The building was still a blazing inferno.

'Once the storm abates, we shall then have to damp the fire down, but that will be a while yet,' said Martin Gibbs.

'In my experience they have been lasting up to twelve hours,' said Longfield.

'How are you and your men spending your time during the night, Inspector?' asked a voice behind him.

Turning around they saw Timothy Doughty standing there.

'Not much we can do at present,' the inspector replied.

'You'd better come along home with me. I'm sure Lily will be able to muster up some hot soup and tea,' he said.

Lily did just that, and for the contingent of firemen as well, coming to the cottage in relays, eating and resting.

'Dreadful business this: losing Lord St John and their home, and Daniel having just become Lord of the Manor. Timothy and I have spent most of our lives here. Their feelings must be ten times worse,' said Lily.

The constabulary officers remained with the Doughtys for most of the night, and managed to get some sleep.

'Thank you for your hospitality. That soup was delicious,' said Longfield.

'You're very welcome. Pleased we're able to do something,' said Lily Doughty.

Outside, the storm had abated. About a quarter of a mile away there was a scene of carnage. The Hall was now nothing but a shell. The fire crews had done a good job damping down the fire. There were just plumes of smoke here and there. Captain Baines was observing the scene.

'Hello, Percy. Thanks for coming,' said Longfield.

'This is absolutely awful. I've got the infantry coming as well. As you see, the Ladies Guild from Eastsea are doing their bit as well, with that kitchen affair they've set up,' said Baines.

'That is thoughtful of them. The inner man needs sustenance to maintain strength,' said Longfield.

'A very profound thought, but a true one,' replied Baines.

Turning to his three constables he said, 'Keep people away from the ruins. Obviously it's dangerous. When the infantry arrive, allocate them to help you. There is a large area to cover. I expect Sergeant Hart will be in charge again. I'm going over to the Hunworths' to see how things are there,' said Longfield.

As Longfield approached the cottage, Professor Bartholomew and his wife were arriving. They had spent the night at a neighbouring property.

'Good morning. I use the salutation out of courtesy, not description,' said Longfield.

'Know what you mean,' the professor answered. 'Thankfully, it is better now though, than early this morning. We've come to see if we can help. Could see the fire from where we were staying. Didn't expect anything of this magnitude though. Where are the Courtenay family?' he asked.

Oh dear! They obviously haven't heard, thought Longfield.

'I'm sorry, Professor, Mrs Bartholomew, there's no easy way to say this. St John Courtenay was killed last night by falling masonry. Came outside at the height of the storm when he heard a terrific bang. Lightning had struck the building. Doctor Moore has the body at the mortuary doing a post mortem,' said Longfield.

'Oh my God. How dreadful! I must go and give solace to Marcia,' said Louise Bartholomew.

'The Courtenay family are with the Hunworths. You know, the architect of the Hall did a fine job building the cottages and the stables, a quarter of a mile away. The horses were restless, but things could have been worse. This way to the cottage,' said Longfield.

They walked along a path and Longfield knocked on the door, which was opened by Amelia Hunworth.

'Come in. Lady Marcia and Jessica are sleeping at the moment. They are devastated, and tiredness has just overtaken them. Doctor Moore is attending later. Helene and Mrs van Rowhe are in the parlour. Daniel, Cedric and Max are out surveying the damage,' she said.

'Professor, I think it's best we leave the ladies for the time being, and find the men,' said Longfield.

They found the three of them at what had been the frontage of

Eastsea Hall. The infantry were in place as well. Leading firemen were in conversation.

'We've done as much as we can. Those embers will smoulder for ages. Alert us if they fly afire. Shouldn't though; been well dampened by the rain and we've put water on as well. The men are weary. Worst call out ever, as you can imagine, so we'll take our leave,' said Martin Gibbs.

'Words cannot express enough our gratitude for your efforts. Brave men – all of you. No one could have asked for more. It is heartbreaking: two hundred years in the building; gone in a matter of hours. What a baptism of fire for me, in more ways than one,' said Daniel.

Longfield then saw Sergeant Hart talking to the constables.

'Morning, Inspector,' said Hart.

'Morning, Hart. Glad you're here. Expect the constables have briefed you. Right, lads, let's get back to Eastsea and home. Be back later, Sergeant Hart,' said Longfield.

'Bye for now,' replied Hart.

When Daniel, Cedric, Max and Professor Bartholomew returned to the cottage, Louise Bartholomew was comforting Marcia Courtenay and Jessica. Helene and Francis were giving their condolences. Amelia Hunworth had sympathy and provided vittles that, hopefully, would comfort the bereaved.

'The priority is accommodation whilst awaiting the inquest and funeral. Long term, hopefully, Francis will agree to accommodate myself and Helene in Eastsea,' said Daniel.

'Of course, and Lady Marcia if she wishes, for the time being,' said Francis.

'Amelia and Max, will you be able to have Jessica and Cedric here?' asked Daniel. 'In time, Mother, you go to stay in London with them,' he said.

'All right with us,' said Amelia.

'And us,' said Jessica.

Both Max and Cedric were in agreement.

'Fortunately, you men have certainly had your heads together, I cannot think about much just at the moment apart from the horror of the past few days,' said Marcia.

'Mother, one matter: we shall need to do some shopping. You, Cedric and I are wearing the only clothes we have after the fire, cosmetics would be useful too,' said Jessica.

'I need to shop as well, I'm now wearing the only garments in my possession,' said Daniel.

'Professor – you and Louise?' asked Daniel.

'Don't worry about us. You've enough to think about. I'm sure we can stay at the Drummonds' still until after the inquest and funeral,' said the professor.

'I think it's about time we all had a good meal,' said Amelia.

'I'll come and help you prepare,' said Jessica.

'And so will I,' said Helene.

'You two are titled Ladies, and should not be doing this,' said Amelia.

'These are troubled times, and anyway I have known my mother to help out in times of strife,' said Jessica.

'I am a very fortunate working class foreign national, who, by love, has been elevated to the English aristocracy, but I shall not forget my roots,' said Helene.

Within half an hour they were sitting down to a meal of roast ham and salad followed by fruitcake and mugs of tea.

'On behalf of the assembled company may I thank Amelia and her two helpers for such delicious fare. We all should feel a little better for the inner person being sustained in such a way,' said Daniel.

'On such an occasion, for it rarely happens, I declare that the men do the washing up. Please signify in the usual manner all those in favour of the proposition,' said Jessica.

All the women voted in favour and so without argument, the

men trotted out to the scullery to do the chore.

After this piece of humour there was an air of cheerfulness within the cottage. Lady Marcia had a smile, and Jessica thought this to be a good time to discuss the buying of replacement clothes with the other women. A shopping trip to Bishops Lynne was then discussed.

Twenty-eighth of August – morning

Doctor Moore was at the police station with the results of the post mortem on St John Courtenay.

'Inspector, the injuries sustained to the head of St John Courtenay are consistent with a heavy blow. There were minute pieces of masonry in the wound, leading me to conclude his death was caused by falling masonry. There are no other injuries. Coroner Lancelot Dunton endorses my opinion,' he said.

'I've got that piece of masonry as an exhibit for the inquest,' said Longfield.

'If that is all, I must now attend to the Courtenay family. No doubt they are feeling rather low at present,' said Doctor Moore. 'Do you know their whereabouts?' he asked.

'When I last saw them they were at the Hunworth cottage and, thank you, Doctor,' said Longfield.

'I'd better take Dunton with me. The inquest needs to be arranged,' said the doctor.

On answering the knock at the door, Amelia Hunworth found Doctor Moore and Lancelot Dunton standing there.

'Hello, Doctor Moore, Mr Dunton; please come in. Can I get you both some vittles?' she said.

'Yes please,' replied Doctor Moore.

Amelia disappeared into the kitchen.

'I'm here to see how you all are bearing up. If anyone would like to have a chat, now's the time,' said Doctor Moore.

'My business can wait until the doctor has finished,' said Dunton.

Amelia reappeared with scones and mugs of tea.

Whilst eating the vittles, Doctor Moore and Lancelot Dunton observed the demeanour of the mourning family.

'I'd like to talk to you, Doctor,' said Lady Marcia.

'Go in the sitting room,' said Amelia.

Lady Marcia and Doctor Moore then retired to the sitting room.

'I'm devastated at present, Doctor. The untimely death of St John and the manner in which it occurred are difficult to comprehend. I'm depressed and unable to sleep. Cedric did give me some mild sedatives. They helped for a while. Maybe you can prescribe me something. They made some humour earlier, which they thought would cheer me up: talked about shopping for replacement clothes and we voted to get the men to wash up. They meant well and I put on a brave face. Thank you for listening, Doctor; it's been a comfort to talk to someone outside the family,' said Lady Marcia.

'You're welcome. Pleased you have gained solace from our conversation. I've some tablets that will help you, and a sympathetic ear is just as comforting at times,' said the doctor.

'In my time, I've said to someone that has a lost a loved one, "I know how you are feeling". In my experience now, it's a myth,' said Lady Marcia.

'It is also said that time is a healer. However, it depends upon how the individual accepts death, especially of a loved one,' said the doctor.

Lady Marcia and Doctor Moore returned to the others in the parlour.

'Anyone else like to talk to me?' asked the doctor.

'No, thank you, Doctor. Whilst you were talking with Mother, we declared our feelings with each other and found peace and compassion. St John Courtenay was a husband we know Mother loved and misses dreadfully. He was also a father, friend and employer to the various of us here, who loved, respected and miss him,' said Jessica.

Professor Bartholomew then stood up and paced the room.

'I had known St John many years. Our initial encounter was during schooldays. With his background of being brought up on a large estate it gave him a certain compassion for nature. Even in those early days nature was of great interest to me. With a common interest, we became firm friends. Recently, as you are all aware, a lot of my time has been at Eastsea, due mainly to the quirks of nature that have been occurring. Although the circumstances were not favourable, the time being spent amongst him and his family meant that, sadly, my dear Louise got rather neglected. Thankfully she is very understanding. To get back to St John, it was a great privilege to have known him,' he said.

Max Hunworth then spoke. 'I was a youngster when I first came to work on the estate. Between them, Lord St John and Timothy Doughty taught me estate management. They saw my interest was in administration. I had for two years to do the heavy manual work of a general estate worker. Lord St John told me that those two years would be beneficial to me for when I became an estate manager. One day Lord St John said to me, "You are ready for a management position. However, it cannot be here; Timothy Doughty has several years before he will retire. I have an acquaintance in Yorkshire, Lord Mountford, who wants a manager. I've told him you are capable enough to do the job." So I went. Upon my return to Eastsea Hall, Lord St John said, "Max, you did not let me down. Lord Mountford wanted you to stay with him, but I wanted you back at Eastsea Hall after Timothy Doughty retired. I have a confession to make: Mountford and I played cards about that time when the Mountfords were staying at Eastsea Hall. Max, you were the prize to the winner." I felt quite honoured that two such men of standing were gambling for my attributes,' he said.

'I didn't know about that,' said Lady Marcia.

'Neither did I until then. Lord St John swore me to secrecy. I should not have said anything now; just got carried away whilst speaking of a wonderful person,' replied Max.

'Too ashamed of what they had been doing, I expect,' said Lady Marcia.

'His Lordship was a real gentleman to work for and I had great respect for him, although life for me would have been so different had Lord St John not won that card game,' said Amelia.

Helene then let her feelings be heard.

'As well as for myself, I speak on behalf of my mother. Ever since disaster brought us to Eastsea, our lives have changed dramatically, mine particularly, in a position within the Courtenay family I could not have dreamt of in my wildest dreams. Sadly, the time with Lord St John was short. Having heard the previous tributes, I would have liked it to have been longer,' she said.

'Thank you all for your words; they are of great comfort,' said Lady Marcia, sobbing.

The room fell silent for a few minutes in quiet solitude, with everyone dwelling on the words that had been said.

'Doctor, later today Helene and I, for the foreseeable future and Mother, until she goes away with Jessica and Cedric after the inquest and funeral, will be residing in Eastsea with Francis. Jessica and Cedric are staying here with Max and Amelia,' said Daniel.

'I'll get a date arranged for the inquest,' said Lancelot Dunton.

Doctor Moore and Lancelot Dunton then took their leave

Thirtieth of August

Henry Matthews, Dick, Isaac Morris and Peter Smith were by the *Canute* sitting repairing nets on the harbour wall along with the other fishing fleet crews.

Daniel arrived on the scene. 'Thank you for keeping the fleet going, Henry, and carry on for the time being. There is so much for me to attend to at present,' he said.

'Right you are, Your Grace,' replied Henry.

'I'm residing at Francis van Rowhe's cottage for the time being,' said Daniel.

'Thank you, Your Grace,' replied Henry.

Daniel then departed.

'Henry, you were moaning about His Grace not so very long ago for not coming to see you,' said Dick mockingly.

'Maybe I was too quick with those remarks. He has got a lot to do,' said Henry. Then as an afterthought, he added, 'Undoubtedly he realised the fleet was in good hands.'

Dick and the other two smiled to themselves.

'What are you lot grinning at? Get on with your work,' said Henry angrily.

Second of September

The coach and four, with Herbert Noakes driving, had almost reached Bishops Lynne, carrying titled aristocracy: three ladies and a lord, namely, Marcia, Helene, Jessica and Daniel.

'It's almost noon. I suggest we have lunch at the Monarch Hotel first, before going about our business,' said Daniel.

The three ladies agreed it was a good idea. As the coach stopped outside the Monarch, a concierge came forward and opened the door.

'Good afternoon, Your Graces,' said the concierge, knowing who they were, for this was the Courtenays' favourite eating establishment in Bishops Lynne.

They thanked him, crossed his palm with a favour, and entered the hotel.

'Herbert, get the horses refreshed, then please collect us from here at four o'clock,' said Daniel, and then he followed the ladies into the hotel.

The concierge also received a favour from Daniel as he passed.

There were words of condolences from both guests and staff to the Courtenays, for the Monarch Hotel was a favourite haunt with the other local aristocracy.

Questions asked were, 'How are you all?' 'When is the inquest and the funeral?'

These were answered by, 'We are coming to terms. Bearing up. We'll let you all know when and where.'

Despite all this attention, they did manage to complete lunch.

The place for getting the horse refreshed was the Ostlers Tavern – water and hay for one shilling per horse and for one penny a tankard of ale for the coachman.

After lunch, the four of them left the Monarch. The ladies headed for the shops and Daniel for the solicitors.

'I have told Noakes to collect us from here at four o'clock. I'll be back at thirty minutes after three. We can then take tea before leaving. Between now and then should give you plenty of time for shopping. Goodbye. I'm going to the solicitors,' said Daniel.

Herbert Noakes enjoyed bringing the coach to Bishops Lynne. The Ostlers was the place where all the coachmen met up from time to time while their employers did business in the town. The topic being bandied about on this occasion was the demise of Herbert's employer.

'Did you see it happen, Herbert? Piece of masonry hit him, didn't it?' asked one coachman.

'Now, listen all of you, because I shall not repeat it. I didn't see it happen and it *was* a piece of masonry, as far I know. I was at home looking after my family in that terrific storm. So, there you are. The inquest is being held in due course, and we may learn more then. Let's get down to drinking ale and playing dominoes. I've not much time now; you all want to know too much,' said Herbert.

Housemans had been the family solicitors for many years.

Daniel was in the office of Hugh Houseman, the senior partner and third generation to have taken articles. The practice had been started by Hugh's grandfather, Cyrus, in eighteen thirty-three, and on his death it was continued by Hugh's father, Garfield, until his retirement a few years ago, when Hugh took over.

'My condolences, Your Grace,' said Hugh.

'Your Grace – that is taking some getting used to, having had it thrust upon me in such an unfortunate and devastating way,' said Daniel.

'The reading of the will shall be conducted after the funeral, and Eastsea Hall was insured for ten million guineas, underwritten by Lloyds of London,' said Hugh with an air of competence.

'How did you know what I wanted to see you for?' asked Daniel.

'Those are two matters that are initially dealt with when something of this magnitude happens,' replied Hugh.

'Hopefully that amount should cover the rebuilding. Not going for anything the size of the original. In the past, the building of a palatial residence could take up to two hundred years and cost a few lives. I want to see the building finished,' said Daniel.

'I'll notify Lloyds of your wishes, and get the paperwork sorted out,' said Hugh Houseman.

'Please, organise Geoffrey Moulton – he's an architect of renown – to come to Eastsea for a consultation,' requested Daniel.

'After all that business, a sherry?' asked Hugh.

'That will do fine,' replied Daniel.

The three ladies arrived back at the Monarch by thirty minutes after three.

'I thought Daniel would have been here now,' said Helene.

They waited another five minutes, still no Daniel. A favour was given to the concierge.

'Please tell Lord Courtenay we are already inside when he arrives,' requested Helene.

Daniel Courtenay and Hugh Houseman chatted for a while. At the offer of a fourth sherry, Daniel suddenly declared, 'Goodness gracious, is that the time? I should have met my wife Helene, Mother, and sister Jessica at the Monarch ten minutes ago,' he said.

'I'll see you again at the inquest,' said Hugh as Daniel hurried out.

'Good afternoon, Your Grace,' said the concierge as Daniel arrived at the Monarch. 'The ladies have asked me to inform you they are in the tea lounge,' he continued.

'Thank you,' said Daniel, making the concierge a favour richer.

'What kept you so long?' asked Helene.

'More business than I anticipated,' said Daniel, telling a white lie.

'Have some tea and scones,' said Jessica.

'No thank you,' replied Daniel.

'Too much sherry and chatter, more like. Don't forget your father used to have business at Housemans,' said Lady Marcia knowingly, with a smile.

The concierge entered the room.

'Excuse me, Your Grace. Your coach awaits you,' he said.

Fifteen minutes later they were on the road to Eastsea.

After supper Daniel conveyed his plans to Helene, Marcia, Jessica and Cedric. Then there was a fashion show of the ladies' purchases.

Under Henry Matthews' management the fishing fleet continued to have its ups and downs, good catches and then low ones. However, Lord Daniel Courtenay was happy with an even balance which kept the ice houses well stocked and provided lucrative auctions.

CHAPTER NINETEEN
1896

Fifteenth of September
THE TOWN HALL was again full for the inquest into the death of Lord St John Courtenay.

High dignitaries of the county were in attendance, with the rest of the Courtenay family in addition to townsfolk.

The coroner Lancelot Dunton brought order to the assemblage.

'My lords, ladies and gentlemen, we are gathered here to ascertain how Lord St John Clarence Lawson Courtenay met his death. Any interruptions during the proceedings, and the perpetrator will be escorted from the building by the Constabulary,' he said.

Lady Marcia Courtenay was seated in the witness area with Hugh Houseman. Inspector Longfield was close by, taking notes. Constables Dawlish and Alexander were seeing all was in order.

'This was an occurrence devoid of witnesses. Lady Marcia Jane Margaret Courtenay discovered the body of Lord St John Clarence Lawson Courtenay after the occurrence. Please, Lady Marcia, take the stand,' said Dunton.

Lady Marcia came forward and took the oath.

'You are Lady Marcia Jane Margaret Courtenay, widow of Lord St John Clarence Lawson Courtenay?' asked Dunton.

'I am,' replied Lady Marcia.

'Please, Your Grace, describe the events of the twenty-sixth of August, eighteen ninety-six,' said Dunton.

Lady Marcia then gave an account of how both she and Lord Courtenay had heard a terrific bang during a violent storm in the early hours. Lord Courtenay went to investigate. He was gone rather a long while, so she went looking and found him lying on the ground outside. Recounting this was clearly distressing to Lady Marcia.

'Thank you, Your Grace. I do appreciate these are difficult times. You may stand down,' said Dunton.

'I could give you an insight into the aftermath of the tragedy,' said Daniel.

'Please do,' replied Dunton.

Daniel Courtenay came to the stand and took the oath.

'My wife and I heard the bang. By the time we got outside my mother, Lady Marcia, was kneeling beside the body of my father, Lord St John. She was soaking wet, in a distressed state. The bang, we assumed, was lightning striking the house, which caused a fire, that was fanned by high winds, which led to Eastsea Hall being burnt to the ground,' said Daniel.

'Thank you, Your Grace. You may stand down,' said Dunton.

'Anybody here present that can add anything more to Lord Daniel's testimony?' asked Dunton.

Max Hunworth then stood up.

'Please identify yourself and your connection with the Courtenay family, if any. Come to the stand and take the oath,' said Dunton.

'Max Hunworth, estate manager at Eastsea Hall. Sir, you may wonder at the lack of witnesses, with the number of staff at the Hall. None of us arrived at the same time as the initial arrivals of Lady Marcia and Lord Daniel,' he said.

Lancelot Dunton deliberated for a few minutes, then gave his verdict.

'From the accounts I have heard and the post mortem report by Doctor Moore, accidental death is the only verdict that can be brought in by me on the demise of Lord St John Clarence Lawson Courtenay, Second Earl of Eastsea,' he said.

Inspector Longfield nodded in agreement.

'I now declare this inquest terminated,' said Dunton.

CHAPTER TWENTY
1896

Seventeenth of September
LORD DANIEL COURTENAY and architect Geoffrey Moulton were riding around the town of Eastsea, getting inspiration for the design of a new Eastsea Hall. They were in a particularly affluent part, Town Green, dominated by large houses – residences of rich merchants. A mansion, known as Town Green House, had taken their eye.

'Horace Wilding, the banker, lives there. The new hall would need to be a larger size, and more palatial looking,' said Daniel.

'There are some wonderful looking properties here on Town Green, but this one I would recommend as a guide to design,' said Moulton.

They then headed back to Francis van Rowhe's cottage.

'The need is great to get a new Eastsea Hall built. I am grateful to Francis, but a person of my standing, Lord of the Manor, living here,' said Daniel jokingly.

In the cottage tea and scones were being enjoyed by Francis and Their Graces Marcia and Helene. The two men joined them.

After refreshment, Daniel outlined his specifications to Moulton.

'As time is of the essence, the building must be of smaller dimensions than usual, though palatial and impressive, covering the ground of twenty acres plus. Ground floor: drawing room, library, dining room, kitchen, pantry, store cupboards, lavatories. Second floor: master bedroom, six others of various sizes, nursery, lavatories, study, store room. There are the guidelines, Geoffrey. Do your best,' said Daniel.

'When is Lord St John's funeral?' asked Moulton.

'Next week: the twenty-fourth,' replied Daniel.

'That gives me a week to get something down on paper that I can bring when I attend the funeral,' said Moulton.

'I'm going up to the estate now. I'll drop you off at the railway station on the way,' said Daniel.

As he was heading for the estate, Daniel met up with Amelia Hunworth walking back home.

'Hello, Amelia,' he said.

'Your Grace. I've been into Eastsea to buy more clothes as I'm getting bigger, and I'm visiting the family,' said Amelia.

'Jump in the trap,' he said.

Daniel was deep in thought as they jogged along.

'Penny for them,' said Amelia.

This shook him from his inner mind.

'Sorry, Amelia, it's discourteous of me. Didn't mean to ignore you. I was wondering if you remember our first meeting. Came to tell you Mother would like to see you,' he said.

'Yes, I do remember, and I expect the rebuilding of the Hall weighs heavy on your mind,' replied Amelia.

'I'd be telling lies if I said it didn't, though seeing you today has put things in perspective. A lot has happened in a short while. Today has brought me back down to earth,' said Daniel.

As Daniel stopped outside the cottage, Max Hunworth approached.

'Good afternoon, Your Grace,' he said.

'Thanks for the lift, Your Grace,' Amelia said.

'The pleasure's all mine. Our chat was inspiring,' said Daniel. 'Max, please get in the trap. We'll take a ride to the site of the new hall.'

They reached the site and Daniel sat pondering.

'Am I asking too much of the men who will be digging the footings? Been consulting with Geoffrey Moulton, the architect, with a view to building a small hall. Even then, it's a monstrous task. I don't want too many years or lives spent on it. Want to see a completion in my lifetime,' he said.

'Hopefully everything will be all right. Have to wait and see,' said Max.

CHAPTER TWENTY-ONE
1896

Twenty-fourth of September
EASTSEA PARISH CHURCH: the setting for the funeral of Lord St John Courtenay, officiated over by the Bishop of Bishops Lynne, assisted by the Reverend Paul Ives.

As would be expected for a man of Lord St John's standing, mourners were dignitaries from far and wide, not least a courtier representing Queen Victoria, and folks he had befriended or who had laboured for him.

The service was opened by the words of the Reverend Paul Ives. 'We are gathered here in the sight of God to convey the soul of Lord St John Clarence Lawton Courtenay to his keeping.'

The service continued with the hymn, "The Lord Is My Shepherd", followed by people of standing paying tributes ranging from St John being a wonderful human being, to 'A man of great fortitude and sentiment'. Max Hunworth, on behalf of the estate staff and workers added: 'A strict but fair person'.

Then the hymn "The Day Thou Gavest, Lord" was followed by prayers.

The bishop gave the sermon, extolling the virtues of Lord St John and advocating the earlier tributes and including words of how birth is the start of life for a soul, and death a journey to meet the Maker.

Condolences were paid to the Courtenay family.

The offering of Lord St John Courtenay's soul to God, and the

Blessing, was followed by the hymn "Abide with Me".

The body was then taken to the Courtenay family tomb.

The town hall housed the assemblage for the wake. This proved to be an offering of fine fare, provided by a purveyor of fine foods from Bishops Lynne with consultation from Amelia Hunworth.

During the proceedings, Professor Guy Bartholomew took Lord Daniel and Inspector Longfield along with the chief constable to one side.

'Gentlemen, I need to speak to you all in private on a matter of great urgency,' he said.

The four of them entered the Lord Mayor's robing room in the town hall.

The professor then said, 'What I am about to tell you, gentlemen, must stay within these four walls for the time being, unless of course it becomes a safety issue. I leave that to the discretion of the Constabulary. Earlier during this week I attended a forum in London. Those present were eminent international scientists and naturalists, who are deeply concerned we are moving towards another Eocene period. Worldwide there have been those tempest-like storms such as experienced here at Eastsea. Apart from the storms, I told them about the *Basilosaurus* activity here.'

'That is frightening. We will need to be vigilant and at the same time not to cause alarm,' said Longfield.

The professor continued, 'Unfortunately, there is more. A month ago two fishing boats were attacked by a creature in the Mediterranean Sea off the coast of Egypt. Some of the fishermen were killed. One or two who managed to escape described the creature as a huge monstrous black fish, and at the time a violent storm had suddenly blown up. The area was the natural habitat of the *Basilosaurus* during the Eocene period over thirty million years ago, and the storms were a feature of that period, hopefully, there will not be a resurrection. Some of this I explained to you at the original *Basilosaurus* activity here. My original theory that the creature was dormant and resurrected by a lightning strike may have been incorrect: it could have been alive all along, until it killed itself hitting the coal boat.'

'My goodness! I can understand why secrecy is paramount for the time being,' said Lord Daniel.

Professor Bartholomew thought for a moment.

'I assume the storm we experienced when your father died was the last of late?' he asked.

'That is correct. Nothing since,' replied Lord Daniel.

'The problem is containing this knowledge. The fishing boat attack was news in the Middle East. Fortunately, likely, due to lack of communication and good fortune, it did not spread this far. The storms have been occurring worldwide and have been news. Governments are concerned. Fishermen in the area where the attack happened are not venturing out. Here at Eastsea, I believe your seafaring folk can carry on as usual. There has been no sign of Eocene features recently. The present climate seems to have contained it,' said the professor.

'Doesn't bear thinking about. Had the Eocene period evolved again, what a drastic effect it could have had on seafaring activities worldwide. The *Basilosaurus* could have made their way from the habitat and spread worldwide, said Lord Daniel.

'Let's hope and pray that is an end to it,' said the chief constable.

The other three nodded in agreement, and all four then returned to the main hall for refreshment.

'Where have you been?' asked Lady Helene.

'I wanted to ask the professor for advice regarding nature matters on the estate, and it was rather noisy in here, so we went in the Mayor's robing room,' replied Daniel.

Lady Helene then gave Lord Daniel a roll of paper, which he opened.

'Geoffrey Moulton left it. Been looking for you, but had to

leave. Said he'll be in touch,' she said.

Daniel opened the roll.

'The plans of the new hall,' he said.

Lady Marcia was already at the door, saying thank-yous and goodbyes as people departed.

Daniel and Helene joined her.

'You found him, then, Helene?' observed Lady Marcia.

'I'll tell you later what happened,' replied Daniel.

Twenty-sixth of September

Lady Marcia, Jessica and Cedric Lewis were at the railway station for their journey back to London, being seen off by Lord Daniel, Lady Helene and Francis van Rowhe. Kisses and goodbyes were the order of the day. A few minutes later the train left the platform.

On their way back to the van Rowhe cottage, Daniel stopped the pony and trap on the harbour wall to watch the fishing fleet unload their catch.

'Good afternoon, Your Graces, Mrs van Rowhe,' said Henry Matthews as he approached them.

'Looks like a good catch,' said Daniel.

'Yes, Your Grace. Been quite a few of late,' replied Henry.

That's a good sign – nothing else eating them, thought Daniel.

'Anything,' said Daniel hesitatingly, 'untoward out there?'

'No Sir. May I know why you ask?' asked Henry.

'No reason. Just making conversation. Good day to you,' replied Daniel.

Daniel returned to the trap and the ladies, and then drove away.

A damn strange remark to make in conversation, thought Henry as he returned to his task.

CHAPTER TWENTY-TWO
1896

Thirtieth of September
LORD DANIEL was once again at the site of the new hall, observing the scene with Max Hunworth and Geoffrey Moulton.

The task of marking out the area for the footings of the new hall would be undertaken by Geoffrey Moulton with his team of workers, plus stonemasons and carpenters to do the building.

'Where will you get the sandstone blocks and mortar?' asked Moulton.

'From local quarries. It will be a long drawn out task. Need to get more men to dig the footings. The estate workers have other work to do, but I'm sure they will put in a few hours to help. I cannot ask more of them,' replied Daniel.

'How about laying up the fishing fleet for a while and using the crews,' said Max Hunworth.

'Not feasible. They are getting good catches at present and that is good revenue to add to the insurance money to help with the building of the new hall,' said Daniel.

'Display notices around the area for labour,' suggested Geoffrey Moulton.

The three of them then walked up to the fish auction. Business was brisk and the fish were making good money.

'See what I mean? A good source of income,' observed Daniel.

'Your Grace, maybe we could announce the work that is available at the site of the new hall here at the auction. Good wages would have to be offered as it will be hard work – say one shilling an hour?' said Max Hunworth.

'One shilling an hour, Max? Are you trying to bankrupt me?' asked Daniel in an exasperated tone.

'As I said, it's hard work and a princely sum will be attractive,' replied Max.

'You're right, Max, and we have the funds. All right, go ahead,' said Daniel.

Max Hunworth went up onto the auctioneer's podium to make the announcement.

'Anyone who would care to dig footings for the new hall, please come and see me after the auction. It will be hard work, requiring physical fitness. Therefore payment will be one shilling an hour,' he said.

There were mumblings of approval in the crowd.

After the auction, Max Hunworth was inundated with applicants. Names were taken.

'As soon as you are required, notices will be circulated and put in the local newspaper. As yet the area has to be marked out first,' said Hunworth.

Herbert Noakes approached the desk.

'Mr Hunworth, you paying casual labour one shilling an hour isn't going to please the regular estate workers on nine pennies. Think you'd better do the same for them, unless you want bother,' said Noakes.

'Are you making a threat, Noakes?' asked Hunworth.

'No, Sir, just trying to make a point,' replied Noakes.

'Do as he says, otherwise we'll get no other estate work done; they'll want to be digging footings instead,' said Daniel.

Within the next few days, Geoffrey Moulton and his crew had begun marking out the area for the new hall, covering just over twenty acres. This work was expected to take a few months.

CHAPTER TWENTY-THREE
1896

Second of October
ARCHIE LONGFIELD and Percy Baines, both off duty, were in the Cockleshell drinking ale, socially, with a few of the townsfolk present.

The door opened and Jonathan Lambert entered. He was home on leave in Eastsea. He was an attaché at the British Embassy in Cairo.

'Jonathan, good to see you! Didn't know you were in town,' said Longfield.

The pair shook hands. Percy Baines then made his welcoming retort.

'Arrived yesterday afternoon. Took a month to reach England. We're staying with my wife Agnes' parents, the Smythes, at present and then with mine later,' Jonathan replied, and then bought ale for the three of them. 'The Smythes tell me there's been some strange goings-on here over the past year or so', he said.

Longfield and Baines between them recounted to Lambert the storms, the *Basilosaurus*, the gold treasure and oil phenomena.

'Around here? Extraordinary! The *Basilosaurus* were native to the habitat of the Red Sea. Those storms and the *Basilosaurus* recently occurred in the Middle East. As an officer of the British Embassy, I learnt that international scientists were deeply concerned that the world could be entering another Eocene period from over thirty million years ago. When fishing boats were attacked in the Red

Sea off the coast of the Eastern Desert by ferocious mammals, almost certainly *Basilosaurus*, they were convinced. Fortunately our present climate curtailed the reoccurrence of the Eocene period and after thorough investigation the scientists are satisfied all is well,' he said.

Amongst those in the bar was Henry Matthews. He'd been eavesdropping on Jonathan Lambert's conversation, and was now in deep thought.

It was ten of the clock at night when Daniel Courtenay reacted to the loud banging on the door of Francis van Rowhe's cottage.

Upon opening it, Daniel found an angry and rather drunk Henry Matthews.

'I want a word with you, Daniel Courtenay. Some time ago you asked me after a fishing trip if there was anything untoward in the North Sea. Just realised what you meant, after hearing a conversation in the Cockleshell,' he said.

'What's that got to do with me?' asked Daniel.

'A lot! You thought there could still be *Basilosaurus* activity in the North Sea and you let the fishing fleet carry on working, not sure whether or not it was safe,' replied Henry.

'I'm sorry,' said Daniel apologetically.

'Sorry? Not good enough, playing with lives. The job is dangerous enough as it is,' said Henry.

Henry Matthews then punched Lord Daniel Courtenay on the nose, causing it to bleed. He then hurried away from the cottage.

'Whatever happened to you?' asked Helene, who was sitting with her mother as Daniel entered the parlour.

'Henry Matthews hit me, drunk and arguing about fishing,' replied Daniel.

Helene then set about treating Daniel.

'You'll have to report him to the Constabulary,' suggested Francis.

'No. I feel rather ashamed and probably deserved it to a degree. I put the fishing fleet in what could have been a dangerous situation. I was obsessed with the revenue they were bringing in to help fund the building of the new hall,' said Daniel.

Third of October

Henry and Susie Matthews were having breakfast when there was a knock at the door. When Henry opened it, Daniel Courtenay was standing there.

Daniel spoke before Henry could utter a word.

'I've come to apologise, Henry. Should never have let the fishing go on without certainty. Became so focused with the expense of the building of the new Hall that I'd overlooked the people who graft for my good as well as their own and do a good job. Fishing was bringing in good revenue,' he said.

Henry was pleased and grateful for this encounter.

'I shouldn't have reacted in that way, and sorry you were punched. Thank you for being understanding. Your father was a well-respected employer and you, apart from this matter, are following in his footsteps. Come in and have some vittles,' he said.

Henry and Daniel shook hands and joined Susie in the parlour.

After Daniel had departed Henry noticed a puzzled look on Susie's face and explained what had happened.

CHAPTER TWENTY-FOUR
1896-1897

Fourth of December
TWO MONTHS HAD since passed. The footings for the new Hall were well on the way to completion. Workmen had laboured hard for their wages. However, there was one casualty. Herbert Noakes, a Courtenay family worker for forty-odd years, had delusions that he could still labour as hard as he did when a young man. Sadly, the effort was too much, and one day he collapsed and died of a heart attack. Others suffered broken bones, cuts and bruises.

Lady Helene announced she was with child, which would be born in a few months.

Eastsea life continued busily, the fishing fleet netting good catches, which pleased Lord Daniel Courtenay.

Later in the month the festive season of Christmas was observed.

Sixth of January
For the first time in its history, Eastsea was experiencing prosperity. The payments evolving from the hall footings work was putting extra money into the household budgets of the families of men labouring there daily, working on the estate and farms, in the evening, digging footings by beacon light, at times in cold and wet conditions. Geoffrey Moulton's crew worked by day, thus there was continuous digging.

Prosperity had given local traders a boost. An ironmonger

supplied many shovels and picks to the Eastsea Hall Estate for the digging. Likewise drapers were providing new shoes and clothes for children, fashion dresses for the ladies, and suits for the men. So it went on. Toby Hughes' takings at the Cockleshell increased, for one or two extra tankards of ale could be afforded.

With the footings completed, the next stage was getting the building material produced. Lord Daniel Courtenay and Max Hunworth were planning on opening up a redundant works on the estate. These works were used in the building of the original hall.

Men that had worked on the digging of the footings were worn out and tired, and wanted rest. They hoped that Lord Daniel Courtenay would not be pressing them to get started on the new building for at least a month.

Lady Marcia, Jessica and Cedric visited from London to see the family and the progress that had been made on the rebuilding, staying at the Royal Hotel in Eastsea. Impressed, they returned to London after a few days.

The men organised a meeting amongst themselves with a view to meeting with Lord Daniel Courtenay regarding having a month's break from the building programme. It was agreed that Ephraim Howard and Robbie Dewhurst would be the representatives at the meeting between employer and employees.

Eleventh of January

Four men sat around a table in the estate office.

'What can I do for you?' asked Lord Daniel Courtenay.

Ephraim Howard prepared himself and spoke hesitatingly.

'Your Grace, the men that worked on digging the footings are requesting that the start of the production of building materials is put off for a month. They are worn out and tired,' he said.

Lord Daniel looked at both Ephraim and Robbie Dewhurst sympathetically.

'Don't look so worried, the pair of you. I do agree, and apologise for not thinking of such an arrangement and offering it. A lot of hard work was done and the men responded well. They deserve a break. I'm sure you're in agreement, Max,' he said.

'I am. Sound idea. Hopefully afterwards they will be refreshed for times that will be measured in years rather than months,' said Max Hunworth.

Robbie Dewhurst then put forward a suggestion.

'Maybe breaks such as we are suggesting will be convenient?' he said.

'Of course they will,' replied Lord Daniel.

'Thank you for your understanding. We weren't sure you would agree, Your Grace, knowing how anxious you are to get the building completed,' said Ephraim Howard.

'It will be a very long-term job and I need the co-operation of the workers, so they must be satisfied with things,' replied Lord Daniel.

The four then made cordial exchanges on the outcome of the meeting and agreed that the time off would begin after the proposals had been put to the workers and accepted.

Thirteenth of January

Soon after, a meeting of the workers was convened. Ephraim Howard and Robbie Dewhurst reported the details Some workers accepted the proposals, others were against. Discord entered the proceedings. Jack Brooks, wanting fair pay for hard labour, Larry Granger with a similar attitude, had the support of the majority of the men.

Jack Brooks raised the issue.

'It's going to be a lot harder building that hall. We want more money per hour. Daniel Courtenay wants that hall built. He's going to have to pay for it,' he said.

There was a groundswell of approval from the floor, and

clapping and cheering.

'How much do you want?' asked Ephraim Howard.

'One shilling and three pennies an hour,' replied Larry Granger.

Again there was lots of support from those assembled.

'I'm not sure His Lordship will agree,' said Robbie Dewhurst.

There were mumblings of discord amongst the men.

'Then find out, for no work will be done until we have a satisfactory settlement,' said Jack Brooks.

The next couple of days were taken up with meetings.

'They want what?' shouted Lord Daniel.

Ephraim Howard and Robbie Dewhurst were in a meeting with Lord Daniel and Max Hunworth.

'One shilling and threepence an hour,' replied Ephraim nervously.

'Who incited them to do this,' asked Lord Daniel.

'Jack Brooks and Larry Granger,' replied Robbie.

Max Hunworth looked self-satisfied.

'Thought as much. All of the men worked arduously, especially those two, and want good payment,' he said.

'We shall have to check the finances,' said Lord Daniel.

There was another meeting of the workers. However, on this occasion, Ephraim and Robbie were not addressing them. Before them were standing Lord Daniel and Max Hunworth.

Lord Daniel spoke.

'Gentlemen, I'm prepared to meet your demands. You are all probably aware that I would like to see the new Hall completed in my lifetime. I do realise this may not be possible. The original Hall took around one hundred and fifty years to complete. Let me put things in terms easy to understand. The usual rate for normal estate work, and the building of the new Hall – one shilling and threepence an hour. Two working parties will be convened.

Working for the duration of four hours at a time for fourteen days then a break, for the same period of time. The process for building the hall will not be interrupted. Helene and I await the birth of our first child, who, hopefully, in time, will be able to continue the work, as many of your children will, then their children, and so on. The new Eastsea Hall will be a monument to us all.'

'Are you all in agreement?' he then asked.

The assemblage, even Jack Brooks and Larry Granger, exploded in rapturous applause to confirm their agreement.

The time taken with the various meetings took up almost a month, so was defined as the break.

Twenty-third of February
Work then began in earnest restoring the old works. Daily toil continued. Time sharing labour evenings; the men, a month later, had production of heavy slabs underway. Sand and lime from the estate quarry were mixed to make mortar.

The manufacture of the slabs proved to be even more arduous than the digging of the footings. The slabs must have weighed a ton or more, and were six feet high, two feet wide and four inches thick. Shuttering was made up so as to make six at a time.

Geoffrey Moulton's plans were for the footings to be two yards deep. The slabs would then be built vertically twelve high for the structure of the building and the design to conform to the contemporary fashion of the halls and mansions of England. On completion, the building would be over seventy feet high and covering twenty acres.

The works had been in full production for a month. The men were enthusiastic in making the building materials. Mixing the sand and lime for the mortar proved to be really hard work. The mortar was then poured into the shuttering to make the slabs.

When the mortar had set the shuttering was taken away. Leather straps were then wrapped around the slabs, which were dragged by several men to a storage area. So the procedure continued.

Lord Daniel and Max Hunworth were pleased with the progress.

CHAPTER TWENTY-FIVE
1897

Twenty-seventh of February
DOCTOR MOORE confirmed that Lady Helene was in the condition of being with child. Lord Daniel was hoping for a boy as it was customary for a male to be the Lord of the Manor when the time came to hand on the title. Within his heart, boy or girl, Daniel wished the child good health.

The manufacturing of the slabs continued. Horse drawn carts were used to bring the sand and lime from the quarry.

Sadly, Jack Brooks was crushed to death by a slab when a leather strap snapped. The straps could be weakened over a period of time as a result of the sheer weight carried. Jack's son, Bobby, aged sixteen, took his father's place in the work force.

Geoffrey Moulton's crew had been working on the building of the footings for a while.

With the death of Jack Brooks, the morale of the men waned. Working by day on the estate or a farm, they were worn out. Neither Larry Granger nor Bobby had Jack's charisma to drive the men.

As time went on, fathers grew older and sons took their place. They could see the work was energy sapping, so got less and less enthusiastic on the building and were content with the work on the estate and farms. The extra income had been useful. Families relied on their men. However, their motto was 'health rather than wealth'. Lord Daniel and Max Hunworth tried to encourage them, but to no avail.

Production at the works ground to a halt. Geoffrey Moulton brought in more craftsmen and workmen to keep it going, so as to maintain work on the building.

Geoffrey Moulton, due to the attitude of the estate workers, organised a rota system. In time he had six teams, each consisting of thirty men, rotating, each team working for a week and then having a week off. From time to time, some of the estate workers would help out. Maybe the extra income was useful when a member of a family required new clothes or shoes; or for purchasing household items and luxury food such as chicken.

With the extra labour, building and preparing materials, progress was not going to plan, a matter of great concern to Lord Daniel and Max Hunworth.

'At the present rate, I won't see the building finished,' said Lord Daniel.

'Afraid it appears that way,' replied Max Hunworth.

CHAPTER TWENTY-SIX
1897

Sixth of March
'WHAT WAS that noise?' asked Lord Daniel, waking up startled.

The cottage was shaking, but this ceased after a couple of minutes.

Lady Helene and Francis were soon about.

'What's happening?' asked Helene.

Daniel thought for a moment.

'I can only assume, considering the movement, an earth tremor,' he replied.

There were anxious townspeople outside.

Daniel told them his assumption.

'Everyone go back indoors and stay up for an hour in case it happens again, and then when that time has passed and all of you are satisfied it is safe, go back to bed,' suggested Daniel.

'What is going to happen next?' said a rather frightened Francis.

Inspector Longfield was active in the town with his constables, reassuring townsfolk after the tremor. Captain Baines was also around. Longfield more or less gave the same advice as Lord Daniel.

The occupants of the van Rowhe cottage were still asleep later that morning and were woken by someone at the door.

Upon answering, Daniel found Max Hunworth standing there.

'My apologies for disturbing you but I think you would want to know that the tremor last night caused some damage on the estate,' he said.

'Come in, Max, and have some breakfast,' said Daniel.

Helene and Francis entered the parlour.

'Good morning, Max,' said Helene. This salutation was echoed by Francis.

Francis prepared toast and mugs of tea.

'The parts of the new Hall already erected have collapsed, and the works is a pile of rubble,' said Max.

On their way to the estate, Lord Daniel and Max Hunworth met Longfield and Baines.

'Anything to report, Your Lordship?' asked Longfield.

'Going up to the estate to look at some damage,' replied Daniel.

'Strangely, and fortunately, there were no injuries or damage in the town. Looked in the Constabulary records and discovered one occurred seventy years ago — a fact confirmed by some elder townsfolk. Again no injuries or damage,' said Longfield.

'What is going to happen next?' remarked Captain Baines.

Lord Daniel and Max Hunworth were observing the damage.

'Fortunately just this,' said Daniel. 'Why, Max?' he asked.

'The foundations at the front of the hall needed more time to settle. Regarding the works so we concentrated on the inside. Outside the mortar needed repointing,' replied Max.

Henry Matthews and the crew were preparing the *Canute* for a fishing trip.

'Father, do you think it is safe to go out today, considering the tremor last night?' asked Dick.

Isaac Morris and Peter Smith were of the same mind.

'It'll be all right. That was hours ago. We need to keep up the good catches. I hope it's not driven the fish away. They may well have survived here,' replied Henry.

The fleet then set off for the fishing grounds.

Lord Daniel was looking deep in thought.

'A penny for them, My Lord,' said Max Hunworth.

'I've heard that Horace Wilding the banker has died.'

'That is giving you food for thought, My Lord?' asked Max.

'With respect, Max, I'll keep my thoughts to myself for the time being,' replied Daniel.

The fleet was in the fishing grounds.

'Two hours, and hardly anything,' said Henry Matthews.

The rest of the fleet were just as unsuccessful.

'Let's give it another couple of hours,' suggested Dick Matthews.

The fleet agreed.

Those hours passed without much success.

'That's it. In my opinion the earthquake has affected the fishing, and Lord Daniel will not be happy. The success we were having before helped to finance the rebuilding of the Hall,' said Henry.

Eighth of March

Lord Daniel, Max Hunworth and Geoffrey Moulton were at the scene of the collapsed structures of the new Hall.

'I'm not going to be able to start again. A quantity of the insurance money has been used getting as far as we have. The revenue from the fishing fleet has diminished, again due to the earthquake. Shoals have left the fishing grounds,' said Lord Daniel.

'That is a shame, My Lord, but I do understand. With help you may be able to continue. Try the insurance company, or get a bank loan,' replied Geoffrey Moulton. 'If not, what will you do?' he asked.

'It's devastating after all that hard work,' interjected Max Hunworth.

'I'm deliberating options at present,' replied Daniel.

On his arrival back at the cottage, Daniel discovered he had a visitor. Professor Bartholomew was in the parlour having vittles with Helene and Francis.

'Hello, Professor. What a pleasant surprise,' he said.

'My Lord, decided to see if I could help in any way on hearing of the earthquake, though I'm not sure what I can do,' he said.

'Thank you for your concern, Professor,' said Daniel, and he explained his reasons for not being able to start building again.

'That is absolutely awful. I met Inspector Longfield on my way here and he gave me an insight into the earthquake situation. Nothing like it for seventy years, apparently. Phenomenal how terra firma can be disturbed for a few minutes,' said the professor.

'We have not got enough room to accommodate you here at the cottage,' said Daniel apologetically.

'No problems; I'm already booked in at the Cockleshell,' replied the professor.

Tenth of March

Lord Daniel, Max Hunworth and Henry Matthews were in the estate office discussing the situation regarding the fishing fleet.

'Not much out there at the moment then, Henry?' asked Daniel.

'No, My Lord,' replied Henry.

Lord Daniel and Max Hunworth thought for a while.

'We could find work for the fishermen on the estate during the lean time,' suggested Max.

Henry looked disconsolate, due to not being keen on estate work.

'All right, if it has to be,' he said.

'You've not been out for a couple of days, have you?' asked Daniel.

'No, My Lord,' replied Henry.

'Go tomorrow. Professor Bartholomew suggests that without

further disturbance, the fish could be back just as quickly as they left,' said Daniel.

Thirteenth of March
Eastsea Town Hall was full of townspeople listening to Professor Bartholomew give a talk on the whys and wherefores of earthquakes. This was the result of Lord Daniel taking the professor to task after the remark the professor made that he wasn't sure how he could help. He hoped that his talk would reassure the townspeople.

The townsfolk appeared to be comfortable with the professor's explanation, and normal life returned. This was also the case with the fishing fleet.

CHAPTER TWENTY-SEVEN
1897

Seventeenth of March
DANIEL COURTENAY entered the cottage with an air of confidence.

'Why are you looking so pleased and satisfied?' asked Helene.

He was pleased, though this feeling was tinged with sadness.

'Horace Wilding has died, and Town Green House is up for sale,' he replied.

'Why would that concern you?' asked Helene.

'I'm thinking about putting in an offer,' he replied.

Helene looked thoughtful.

'I see. As we are now unable to rebuild the Hall, Town Green House would be the next best thing,' she said.

'When Geoffrey Moulton and I were looking at houses on Town Green, this one caught his eye,' said Daniel.

'Can we afford to make an offer?' asked Helene.

'Max Hunworth and I have checked our finances, and Gilbert Harrison has also, and we can. There is still some insurance money, and revenue from the wood yard; and the fishing picking up again will help,' replied Daniel.

'It's a wonderful idea, Daniel. There will be fixtures and fittings to be considered. Both mothers could live here,' said Helene with excitement.

'I shall instruct Hugh Houseman to make an offer of five hundred guineas,' said Daniel.

Twentieth of March
Geoffrey Moulton gave his full support for the purchase, and the offer was accepted by the Wilding family.

Inspector Longfield conducted a security assessment of Town Green House at the request of Lord Daniel. Having been the former residence of a banker, very little needed updating.

Twenty-seventh of March
Following the security assessment, another trip was made to Bishops Lynne for the purchase of fixtures and fittings. Town Green House was then prepared by the respective craftsmen.

By the end of July, the residence was ready for occupation. Thus Town Green House became the ancestral home of the Courtenay family. Lady Marcia and Francis van Rowhe would also reside there.

However, destiny decided that this would not be the case for one of these ladies. Several business visits to Town Green House by Hugh Houseman proved that pleasure was also mixed in with Francis van Rowhe. Houseman had divorced his wife Clara on the grounds of adultery with a businessman in Bishops Lynne. Shortly after, Hugh married Francis, with the blessing of Helene, and Francis went to live in Bishops Lynne.

During the following months life in Eastsea continued as normal, with nothing phenomenal manifesting. Occasional criminal activity or drunkenness was dealt with by the Constabulary. The fishing fleet were bringing in good returns.

Twenty-seventh of September
Lady Helene gave birth to a son, an heir for Lord Daniel. He would be named Lancelot Algernon Daniel. Lord Daniel was happy; the birth had been straightforward, the greatest joy being mother and child in good health.

The Hunworths had quarters at Town Green House. Amelia carried on with her housekeeping duties and the two maids, although their families lived in Eastsea, continued to live in. Max would commute to the estate office either by pony and trap or horseback. Outhouses at the property had been converted to stables. Upon the death of Herbert Noakes, Sam Morgan became the ostler.

The fishing fleet had a slow period, but things quickly picked up again, and the fleet was making good catches once more – a fact that pleased Lord Daniel and Henry Matthews.

Twentieth of October

Lady Marcia, Lord Daniel and Lady Helene were in the drawing room of Town Green House.

'Mother, you wish to speak to us?' asked Daniel.

Marcia composed herself and began.

'As you are both aware, Gilbert Harrison's wife died a few months ago,' she said.

Daniel and Helene looked thoughtful.

'We are,' replied Helene.

Daniel interjected.

'Why would that be a matter for our deliberation?' he asked.

'Gilbert has opened a practice in Lincoln's Inn Fields in London and will be living there most of the time, but will continue to service us and the rest of his clients around here,' replied Marcia.

'So this is what you have to tell us, Mother? Rather dramatic of you, is it not?' asked Daniel.

Marcia hesitated, unaware of what the reaction would be to her next piece of news.

'No, there is more. Gilbert has asked me to marry him,' she replied.

Daniel and Helene were taken aback.

'Although we are sorry that you are going, it's wonderful! My mother has found happiness, never expected again, and now you. I'm delighted, as Daniel should be,' said Helene.

Marcia looked questioningly at Daniel.

'Well?' she asked.

Daniel thought for a moment.

'Did you agree to do so?' he asked.

'Of course I did,' Marcia replied.

Daniel sat quietly, with a playful kind of look.

'It's a bit of a shock, Mother. I like Gilbert and would be honoured to have him as a stepfather. You have my blessing,' he said.

'Thank you for your understanding, both of you. I have always liked and respected Gilbert, even before he asked me to marry him. He was so compassionate when your father died,' she said.

'Have you told Jessica and Cedric?' Daniel asked.

'We are going to London tomorrow. Gilbert has some business and I shall see them then,' said Marcia.

'I'm sure you'll get their blessing,' said Helene.

'So am I, Mother,' said Daniel.

The Hunsworths and the rest of the staff were delighted on hearing of the forthcoming marriage of Lady Marcia and Gilbert Harrison.

As expected, Jessica and Cedric gave their blessing to the couple.

Gilbert and Marcia married a month later.

CHAPTER TWENTY-EIGHT
1897

Fifth of December
INSPECTOR LONGFIELD and Captain Baines were walking the Eastsea foreshore after checking for damage in the town following a ferocious storm in the early hours, similar to those experienced in the past.

'Can't see any damage or phenomenal activity,' said Longfield.

Captain Baines looked relieved.

'Thank God for that,' he replied.

On the other hand, Lord Daniel Courtenay and Max Hunworth were on the estate observing an amazing sight. About four acres of land was spouting steam high into the air.

'What on earth is happening?' asked Daniel.

Max looked thoughtful.

'They, I believe, are called geysers. That is about as much as I know,' he replied.

'None of the storms of late, then after last night, we discover this activity. It's frightening and weird,' said Daniel.

Longfield and Baines arrived on the scene.

'Good afternoon, My Lord, Mr Hunworth,' said Longfield.

Lord Daniel and Max Hunworth turned around and appeared surprised.

'Hello, Longfield, Baines,' replied Daniel.

Longfield and Baines both gave respective salutations.

'I can see you're surprised to see us. Heard about it in the town. Checked the foreshore earlier; nothing untoward. Thought we had got away with it this time,' said Longfield.

The news had certainly reached the town. A crowd were making their way towards the estate.

'Don't let them get too close; the steam is boiling hot,' said Captain Baines.

Longfield was looking thoughtful.

'Shall have to get the infantry here, posthaste. Your Lordship, Captain Baines, Mr Hunworth: please keep the people at bay for the time being. In the meantime, I'll get the constables here to take over. Good afternoon,' said Longfield, who then headed off to Eastsea.

'I shall have to contact Professor Bartholomew,' said Daniel.

The fishing fleet had been out and had made successful catches.

'When the catch has been unloaded onto the carts for it to be taken to the ice houses on the estate, we'll hitch a lift to have a look,' said Henry Matthews on hearing of the geysers.

Most of the fishermen were interested, and sat on the top of the loads of fish. On their arrival at the estate they found a mass of people had congregated to see the phenomenon. By this time the infantry were in control, along with Inspector Longfield and the constables.

Seventh of December – afternoon

Lord Daniel and Max Hunworth were at the railway station awaiting the arrival of Professor Bartholomew. The train arrived and they looked out for him as the passengers alighted.

'Lord Daniel Courtenay?' asked a voice behind them.

They both turned around. To their surprise, standing there was an attractive young woman.

'You were expecting Professor Bartholomew?' she asked.

'To be frank, we were,' Daniel replied.

'He sends his apologies. Unavoidably detained at the last minute. I'm Vivien Stanwell, an undergraduate at the museum. The professor believes I shall be able to advise on this matter,' she said.

'By the way, this is Max Hunworth, the estate manager,' said Daniel.

Salutations were exchanged.

Lord Daniel, Max Hunworth and Vivien Stanwell arrived at the scene. She made some observations, took some books out from her case, and studied a few pages.

'They are geysers, caused most likely by the disturbance of sulphur under the surface, steam is produced, then blows due to pressure. These geysers occur in New Zealand and certain other areas of the world, but, as far as I know, never in this country,' she said.

'We'll accommodate you at our home in Eastsea,' said Daniel.

This offer pleased Vivien Stanwell for she had been wondering where to stay, though Professor Bartholomew had told her that she would most likely receive the Courtenays' hospitality.

'Thank you. The professor had spoken of your circumstances and the tragedy surrounding your family,' she said.

The initial novelty of the geysers slowly waned, and the crowd dispersed.

Lady Helene was just as surprised on being introduced to Vivien Stanwell.

'Don't be embarrassed, Your Ladyship. His Lordship and Mr Hunworth were just as surprised as you,' she said.

'You're most welcome,' replied Lady Helene.

The geysers had now been active for a week or more. Lord Daniel, Max Hunworth and Vivien Stanwell strived to reach an explanation. Around this period of time, Max Hunworth made a suggestion.

'Why don't we try and harness this steam and power to some practical use?' he asked.

Lord Daniel took up this idea.

Two steam engineers from the railway company, which was pioneered by George Stephenson, came and assessed the situation, and put forward the idea that heating the estate workers' cottages could be achieved. However, this was discounted when the geysers began activating only periodically.

Unable to give any further advice or explanation, Vivien Stanwell returned to London.

Fifteenth of December

The geysers continued to activate spontaneously.

Eastsea was preparing itself for Christmas. Snowfall was helping to give a seasonal atmosphere. After the past tumultuous few months people were hoping for a troublefree time and were going to celebrate with enjoyment. Shops and houses were all decorated.

Town Green House was also getting into the spirit of things. Although not the same as being at the Hall, there was a joyous atmosphere within the house.

Amelia Hunworth was supervising the arrangements in the kitchen. A full house would be the order of the day in due time.

Apart from Lord Daniel, Lady Helene and Lancelot; Lady Marcia Courtenay-Harrison and Gilbert, Jessica and Cedric, and Francis and Hugh Houseman would be staying. Also staying would be Professor Bartholomew and his wife Louise, the professor wishing for a hassle-free visit and invited on this premise.

Amelia, Max and David Hunworth would be celebrating in their quarters, with Henry, Susie, Dick and Mary – who was now heavy with child – and their son Cedric.

Inspector Longfield and the constables were hoping for a quiet Christmas period to spend more time with their families, although each officer would be required to spend some time manning the police station. Sentiments endorsed by Captain Baines.

This proved to be an exceptionally quiet period with only a few cases of disturbing the peace or felons unable to afford presents.

Twenty-third of December

Town Green House was now fully decorated for the occasion. Log fires were burning in all the rooms. The Christmas tree stood majestically in a tastefully decorated drawing room.

All the guests had arrived.

Later in the day they were gathered in the drawing room, drinking mulled wine and eating hot mince pies.

There was chatter amongst them.

The wine and the heat of the fire were making some folk sleepy. Thoughts and opinions would be to the fore with others.

'It is my belief that women should be given the vote in Great Britain,' declared Lady Marcia.

The rest of the party were taken aback.

Gilbert Harrison, who was asleep, or appeared to be, as Lady Marcia assumed, piped up, 'I've told Marcia to keep those ideas to herself, although there has been a lobby in America for fifty-odd years, and other countries are getting involved. Hopefully this policy will never be adopted here. Wife of a solicitor mixed up in this nonsense. Could ruin my reputation.'

Lady Marcia then stood up to her full height.

'Gilbert Harrison, that is just the sort of attitude from most of the male species. You think that women do not have the acumen, but they have to use their sense each day running a home, bringing up a family; and they should be given the right to vote for what they believe in and who should represent them in Parliament… and female Members of Parliament would not be out of order,' she said.

The other ladies in the room gave their endorsement, with clapping and cheering. Marcia then fell back into her chair.

The men tried to give their various opinions but Daniel interjected.

'I don't want to hear any more of this over Christmas, or any other time,' he said.

The appearance of Amelia Hunworth to announce dinner was ready to be served brought serenity to the proceedings.

For the remainder of Christmas, nothing more was said of the issue, although when there were no men present, the women gave their opinions to each other. They all wanted to be able to vote.

Christmas Period

As expected, the Constabulary were kept busy, with the usual over indulgence of ale causing merriment and mayhem together with an odd shoplifting spree.

The folk of Eastsea were enjoying a time of spiritual uplift, entertaining their relations and friends at each of their respective abodes.

This was the case at Town Green House, Lord and Lady Courtenays' guests receiving the best of hospitality with fine Christmas fare and party games.

Max Hunworth made a daily trip to the estate and each time reported that the geysers were still active from time to time.

Each day, after supper was finished, and the clearing away and washing-up completed, Amelia and Max Hunworth, along with their guests, would join Lord and Lady Courtenay and their guests

– the ladies staying in the drawing room eating mince pies and drinking wine whilst the men retired to the library for brandy and cigars.

When on their own the men would discuss, amongst other matters, the subject of women wanting the vote.

'I suppose it could happen in time,' said Lord Daniel.

'They should be allowed. There are strong-willed women with a lot about them. Take Vivien Stanwell as an example,' said Professor Bartholomew.

'Men vote, not women, their place is at home bringing up children, preparing vittles,' said Henry Matthews. 'What are you two thinking about?' he asked.

However, still the ladies would discuss the matter amongst themselves. Their opinions did not vary. They wanted to be able to vote.

During the middle of this period, on one of his daily visits to the estate, Max Hunworth discovered there was not any geyser activity, and there did not appear to have been any recently as the snow around the area was packed hard. As he proceeded he met Sam Morgan and some other estate workers, and asked them about the geyser activity.

'Well, Sir, a while after you left yesterday the geysers, as usual, stopped spouting. I thought it to be merely one of the inactive times. However, since then they have not been active at all. Most probably that is the end of them,' Sam replied.

'Hopefully you are right. They were not of any practical use,' replied Max Hunworth.

Upon his return to Town Green House, Max reported to Lord Daniel the matter regarding the geysers.

'Another of those phenomenal happenings after that recent storm,' said Lord Daniel.

New Year's Eve
The party was in full swing at Town Green House. Everyone was in good spirits and looking forward to a settled future.

Things were in much the same vein in the rest of Eastsea.

Throughout the evening the parties proceeded.

On the stroke of midnight cries of 'Happy New Year' could be heard, and again that spirit of hope could be felt.

CHAPTER TWENTY-NINE
1898

Second of January
The usual busy period for the Constabulary dealing with public disorder and burglary offences, which were being heard by the town magistrate, Stacey Oldman. Fines of a few shillings were imposed upon the drunks. The felons, apart from fines, could expect to spend a week or two in the Constabulary cells.

Mary Matthews gave birth to a second child, christened Susan Amelia, so named after both grandmothers.

Fifth of January
During the afternoon, Amelia Hunworth answered the bell ringing at the door of Town Green House.

A visitor was shown to the drawing room.

'Miss Vivien Stanwell,' announced Amelia to Lord Daniel and Lady Helene.

'This is a pleasant surprise,' said Daniel.

Vivien Stanwell then explained, 'First of all, apologies for turning up without prior word. I'm in Eastsea for an interview at the museum. Whilst here recently regarding the geysers, I discovered the curator was retiring and there would be a vacancy, and I made an application. Me having since graduated, Professor Bartholomew has given me a reference, and I meet with the trustees tomorrow. By the way, I understand the geyser activity is dormant.'

'Yes it is, and I do hope you are successful,' said Daniel.

'Have you arranged accommodation?' asked Helene.

'At the Cockleshell,' replied Vivien.

'It would be marvellous to have you live in Eastsea, not only for your company, but it would be helpful that an expert is around with all these phenomenal things happening. Won't have to keep troubling the professor,' said Daniel.

'You could have stayed with us,' said Helene.

'The professor said as much but I did not want to intrude,' said Vivien.

'I'll get some tea and scones organised,' said Helene as she left the room.

'Were I to be successful, there is accommodation with the job,' replied Vivien.

The door opened and Helene entered, followed by Amelia with the vittles.

Tea and scones finished, an hour or so of chatter, and it was time for Vivien to leave.

'Good luck for tomorrow, although I don't think you need it,' said Helene.

This sentiment was echoed by Daniel, who added, 'Let us know the outcome of the interview.'

'Thank you for your hospitality,' said Vivien as she departed.

On her arrival back at the Cockleshell, Vivien turned a few heads, especially those of Toby Hughes' son Michael and Peter Smith's son Saul.

There was still a lobby proceeding to get votes for women. However, Parliament did not get a bill put forward and so the issue went on. Women vowed to fight on, and were getting militant in their frustration.

The fishing fleet was still a good source of revenue for Lord Daniel, having successful trips and keeping the fishermen gainfully employed.

The lifeboat the *William Cartwright* had proved its worth over the previous months, making several rescues of crew from stricken vessels and on one occasion getting a captain's wife, who had gone into labour, ashore to hospital. Indeed the captain and his wife, who had a boy, were so grateful that they named him Henry after Henry Matthews, the coxswain.

Life in Eastsea was deemed to be settled for a while as folk went about their everyday business, and the remainder of the year proved to be peaceful.

CHAPTER THIRTY
1899

January
VIVIEN STANWELL stood outside the museum taking in the scenery and the crisp cool air of the early morning, thinking how fortunate she was at what had been achieved: living in a beautiful part of the country and the proverbial country cottage in which she resided; the friends she had made; the advances from Saul Smith and Michael Hughes, rebuffed by her, although they were kindly lads; a career in an environment she loved; the prejudices of the museum trustees that had been overcome. Common sense had prevailed as they realised her potential.

Seventh of March
Lady Marcia Courtenay-Harrison and husband Gilbert were on a visit to Eastsea, partly to see the family at Town Green House, but also to give substance to the Votes for Women campaign at a meeting in the Town Hall.

Originally the Town Council were unsure as to whether to allow the meeting to proceed, but after a lengthy debate they decided to let it go ahead for, strange as it was, there were councillors who thought ladies should be given the chance to put their points over locally. A ballot was taken, proving equal votes for and against. The chairman had his casting vote, allowing the meeting to go ahead. Considered by some male traditionalists that the wrong decision had been made.

'I hope he knows what he's doing,' said one opinionated gentleman.

'Votes for women must never be upheld by the government, the consequences will be unthinkable,' remarked another gentleman.

These views were endorsed by others.

The meeting was now in session and chaired by the Mayor.

Inspector Longfield and the constables were in attendance, expecting arguments and prepared to quell any.

'My Lord, ladies and gentlemen, please let Lady Marcia have her say, and then afterwards you may make any comments,' said the Mayor.

Lady Marcia stood up to a mixed reception and began.

'The issue of votes for women must be dealt with with some urgency, for us women are far more resourceful than given credit for. Keeping house and bringing up a family requires a great deal of tenacity. On the other hand, women have other qualities. Take, as an example, Miss Vivien Stanwell, curator of the museum. She worked in the mainly male dominated British Museum in London, but by her tenacity and competence she won the confidence of the men. An occurrence of a natural phenomenon first brought her to Eastsea. The rest is history. Please make yourself known, Miss Stanwell.'

At this Vivien Stanwell stood up, to loud applause from the women. The men had mixed feelings.

Lady Marcia continued, 'If the Whigs and peers of Parliament do not acknowledge our cause soon, there will be riots and mayhem on the streets of this country. There are groups who share our feelings, and they are growing in number, and will in time have an organisation with strength and ambition. Ladies, please, think about the cause for women to have the right to vote. I do not want arguments to occur in households – men do have a strong opinion – but rational discussion, for one day in the not-too-distant future, hopefully, women will get the chance to vote. Make no mistake, we are a determined species. Thank you.'

There had been the occasional bout of barracking but the

assemblage was now in uproar, with a mixture for and against the argument.

Most likely heated debates would be the order of the day from now on.

'Has anyone got any comments?' asked the Mayor.

'Yes. I have,' said Henry Matthews. 'It cannot be allowed to happen. Men have always been the breadwinners. A woman's place is in the home,' he said.

This sentiment was echoed by a large number of men.

Susie Matthews stood up in defiance and shouted, 'Votes for women.'

She received a look from Henry that said it all: just wait until we get home.

Lady Helene, Francis Houseman and Amelia Hunworth gave support to the campaign, having made their opinions heard in the past. Lord Daniel, Hugh Houseman and Max Hunworth were aware of this. Gilbert Harrison came in for some ridicule for allowing his wife to advocate such an issue.

'Your practice could suffer, Harrison,' said one of his clients.

Harrison shrugged his shoulders.

'You've seen how strong-willed Lady Marcia is, and there are many more of the same mind. You'll see, in time women will achieve the vote. They have the determination to succeed, and will not falter until they do,' he replied.

Francis Houseman organised another such meeting in Bishops Lynne for Lady Marcia to address. The same sentiments manifested – women with their opinions, and men making their voices heard in opposition.

Meetings were arranged around the country as the campaign lifted the spirits of women, especially those with ambition.

CHAPTER THIRTY-ONE
1900

March

THE SOUND OF a newborn child could be heard coming from the cottage of a young man and his previously pregnant young wife.

In attendance was the self-appointed town midwife, Dolly Byrd, who had declared that the young woman had given birth to a boy.

Having taking over from her mother, Dolly had been providing this service for many years and was still going strong although in her seventies. She had delivered many children and both the young man and his wife in her time as well as other parents and their children.

Earlier during the day, the young man had run to Dolly's cottage.

'I'm on my way. Have towels and hot water ready,' she said, as she would always say on these occasions.

Dolly had no real medical qualifications. Doctor Moore had many times chastised her, asking for the practice to stop. Dolly took no notice, and women were comfortable with her bedside manner.

When he became aware, Doctor Moore would visit the latest additions to the Eastsea population. Dolly, on hearing of his interference, always confronted him.

'Don't you think I'm capable of caring for a mother and child?'

she would say, to which Doctor Moore would reply, 'No, I don't believe you are.'

Both had utter contempt for each other.

Doctor Moore had even got the Medical Council involved at one time, to no avail.

Dolly had talked her way out of this, make no mistake. She had a silver tongue where midwifery was concerned. Add to this the backing of the Eastsea women, and Dolly was victorious.

May

Lord Daniel Courtenay was in the office of Hugh Houseman in Bishops Lynne. Along with Helene and Lancelot, they were visiting the Housemans for a couple of days. Daniel had got out of the carriage at the office and Helene and Lancelot had carried on to the Houseman residence.

'What is that?' asked Daniel.

He was pointing at a device which stood about eight inches high, surmounted by what could be a mouthpiece, and, attached on the side, most likely an earpiece.

'That, my dear boy, is a telephone, invented by Alexander Graham Bell,' replied Hugh.

He could see that Daniel was puzzled.

'It's quicker than telegraph. I'll show you how it works,' said Hugh.

He picked up the device, pushed down the arm holding the earpiece, and spoke into the mouthpiece.

'Please can I have Bishops Lynne twenty-three?' he asked.

Daniel was not aware who was receiving this question from Hugh.

Suddenly he said, 'Hello, Francis, it's me, Hugh. Daniel is here with me at the office. Helene and Lancelot will be with you now, I expect. We'll be home later,' he said.

Francis had made a reply of some sort as Hugh then replied,

'Thank you, Darling. Goodbye.'

Daniel stood open mouthed.

'I've had it a week. Waited until we met to show you. You noticed it before I could explain,' said Hugh.

Daniel still looked mystified.

'Let me explain,' said Hugh.

He took Daniel to the window.

'See that wire above leaving the building and crossing the square to the post office? Within the telegraph office is the telephone exchange for the privileged few of us in Bishops Lynne that have these telephones. I'll take you over there and show you the workings.'

They went across to the post office.

People were waiting to be served by two ladies. Stamps were being bought and letters sent.

When it came to their turn to be served, Hugh was about to ask to see the postmaster, Reginald Holme, when he appeared from a room at the back of the counter.

'Hello, Hugh,' he said, and carried on towards another room.

'Reginald, I'm not here for counter business,' called Hugh.

At this Holme turned around.

'If it's convenient, I would like you to meet someone,' said Hugh.

Houseman and Holme had been friends since schooldays, and Holme had once worked for Hugh.

'Of course! Come through to my office,' said Holme.

He opened a hatch at the end of the counter.

'Thank you, Reginald,' said Hugh.

In the office Daniel and Houseman stood facing Holme.

'I have great pleasure introducing Lord Daniel Courtenay of Eastsea Hall – Francis' son-in-law,' said Hugh.

Daniel and Reginald shook hands and exchanged the usual salutations.

'What can I do for you?' asked Holme.

'I want to show Daniel the workings of the telephone facility,' replied Houseman.

Holme took them through to the room that housed the telephone exchange.

A lady sat in front of a small upright unit, answering as a phone rang, and placing a plug in a socket and speaking.

Daniel was really interested.

The exchange phone rang.

'Watch and listen,' said Holme.

'Exchange,' said the operator.

She listened and then replied, 'One moment please. I'll connect you.'

Holme could see that Daniel was bursting to ask questions and pre-empted him.

'The caller asked for a number. The operator then plugged in the socket for that particular number. It works like this. Firstly, let me explain. A scientist, Thomas Edison, has invented a method to produce light, called electricity, which could replace gas mantles and oil lamps,' said Holme.

'How was the name electricity contrived?' asked Daniel.

Holme stood for a moment to gather his thoughts to explain.

'From my understanding, Edison studied thunderstorms and the effect lightning strikes had, and believed if a man-made spark could be made such as that, the result would be of advantage to mankind. Greek philosophers had referred to those storms as electro storms, meaning heat and light. Edison tried to find out if a mineral of some kind could be found to produce that spark. After much research and testing, he discovered copper was a good conductor of that spark, made by two pieces of that mineral being touched together. Thus the way to get the signal along the wire was found, and the copper was then protected by a rubber coating. This is the theory of how the telephone system works,' he said.

'Absolutely amazing! What a clever invention! Hope we can get connected at Eastsea as soon as possible,' said Daniel.

'It will take a long time to go countrywide. At present, it is being developed in only a few towns, and men are still being trained,' replied Holme.

'Thank you very much, Reginald,' said Houseman.

'My thanks too. Very enlightening,' said Daniel.

'Pleasure was all mine,' replied Holme.

Daniel and Hugh then took their leave.

CHAPTER THIRTY-TWO
1901

January

SERGEANT WALLACE HART of the infantry was browsing around the Eastsea Museum.

'Good morning, Sergeant,' said a voice behind him.

Turning around, he was facing Vivien Stanwell.

'Good morning to you, Miss,' he replied.

There was a silence as they both needed to find words to continue conversing. Although Hart was used to being authoritative there was a trace of shyness towards the opposite sex. This was also the case with Vivien Stanwell.

Hart broke the silence.

'Very cold with the snow today,' he said.

'I have not yet ventured out but will have to later for provisions,' Vivien replied.

Silence again then.

'Maybe I could do the shopping for you,' said Hart.

'Thank you, but that will not be necessary as I do need to get some air,' she replied.

Hart turned away nervously to look at some armoury.

'Not seen you in here before,' said Vivien.

'No, but I recently heard there was ancient armoury on show. Interesting to a military man,' replied Hart.

Truth was, although interested in armoury, he had seen Vivien Stanwell in town from time to time and was taken with her.

'I am off duty today and shall now go to the Cockleshell for refreshment and ale,' he said.

Vivien had seen Hart in town on military duties and admired him from afar. Now, she wanted to ask him to stay for vittles at her cottage, but then held back, thinking ladies should not be so forward.

'I'm pleased you found the armoury interesting,' said Vivien.

Hart hoped that she would invite him to stay after letting her know he would be taking refreshment at the Cockleshell.

'Goodbye, Miss Stanwell. Will be pleased see you again,' said Hart.

Hopefully a lot sooner than you expect, Hart thought to himself.

The Cockleshell was situated directly opposite the museum. A window seat was a good vantage point for seeing comings and goings. Fortunately it was unoccupied, and Hart sat down there.

'Tankard of ale and vittles please, Landlord,' he said to Toby Hughes.

The reason this seat was not in use became clear. There was quite a draught but Hart took solace that enduring this would be worth it to see Vivien Stanwell again.

'Don't often see you in here,' said Toby.

'Been busy of late with military duties,' replied Hart.

A few tankards of ale to give him Dutch courage, Hart sat patiently for Miss Stanwell to appear.

Early afternoon his wish was granted. Vivien Stanwell emerged from the confines of the museum.

Hart rushed out of the Cockleshell.

Toby Hughes smiled to himself, realising Hart's intentions, for he had seen him entering the museum earlier.

'Good afternoon, Miss Stanwell,' said Hart, attempting to make the situation appear as a chance encounter.

'Why, Sergeant Hart! I expected you to have been long gone

back to barracks,' she said.

'I like to spend as much time away as possible,' he replied, thinking to himself, I shall endeavour to do more in future.

Vivien Stanwell walked on, once again not wanting to appear too forward, but was secretly pleased when Hart said, 'May I help with your shopping?'

'Of course,' she replied, but then realised maybe that was being too forward.

They walked together into the town, both feeling pleased.

On return, goodbyes were said on the doorstep of her cottage, an act that did not go unnoticed by Toby Hughes. Had he been within earshot he would have heard the following conversation.

'Thank you for your help, Sergeant Hart,' said Vivien, wanting to invite him in for vittles, though that would be unseemly for a single lady with a certain standing in the community.

'My pleasure,' said Hart, wanting that invitation, but he took his leave.

During this period, the suffragettes were fighting their cause with determination by mutilating paintings in the Manchester Art Gallery and inciting destruction of the Chancellor of the Exchequer's home – acts that caused the Home Secretary to warn that if such protests did not cease, the group would be charged with anarchy.

Two days after their first encounter, Hart was back at the museum.

'Good morning, Sergeant Hart,' said Vivien with a knowing smile.

He felt embarrassed. She had realised he had taken a fancy to her and there were a few people around.

'Wanted a second look at the armoury,' he replied.

Vivien smiled, knowing that was not the full truth, and she had her own feelings for him.

Hart stood looking at the armoury, trying to show interest, really wanting to find the right words.

'Miss Stanwell, would you do me the honour of eating out with me tonight at the Cockleshell?' he asked.

Vivien glowed with happiness, for this was something that gave her an indication of his intentions.

'I shall be very pleased to accept your offer,' she replied.

On entering the Cockleshell, Wallace Hart and Vivien Stanwell were the centre of attention.

Toby Hughes was not too surprised, having watched this relationship unfold before his eyes from a vantage point through a window behind the bar. He thought the two were well suited.

Michael Hughes and Saul Smith looked decidedly disappointed.

'Good evening, Miss Stanwell, Sergeant Hart,' said Toby with a cheerful smile.

'Thank you, Mr Hughes. Wine for the lady and a tankard of ale for me,' said Hart.

'Michael, please take this wonderful couple to their table, and I will bring the drinks through,' said Toby.

Miss Stanwell and Sergeant Hart enjoyed a meal of vegetable soup, venison served with vegetables, and suet pudding.

Anyone observing them could tell they were happy together.

At the end of the evening Hart escorted Miss Stanwell home.

'Thank you for a lovely evening,' said Vivien.

'Pleasure was all mine,' replied Hart.

He went to kiss her and she proffered her cheek.

Hart did not appear at the museum for a week or so. Vivien believed conversation during their evening together had revealed their real ambitions and feelings: Vivien's for the museum and Wallace's for the military commitment and these had compromised the relationship.

Vivien answered a knock at the door one evening. Standing there was Sergeant Hart.

'Wallace,' she shouted with excitement, but then realised she was being forward, and this maybe was not the reaction he wanted.

'Vivien,' Hart replied, 'may I come in?' he asked.

At the precise moment she discarded her inhibitions and allowed him to enter the cottage.

April

Lord Daniel and Lady Helene were walking in the garden of Town Green House. Her Ladyship was pushing a baby carriage. Their daughter, Charlotte, was a month old. Lancelot was with them, pulling along a wooden trolley. They were laughing and chatting after hearing of the lengths Doctor Moore went to attend the birth of Charlotte by himself.

The usual disagreement between Doctor Moore and Dolly Byrd had occurred.

Dolly was never allowed to attend births within the aristocracy. Determined as she was, Dolly never managed to overcome Doctor Moore insisting that he kept any such confinements to himself.

On the occasion of Charlotte's birth, he had let it be known that such a birth was imminent at a country estate a few miles away. Dolly took five hours to walk there only to find it was untrue. One of his other ploys on such occasions was to take Dolly, who was partial to whiskey when someone else was buying, to the Cockleshell and get her drunk. No one could ever work out whether she realised what he was doing but had nevertheless submitted for the sake of a few whiskeys.

July

The Eastsea church bells were ringing for the wedding of Vivien Stanwell and Wallace Hart.

That week in January when Hart did not appear was to prove

whether or not they were for each other. He had wanted to go to her, but beat temptation. Vivien had grown despondent, thinking she had lost him.

Both sets of parents were in attendance along with the Courtenays, the Hunworths, the Bartholomews, Vivien's former colleagues from the London Museum, Hart's military colleagues, and various townsfolk they had befriended.

CHAPTER THIRTY-THREE
1902

February

INSPECTOR LONGFIELD and Captain Baines were walking along the harbour wall after another ferocious storm had abated. Crowds had gathered, looking at a strange vessel moored up.

'That must have appeared during the night,' said Longfield.

'Good morning, gentlemen,' said a voice behind them.

They turned to the direction of the sound.

Facing them was a young gentleman with long hair and beard.

'I can see by your uniforms you are in authority. My name is Mr Noah and I can see both of you are mystified. Let me explain. I needed to get shelter. On board is my wife, with animals, mammals and birds.'

Longfield and Baines still gave the impression that they wanted further evidence.

'I can't explain or understand, but this must be another phenomenon – Noah's Ark,' said Longfield.

'Would you like to go aboard to look around?' asked Noah.

'Please,' replied Longfield.

Baines noticed that Vivien Hart from the museum was in the vicinity.

'Mrs Hart, a naturalist, would like to accompany us. Would you mind?' asked Longfield.

'Not at all,' replied Noah.

Longfield went over to Mrs Hart to explain. By the look

on her face, she found the situation hard to comprehend, but she accepted the invitation to go aboard the vessel.

The four of them walked up the gangplank and into the cabin, where the three Eastsea residents were introduced to Mrs Noah.

'Come. I'll show you around,' said Noah.

Below deck an extraordinary sight befell the three of them: enclosed stalls of animals, two in each; birds in cages, of every species imaginable; and then one shocking discovery – in a large water container, two small mammals.

Longfield, Baines and Vivien stopped in their tracks.

'Anything wrong?' asked Noah.

'These mammals you referred to are *Basilosaurus*, the most terror-active of mammals. They have been extinct for thirty million years. Here in Eastsea, by a quirk of nature one arrived a few years ago. The locals were able to destroy it. There was a discovery of some in the Middle East later but they seemed to have died out,' said Vivien.

Noah looked aghast.

'You're not suggesting we destroy these?' he said. 'Doing so would be going against God's will,' Noah added.

The looks on Longfield's and Baines' faces said it all.

'Where did you find these?' asked Vivien.

'Not going to tell, because of your intentions,' replied Noah.

'Thankfully, the other creatures that terrorised, such as in the Jurassic period, have not manifested,' said Vivien.

Longfield looked thoughtful.

'One matter that makes me wonder: How can you be sure male and female gender will be born?' he asked.

Noah composed himself.

'The Lord will provide. Remember Adam and Eve in the Garden of Eden, and the birth of Jesus to the Virgin Mary and Joseph,' he replied.

'He has a point,' said Vivien.

The three of them then left the vessel.

'How can we destroy the *Basilosaurus*?' asked Baines.

'Have to think about that one,' replied Longfield.

'I'll have a word with Wallace. His military mind may have an answer,' said Vivien.

The next day, Longfield, Baines, Vivien and Wallace Hart were standing looking at the empty space where the Ark had been moored.

Henry Matthews, Lord Daniel Courtenay and Max Hunworth arrived on the scene.

'The vessel has gone,' remarked a surprised Daniel.

'So, was it Noah's Ark,' asked Henry, 'as the Reverend Ives would have us believe?'

Longfield answered without giving away too many details, for if it had been known certain mammals were on board…

'It appears so,' he replied.

'To get into the harbour without any assistance from the lifeboat is truly remarkable,' said Henry.

Within a few hours, Professor Bartholomew had arrived, after being summoned by Vivien Hart.

The professor was now chairing a meeting in the town hall, which was full of townspeople and newspaper reporters eager for an explanation. Eminent scientists were also to give their input.

The professor and the scientists were able to give one theory – a mirage.

'One of God's miracles,' proclaimed the Reverend Ives.

'This idea put forward by the parson is his own view. I and my colleagues can give no other scientific manifestation, other than that of a mirage. We wish that it was possible to give more,' said the professor.

These were the only two acceptable outcomes the assemblage could grasp.

Long after the people at the meeting had dispersed, a group consisting of Longfield, Baines, the Harts, Professor Bartholomew, Daniel Courtenay and Max Hunworth were still in the Town Hall.

'After we'd been on board, that put Noah on his guard,' said Longfield.

'There was no way possible, that I know of, those Basilosaurus could have been destroyed,' said Wallace Hart.

'Going to find him is out of the question. The advantage of surprise has gone. The Ark has most likely disappeared as quickly as it appeared,' said Longfield.

'We can only hope upon hope that another Great Flood does not occur,' said Baines.

'Great Flood? Surely there is not something worse than the storms we have been experiencing?' said Longfield.

'The mirage theory, Professor – is that possible?' asked Vivien.

The professor thought for a moment.

'A mirage is an illusory phenomenon and for so many people to have experienced it is possible, I suppose. Don't forget, you, Inspector Longfield and Captain Baines actually went inside,' he replied.

'It was so realistic,' said Vivien.

Longfield and Baines were both of the same opinion.

'There have been other unexplained occurrences around here over the past few years,' said Max Hunworth.

'Although the opinion is that it has vanished, I'll ask the fishing fleet to watch out for the Ark. But one never knows these days,' said Daniel.

'Professor, you look as though you have something on your mind,' said Longfield.

Professor Bartholomew hesitated.

'You're right; I have. What I'm now going to tell you must stay within these four walls,' he said.

All agreed.

'Remember when the geyser matter arose? I could not attend, and sent Vivien. Well, I was called to an urgent meeting of eminent international naturalists and scientists. There had been a supposed sighting of *Basilosaurus* in their Middle East natural habitat. Travelled out there but found nothing to substantiate the allegation. We all agreed the sighting needed total secrecy. Then this Noah fellow turns up with these mammals on board. Makes you think they could have been the ones seen out there and if there is not another Great Flood, what will Noah do with his cargo?' he asked.

'A worrying aspect,' said Longfield.

They then departed from the Town Hall, all with various ideas and explanations on their minds.

CHAPTER THIRTY-FOUR
1903

THE PHONE WAS ringing in Town Green House at Eastsea.

'Good morning, Eastsea 229,' said Daniel Courtenay.

Recently the phone network had been connected to a privileged few in the town and to the hospital.

'Good morning, Daniel. Hugh speaking,' came the reply.

'Hello, Hugh,' Daniel replied. 'What can I do for you?'

'More to the point, it's what I can do for you,' replied Hugh.

The campaign to get votes for women had gained momentum over recent months. The Women's Social and Political Union, as it was now known, and other groups across the country, were actively demonstrating, with militant tendencies. An office established in London and a committee headed up by Emmeline Pankhurst had organised further acts such as attempting to enter Parliament to demonstrate. On one occasion, Emmeline had been imprisoned for inciting riots and went on hunger strike, relenting only when pleas from followers persuaded her they still needed her leadership.

Lady Marcia Courtenay-Harrison had encouraged Lady Helene, along with Vivien Hart and Amelia Hunworth, into forming a group in Eastsea, to the displeasure of their men; though few in numbers, being strong-willed, the women persevered: men ruled the roost and women did as they were told. This attitude of certain males, the Women's Social and Political Union were determined to overcome. Francis Houseman had joined a union group in Bishops Lynne, at the displeasure of husband Hugh.

A few days after their telephone conversation, Daniel was in the office of Hugh Houseman after being invited to bring the family to visit. Helene arrived with Lancelot and Charlotte at the Houseman residence with Francis, where they would be joined later by the men for afternoon tea.

'What is that clicking noise?' asked Daniel.

Hugh smiled.

'That is what I wanted to show you,' he replied.

Hugh took Daniel to a side office where Matilda, the secretary, was working, sitting facing a device which proved to be producing the noise.

'A typewriter,' declared Hugh.

Daniel watched Matilda pushing keys with great panache.

Hugh then explained.

'The machine was invented by Isaac Pitman, who also produced a system called shorthand. Matilda is proficient in both the typing and shorthand after attending Pitman's college in London.

Daniel looked on in amazement, just as he did at the time when he was being shown the telephone.

Hugh further explained.

'Each individual key has either a letter, number or punctuation etched on it. Pushing a key takes it onto an inked tape to the paper, producing an image. A clearer, tidier-looking letter is the result. Shorthand is a quicker method of taking notes, using symbols to represent words, letters or phrases when I'm dictating. Businesses are taking this up. Soon the quill, inkpot and writing longhand will be largely out of use,' he said.

Later that afternoon, Daniel told Helene of the typewriter.

'Sounds useful. Must get one for the estate office. I would like to learn to type and take shorthand,' she said.

'You would?' queried Daniel. 'Well, you do the bookkeeping already. Maybe Max and Amelia should also be taught in time,' he said.

'Come over more often. I'm sure Matilda would be pleased to teach you,' said Hugh.

'I would like that, and we shall be able to spend more time with Mother and you,' replied Helene.

'Come now; enough of business. The children are getting hungry and so am I,' said Francis.

CHAPTER THIRTY-FIVE
1904

'THOSE CLOUDS ARE threatening,' said Margery Longfield, watching out of the window.

Archie Longfield joined her as Dominic arrived home from school.

'Hope they are not a sign of times past,' said Archie.

'Glad you're home, Dominic,' said Margery, observing the weather again.

A few minutes later Archie Longfield's fears were justified.

Another ferocious storm had erupted.

Several hours later the storm had abated. Inspector Longfield and Captain Baines were checking around the town for damage, and met Vivien and Wallace Hart.

'Fortunately not too much damage – a few fences and trees down,' said Longfield.

'The manifestation of the ark gives me cause for great concern. Could one of the storms evolve to a Great Flood?' said Baines.

The Harts had the same concerns.

Turning the corner onto the harbour wall, they saw that in front of them a large vessel was moored.

As they were walking past the Cockleshell, a tall figure with one arm, dressed in sea captain's attire, came out with some sailors.

'Good afternoon, Sir,' said Longfield. 'You off the boat?' he asked.

The stranger held out his good hand and shook hands with Longfield.

'Inspector Archie Longfield of the Constabulary,' Longfield said.

'Captain Henrik Larsen, at your service,' the seaman replied.

Longfield looked at Larsen inquisitively.

'Wondering why we are here?' asked Larsen.

'Crossed my mind,' replied Longfield.

Captain Baines spoke. 'Captain Percy Baines, Customs and Revenue officer. What is your cargo?'

'Whale meat and oil,' replied Larsen.

Vivien Hart looked deep in thought.

'Of course, Henrik Larsen, one of the greatest whale catchers,' she declared.

'Captain Larsen. Thought I recognised that name,' said Wallace Hart.

'Had to find shelter from that storm. Been looking for a vessel that has a cargo of animals, particularly some rather ferocious mammals,' said Larsen.

'Have you seen it?' asked Longfield.

'About two months ago in the Atlantic,' replied Larsen.

'Still around. About eighteen months ago the vessel was here, sheltering from a storm,' said Longfield.

'Waiting for one of those storms to evolve to a Great Flood,' said Baines.

Larsen gathered his crew together.

'Come on, lads, let's continue our search,' he said.

Longfield grabbed Larsen's good arm.

'Wait. Did you mention any of this in the Cockleshell?' he asked.

'Thought best not to. Told them we were just taking shelter from the weather,' Larsen replied.

'Thank you. Very wise. Wouldn't do for folk to know of this.

Could cause panic. Bon voyage, and I wish you good fortune in your quest. Finding the ark and Basilosaurus would be a great service to mankind, Captain Larsen,' said Longfield.

'Goodbye to all of you,' said Larsen.

He and the crew then ascended onto the vessel.

'Well what do you make of that?' asked Vivien Hart.

'Vivien, my love, I wish I knew what to think,' replied Wallace.

Longfield and Baines echoed these sentiments.

'By the way, I noticed the rest of you looking at Larsen's disability. Legend has it he lost the arm during a whaling trip. One of the whales took offence at being harpooned,' said Vivien.

CHAPTER THIRTY-SIX
1905

LORD DANIEL COURTENAY and Max Hunworth were chatting in the estate office.

'I'm going to diversify the estate business,' said Daniel.

'What's on your mind?' asked Max.

Daniel gathered his thoughts.

'I am thinking of progressing the estate into cattle but continuing with arable farming. Cattle will allow us to enter the dairy business. We already have oxen for the ploughing of the land. I shall sell the fishing fleet, for which I already have an offer from Luke Dean over at Looseley,' he said.

Max appeared surprised.

'Selling the fishing fleet? What does Henry Matthews have to say about that?' exclaimed Max.

Daniel smiled.

'I can understand your reaction, Max, and no doubt I shall receive as much from others. Let me explain. John Drummond has over the years provided milk and butter for the area with his dairy business. He is retiring in a few months' time and has offered the business to me, along with the herdsmen and dairy maids,' he said.

'Sounds a good proposition to me,' said Max. 'Will you buy?' he asked.

'I have discussed the matter with Hugh Houseman. He, myself, John and his solicitor are meeting to negotiate terms,' replied Daniel.

'Why the need really to do this?' asked Max.

'Sustainable revenue is required. The fishing fleet is costly to maintain. The money from the sale will help to finance the purchase of the dairy business, and the crews can be utilised working on the estate. I want to try to build another hall here on the estate. Sadly, I don't suppose it will be on the same grand scale as the former, though there is still money from the insurance when it was disastrously destroyed. I am greatly appreciative of being able to live in Town Green House but the ancestral home needs to be here on the estate, as it had been before,' said Daniel.

'Do you think it's a good idea?' asked Max. 'We've tried to rebuild already, and not successfully. It was unfortunate that the earthquake occurred and I don't believe the men would labour again in view of how hard the work had proved, along with the deaths of Herbert Noakes and Jack Brooks,' he said.

Daniel sat thoughtfully for a few minutes.

'Yes, you are right, Max' said Daniel.

'I can understand how you feel but you have a fine home in Town Green House, a wonderful wife in the form of Helene, and the children are adorable. Make the best of the wonders that you already have,' said Max.

'Thank you, Max; it is sound advice,' said Daniel.

There was a knock at the door of the Matthews' cottage, which was opened by Susie.

'Good afternoon, Sir,' she said.

'I'm Luke Dean,' he said. 'Is Henry about?' he asked.

A few days later, Daniel and Max were in the estate office after the meeting with John Drummond.

'Well, how did it go?' asked Max.

'The estate is now the owner of a fine herd of dairy cows,' replied Daniel.

'The next move then?' asked Max.

'Within the next few weeks, the herd will be moved onto Eastsea Hall Estate. Dairy sheds will have to be built. The herdsmen George Laidlaw, Dennis Bannister and Martin Wilson are highly experienced, energetic and strong, with a total of eighty years' service between them to the Drummond family, and will continue for the time being working for Eastsea Hall Estate, though obviously they are getting older and will have to retire some time. The dairy maids Doris Stone, Wilhelmina Bannister and Molly Wilson – the latter two being the wives of Dennis and Martin – are in the same position. With that in mind, the next few weeks will be taken up with the training of men to work alongside the existing Drummond herdsmen to learn the craft of looking after cattle, and women taught the skill of milking cows and producing butter,' replied Daniel.

'Sounds an exciting new era for the estate,' said Max.

Daniel's mood then changed.

'Yes, but there are rumours I heard from John Drummond that nationally there is unrest, men want working conditions and pay to improve. The rumblings of poor old Jack Brooks and Larry Granger spring to mind. Obviously Ephraim Howard and Robbie Dewhurst will take up the cause and get involved. Shall have to watch out for any developments,' said Daniel.

The following weeks were taken up with recruiting and training. As present workers on the estate were already employed, the task of finding suitable workers to learn the dairy business was focused in Eastsea. After careful consideration, Saul Smith aged thirty, Michael Hughes, twenty-seven and Dick Matthews, thirty-three, who were all muscular and healthy and in the prime of life were appointed as trainee herdsmen whilst Mary Matthews, twenty-nine, Bridget Morris, twenty, and Doreen Hughes, twenty-five, all had the attributes to be dairy maids – fine looking but with the physical strength required. As time progressed, other young men and women were employed in the dairy business. They were all taught their various roles: the men how to herd cattle and look after them; and the women to milk the cows and make butter. During this learning curve accidents were commonplace, especially when Saul Smith was a little heavy with a stick and got kicked for his trouble when herding, which put him off work for a couple of days with a bruised leg. Whilst having a go at milking Doreen Hughes got slapped in the face with a tail, though no real damage was done to her attractiveness.

This estate venture had opened up opportunities for employment in Eastsea, especially Toby Hughes finding two waiters.

Keir Hardie, politically ambitious and having worked at times in the depths of arduous toil, felt that there were flaws in the rights of working men. Motivated by him, men gave support for the cause as protestations spread around the country. Further on from this a political party was born, the Labour Party, led by Hardie to oversee and instigate those rights, opposing the Whigs and peers.

Later in the year, Daniel Courtenay had become the owner of the dairy business on the retirement of John Drummond. The young herdsmen and dairy maids had become adept at their respective roles and the business continued to thrive. Milk deliveries were made around the area by pony and trap. At each cottage, the delivery man would deal out the milk from the churns into the customers' jugs. Deliveries could be hazardous, especially during the winter months, with occasional long spells of snowfall resulting in deep drifts. Whatever the weather, folk still wanted milk daily, but the odd occasion arose when it was too dangerous to venture out on the round. Summer was not without its problems either. On hot days, the churns of milk would stand in tanks of cold water whilst on the round to prevent it going sour, and on delivery to the doorstep the customer would stand the jugs of milk in buckets of cold water in a cool scullery.

The Labour Party, under Keir Hardie, had become a force to be reckoned with by getting elected to Parliament through mainly the vote of the men of the working classes. The opportunity to oppose the Whigs and peers, many of whom had lost their seats, had been achieved when one hundred and fifty or so Labour candidates had won them. The party advocated votes for women, thus becoming a popular choice among the suffragette movement, which had now become stronger.

Landowners – Daniel Courtenay among them – bankers and other prosperous businessmen were becoming increasingly alarmed that their profits would soon probably have to be fairly distributed.

Daniel Courtenay and Max Hunworth were sitting around a table with Henry Matthews in the estate office.

Daniel had explained his plans to Henry, and the reply surprised him.

'Won't be working on the land, and neither will the other fishermen, apart from Dick, who you've already blinded with your big ideas,' said Henry.

'Then you won't have a job. Dick has made a wise choice and is doing well at his job, which he tells me is enjoying,' replied Daniel.

'Oh yes, I will have a job,' said Henry.

Daniel was getting rather agitated with Henry.

'What do you mean by that?' he asked.

'You sold the fishing fleet to Luke Dean behind our backs. First I knew of it was when he came to see me to ask if I would continue to run the fleet at Eastsea, as there weren't enough berths at Looseley. He wanted the same experienced crews, just as you did when the dairy business was bought from John Drummond. As far as the both of us were concerned the only change would be the owner,' replied Henry.

Daniel was now really angry, and stood up to his full height.

'Luke Dean gave no indication of his intentions when he bought the fleet,' he said.

Henry stood up, pointing his finger at Daniel.

'With due respect, M' Lord, what he did afterwards was none of your business,' he said.

Max Hunworth looked at Daniel and interjected. 'Basically, he's correct in what he says, M' Lord,' he said.

'Now look here, Matthews. My family have kept you and yours and families of fishermen employed over the years,' said Daniel.

Both Daniel and Henry were getting even angrier.

'M' Lord, Henry, please, both of you calm down. We'll get nowhere if you continue in this vein. Both of you sit down,' said Max.

They both sat down.

'M' Lord, we do appreciate how we've been employed, but you must appreciate us as well, having had a good fleet and experienced crews. Remember the high price paid when two were lost at sea, and the sacrifices made by lifeboatmen over the years. I'm a man of the sea, as the others are, and our sons will follow, although Dick has fell by the wayside. It's in our blood, as it was in our fathers' and their fathers', and that is why they need to continue this dangerous and arduous work,' said Henry.

Daniel sat thoughtfully, looking slightly ashamed.

'I take your point, Henry. Once again I have to apologise for letting my head rule my heart. Best wishes for the future,' said Daniel.

'Apology accepted. Circumstances can blind one to real issues, as they did on this occasion,' replied Henry.

They both shook hands with conviction.

Max Hunworth breathed a sigh of relief.

CHAPTER THIRTY-SEVEN
1906

THE WIND WAS whistling through the framework of the aeroplane at one thousand feet. Below, people were looking up in awestruck wonder at a most unusual sight.

In Eastsea, Longfield and Baines reacted in similar vein.

'What on earth is that?' queried Longfield.

Baines looked questioningly upwards at the flying machine.

'Most likely one of those machines being developed in America, although a long way from home,' he replied.

The machine then flew off out of sight.

An hour or so later on his return to the police station, Longfield found an agitated Constable Palmer.

'I'm glad to see you, Inspector. Been several reports of a strange flying machine over Eastsea,' he said.

'I know. Myself and Captain Baines saw it ourselves earlier. Since then we've been trying to trace it, but to no avail,' he replied.

'Among those reporting it were Lord Courtenay and Max Hunworth, and they would like to see you,' said Palmer.

Lord Daniel Courtenay and the estate manager Max Hunworth were in the estate office with Longfield and Baines discussing the appearance of the flying machine.

'People are perturbed by this flying machine,' said Daniel.

'I can understand that; it is causing concern to me,' replied Longfield.

There was a knock on the door.

'Come in,' commanded Daniel.

Two estate workers entered, appearing to be quite shaken.

'What is it, Dixon? Murphy?' asked Daniel.

'M' Lord, up on Longmeadow pastures, a flying machine,' Dixon replied.

'That's where it is then,' said Baines.

They all left the office and boarded the wagon being used by the two workers. A few minutes later, they arrived at the pastures.

'It's quite extraordinary. Those phenomenal storms we experienced have not occurred for a year or two but strange happenings are still manifesting,' said Max Hunworth.

The flying machine was unoccupied.

'M' Lord, look,' said Murphy, pointing.

Everyone turned to the direction Murphy had indicated. Out of the woods two figures were emerging.

Longfield approached them.

'Good afternoon, gentlemen,' he said.

They returned the salutation.

'Who are you, and would you please explain your reasons for being here?' Longfield asked.

The men introduced themselves.

'We are the Wright brothers, and this is our flying machine – the first heavier than air. I'm Orville and he's Wilbur,' replied the elder of the two.

'You've given people around here rather a fright,' said Longfield.

The brothers appeared remorseful.

'We do apologise. The craft has brought us all this way to England from America – North Carolina, actually.'

'What are your plans now?' asked Daniel.

'We are not sure,' replied Wilbur.

Daniel Courtenay looked thoughtful.

'You are most welcome to stay with my family,' he offered.

Orville and Wilbur went to one side, chatting to decide.

They returned to the others.

'Thank you; we'll take you up on your offer,' said Orville. 'What about the machine?' he asked.

'I own this land and have an outhouse about a mile away that can be used for the time being. We can, between the eight of us and the horse and wagon, tow it there,' said Daniel.

The journey to the outhouse and getting the machine secured took some three hours or more, after which Max was sent ahead to Town Green House to warn of the imminent arrival of their guests.

After a meal of pheasant, potatoes and swede followed by egg custard, the Wright brothers were relaxing in the drawing room with the Courtenays.

'Thank you for a fine meal. However, we should not eat many more like that for we shall be putting on extra weight and the machine will be struggling to lift off when we leave. As you can see, we are at an appropriate size – both of us have a combined weight of twenty stone – which has to be adhered to for the weight is a big factor for the take-off and in flight, when fuel consumption is a major factor,' said Orville.

'You are very welcome, gentlemen. We are blessed with a marvellous housekeeper and cook in Amelia, Max's wife, and the servants are good. Stay as long as you like, but you'll be tempted by the food,' said Helene.

'I do echo my brother's sentiments,' said Wilbur.

Max and Amelia then joined them.

'I'm sure you have an interesting story to tell,' said Daniel.

'Let me begin,' said Orville.

Orville did but not until the men had been served with brandy, and the ladies with wine.

'As was mentioned earlier, the craft has brought us from North

Carolina – a journey of several thousand miles and several days, with a few stops on the way. At first we owned a bicycle shop although it had always been a longing for both of us to build a craft to fly. It took us three long years to succeed in getting the craft to fly. It is powered by high octane, a liquid hydrocarbon found in petroleum, that exists structurally in various forms. It was developed by some very clever scientists in America. The rest of the engineering, Wilbur and I did,' said Orville.

The others listened in awe to Orville and Wilbur's story.

'A truly extraordinary tale,' said Daniel.

Helene looked thoughtful.

'What about your families, won't they be concerned at your wellbeing, flying a craft that is on its maiden flight and a long way from home?' she asked.

'Not a problem; there are no wives or children. We're both bachelors. Not had time for marriage,' replied Wilbur.

Orville and Wilbur then looked at each other as though something was troubling them. They wanted to ask a question.

'I trust this is not an impertinent question. Flying around over the estate we noticed some ruins. On landing we went to find them and were on our way back to the machine when we met,' said Wilbur. 'What are they?' he asked.

'Not at all; it's a fair question,' said Daniel. The story of the misfortunes of the Courtenay family was then conveyed to the brothers

'That must have been absolutely awful,' said Orville.

'That is how Town Green House became our ancestral home. Sadly, my efforts to rebuild on the estate were unsuccessful. Maybe one day, if not me, one of my heirs will be able to,' said Daniel, sounding rather downhearted.

Max and Amelia then took their leave to retire for the night.

'Another observation I hope you won't find impertinent: although Max and Amelia are very nice people, in America servants would not spend time socially with their employers,' said Wilbur.

'Apart from being employees, Max and Amelia, as you point out, Wilbur, are nice folk and our dear friends,' replied Helene.

Wilbur and Orville thanked the hosts for their hospitality and they too retired for the night. Daniel and Helene followed later.

Next morning at breakfast, Orville and Wilbur announced they would be leaving later that day.

'We have decided not to attempt the return trip by air. Instead, we shall fly to Southampton to arrange passage on a ship. Fuel stocks are getting low and, although enjoyable, we hope we have not put on too much weight from the fine fare received,' said Orville.

'I shall let Inspector Longfield know of your plans,' said Daniel.

In the afternoon sun, as planned, Orville and Wilbur Wright were on the estate preparing the flying machine for the flight to Southampton. The Courtenays and the Hunworths were in attendance and, judging by the number of townsfolk present, word had spread.

A pre-flight check after which the aeroplane was ready to leave. A piece of land close to the outhouses would be used for the take-off, thankfully not far to tow the aeroplane after the efforts a few days earlier.

Inspector Longfield and Captain Baines approached the brothers as final adjustments were being made.

'Thank you for letting me have details of the flight path to Southampton. I've contacted the relevant constabularies to warn them of your existence,' said Longfield.

Orville and Wilbur gave their thanks and salutations and climbed into the cockpit, sitting for a few minutes going through a flight check plan. The moment came to ignite the engine. After several false starts it roared into life. A wave of their hands, and the brothers motioned the craft forward for take-off. The crowd held their breath as the craft rolled over the ground and picked up speed. There were one or two hairy moments as the plane did not appear to lift. Suddenly there was a tremendous roar, and the craft rose up into the blue sky yonder.

The crowd broke into an almighty cheer.

'More excitement over and done with,' said Daniel Courtenay.

'You're correct there, M' Lord,' said Longfield.

The craft was now slowly becoming a distant dot in the sky.

'I am of the belief that what has occurred over the past few days can only be described as phenomenal,' said Baines.

'What do you mean by that, Captain Baines?' asked Max Hunworth.

'Let's go and find somewhere to sit down and listen to Captain Baines' explanation,' said Daniel.

They found benches in an outhouse.

Captain Baines began his theory regarding the Wright brothers and their journey. 'Thinking about it, according to them it took several stops and days to reach England and Eastsea. Consulting the atlas, my conclusion is that starting in North Carolina, they then flew maybe north to Newfoundland or south to the Bahamas or west to the Azores, then Madeira, Canary Islands, Europe – in a flying machine as yet unproven over an extremely long-distance flight. They will have had a directional aid such as a compass, although they would have been at the mercy of the wind and been buffeted here, there and everywhere. To my mind, these are two very brave and resilient men who could well be pioneers of future air travel. Probably not in our lifetime, but who knows? It's difficult to ascertain, just as in the matter of the appearance of Noah's Ark and Captain Larsen.'

The other three looked thoughtful.

'Profound and conceivable, not beyond possibility,' said Max Hunworth.

'That's as maybe. All this deep thinking is making me hungry. The crowd has dispersed, so let's make our way back to Eastsea,' said Longfield.

Lady Helene and Amelia Hunworth were collected from the field where the children were playing, and they did just that.

A few weeks later Professor Bartholomew visited the Courtenays, bringing with him a London paper with a report on two brothers, Orville and Wilbur Wright, who were claiming they had crossed the Atlantic from America with a flying machine and ended up in England at a place named Eastsea. The paper wanted witnesses to verify their story.

'Well, is it true?' asked the professor.

'Yes. I'll take you to see Inspector Longfield, who I'm sure will be interested,' replied Daniel.

Longfield certainly was, as was Captain Baines, who was also at the police station.

'The newspaper report questions your phenomenon theory, Percy,' said Longfield.

Longfield and Baines were deep in thought.

'Shall we acknowledge that we were witnesses?' asked Daniel Courtenay.

'Don't want to be too hasty. Baines and I are still thinking about it,' replied Longfield.

'I think we should. They obviously got back to America,' said Baines.

Longfield was still not convinced. 'I know what we saw, such as Noah's Ark and Captain Larsen, and then this. We could be victims of ridicule were our stories without substance. However, our input would be helpful in the progress of future development of flying machines. Let's do it,' he said.

'I'm sure Max Hunworth will agree, and maybe some townsfolk

as well,' said Daniel.

Max agreed with enthusiasm, as did a few townsfolk.

A letter was then sent to the American Embassy in London, signed by the dominant Eastsea four and several townsfolk, endorsing the Wright brothers' claims.

An invitation was received to visit the Embassy, which Lord Daniel, Max Hunworth, Inspector Longfield and Percy Baines accepted.

A week later they, the four of them made the journey to London by rail. On arrival at King's Cross, a carriage conveyed them to the Embassy, where a cordial welcome was given by the attache, who took the four to meet the ambassador.

The ambassador greeted them courteously. 'Thank you, gentlemen, for making the long journey and with this in view, apartments have been put at your disposal for you to stay overnight. Now, luncheon and a glass of port, then business later,' he said.

Later that day, the chain of events surrounding the Wright brothers' escapade at Eastsea was conveyed to the ambassador.

A few months later, Daniel Courtenay received news from the Wright brothers thanking him for the support from Eastsea and informing him that an engineer named Boeing had joined forces with them.

CHAPTER THIRTY-EIGHT
1907

THE TOWN HALL in Bishops Lynne was full of vociferous chatter created by a large multitude of people. They were attending a meeting to hear Keir Hardie speak of his vision of the forming of a political party with the interests of the working classes as the portfolio.

Sitting at a table on the stage were the Lord Mayor and Town Clerk of Bishops Lynne, Keir Hardie and Emmeline Pankhurst. She, along with members of the Women's Social and Political Union, had given support to Hardie since his declaration that he advocated the right for women to have a vote. The assemblage consisted of local dignitaries and businessmen, among them Lord Daniel Courtenay, Gilbert Harrison and Hugh Houseman; and a large number of the working classes. The dignitaries' spouses – Lady Helene, Marcia and Francis – and various other members of the Women's Movement, which had at the time caused heated exchanges between them and their husbands, were in attendance.

The Town Clerk introduced Keir Hardie, who received a welcome that clearly showed who were the bosses and who were the workers.

Hardie stood up and began, 'Ladies and gentlemen, thank you for the welcome. Coming straight to the point, I am well placed to deliver my hopes for the working class, having been born in the areas of the Scottish coalfields, working from the age of seven, and into the coalmines when I was ten. During my time there I realised the miners needed better working conditions, and championed for the owners to halt the victimisation. I later managed to get educated and left the mines to become a journalist, which enabled me to become involved in politics and advocate the cause. Spasmodic periods as a member of parliament. As there was no real voice for the working class, I decided to attempt the founding of a political party, namely, the Labour Party. As at previous meetings, judging by the occasional heckling there are those opposed to my idea: bosses and businessmen, who will likely have to provide better working conditions and pay. Otherwise I'm inspired by the shouts of approval and the ladies in attendance.'

This brought tumultuous applause, though a few boos.

After the audience reaction had died down Hardie continued, 'Let me tell you: in most of the places I have visited, certain factions attempted to stop the meetings occurring. Having persevered I will, with the support I am receiving, continue the fight to get the Labour Party functioning as a powerful representative of the working classes of this country. Further, my belief is that women should be entitled to have the vote. This is another goal I shall strive for, as the outcome of an election affects them as well.'

Again the audience went into raptures of applause, amid some cries of derision.

CHAPTER THIRTY-NINE
1908–1913

DURING THIS PERIOD of time, Inspector Archie Longfield nurtured Dominic for a career in the Constabulary. Captain Percy Baines encouraged Simon to enter the Customs Service.

However, both sets of parents had to be content with the opposite, Dominic opting for the Customs Service and Simon the Constabulary. The two lads pursued their chosen careers with enthusiasm, pleasing the parents.

Later Dominic married Sybil Palmer and Simon, Laura Dawlish, daughters of constables Palmer and Dawlish respectively, both of whom welcomed the young men into their family circles.

Henry Matthews was gradually handing over the running of the fishing fleet to Saul Smith, who was also being groomed for the position of coxswain of the lifeboat.

Meanwhile, changes at Eastsea Hall Estate were proceeding, with Lord Daniel Courtenay giving Lancelot insights into life as Lord of the Manor and the running of the estate. Max Hunworth showed David the skills of estate management, and Amelia Hunworth was teaching her granddaughter Susan culinary skills and housekeeping matters in relation to Town Green House. At the end of all this, Lancelot had taken a fancy to Susan, and they were walking out together. Of this, Lord Daniel or Lady Helene could give no opinion, for would the future give any reflections of the past?

Keir Hardie had won a resounding victory in a General Election. The Labour Party attracted men of high standing who had won seats. Those of the working class had shown interest and got elected. The workers preferred parliamentary business to their jobs; bosses were unhappy and threatened to dispose of their services. Legislation declared this action as an offence and fines would be imposed were this to occur. Advocating votes for women was still an issue.

The suffragettes were still active, and containing them was proving difficult. There were protest marches, chainings to railings, and one suffragette even threw herself in front of galloping horses at Ascot.

The Labour Party was proving popular and went from strength to strength, and Keir Hardie proved himself to be a good leader.

CHAPTER FORTY
1914

AT THE beginning of this year Lancelot Courtenay married Susan Matthews. Lady Helene then had the task of teaching Susan the way of the aristocracy, just as Lady Marcia had instructed her on her entering the Courtenay family a few years previously.

The sign over the building proclaimed: Wallace Hart – Motor Engineer. Inside, Wallace had the bonnet of a Model T Ford open.

Whilst serving in the military, he had been given the opportunity by the authorities, who had become aware of a vehicle being developed by an American engineer, Henry Ford, which was driven by a combustion engine with intricate accessories, and a fuel called petroleum. Wallace learnt to be a vehicle engineer at Henry Ford's facility in London. Upon his retirement, with savings and remuneration from the military, Wallace had set up this business.

A new age of transport had been born and for some time the vehicle was called a horseless carriage, but later a name more apt: motor car.

The invention proved popular with the aristocracy and businessmen. The car was too expensive to buy or run for the working class of the time. However, the few wealthy people in Eastsea kept Wallace busy giving driving lessons and servicing the vehicles. Lord Daniel Courtenay and Max Hunworth each owned a car.

The garage had a petrol pump, serviced by an underground tank with a capacity of one thousand gallons. Oil was also used to keep the engine components greased for easy running.

Wallace and Vivien had a son, Julian, born in nineteen hundred and three. It was hoped he would take over the business one day.

Lord Daniel Courtenay stood in the drawing room of Town Green House looking rather concerned.

The door opened. 'You wanted to see me?' asked Lancelot.

'Yes, I did,' replied His Lordship.

'You're looking worried,' said Lancelot.

Daniel hesitated, deep in thought.

'My belief is there will be trouble in the Balkans. Archduke Franz Ferdinand, heir to the throne of Austria, has been assassinated. Austria recently annexed Bosnia-Herzegovina. A young Serb, Gavrilo Princip, carried out the killing. The world waits for Austria's reaction,' he said.

'How does that affect us?' asked Lancelot.

'Wait and see, but be aware of the situation,' said Daniel.

Wallace Hart was also keeping an eye on the events in the Balkans. Being an ex-military man, he knew how things could escalate.

Vivien noticed a change in his demeanour.

'What is bothering you, Wallace?' she asked.

'This business in the Balkans,' he replied.

'Do you think we will get involved?' Vivien asked.

Wallace carefully put his mind to the answer, but just replied, 'I wouldn't think so', not wanting to worry his wife.

The Government were also concerned by the happenings in the Balkans. Keir Hardie and the Cabinet had put some contingency plans in place but had not as yet made them public. The situation was being carefully watched.

A few days later it was becoming clear. Austria had blamed Serbia for supporting Princip and his accomplices and, confident of support from their German allies, presented Serbia with a sharp ultimatum. The Serbs rejected it. Austria declared war on Serbia. Serb Slavics in Russia began partial mobilisation to deter the Austrians. Germany warned they would mobilise if they went ahead. Again the world waited.

France became involved. Russia pressed ahead. Germany then declared war. England then gave their allegiance to France. Hostilities spread.

Lord Daniel, Lancelot and Wallace Hart were in the drawing room of Town Green House. Wallace, with his experiences of the military, had been invited. Max Hunworth was also there.

'Thank you for attending, Wallace; your knowledge of military matters will be useful,' said Daniel.

'It's an honour to be asked,' replied Wallace.

Daniel opened the proceedings. 'Gentlemen, as I see it, England has put her support behind France.'

At this juncture, Wallace smiled.

'Mr Hart, you find something amusing?' asked Daniel.

'I apologise, My Lord, but it is ironic that we were fighting them a century or so ago during the Napoleonic wars,' replied Wallace.

Daniel smiled, having understood the point, and continued. 'Quite. As I said, we have our allegiance with France and the word from London is that we shall be mobilising soon. Plans are in place. Wallace, your thoughts please?' he said.

'My understanding is that when the hostilities escalate our regular soldiers in the military will be sent to France, the problem being these are not vast numbers. By your quizzical looks, I assume you are wondering how those numbers will be increased. I guess, by conscription. Men between the ages of, say, eighteen and forty, will be called up,' said Wallace.

The others looked shaken by this.

'Then it could mean that Lancelot and my David…?' said Max.

'It's only my assumption, but it is possible,' replied Wallace.

'Also several other young men from Eastsea,' said Daniel.

'Let's just wait and see for the Government's decision before taking any drastic action. At present, keep what has been said within these four walls; we don't want mass panic,' said Wallace.

They all agreed this would be the best policy.

The womenfolk were getting concerned. Rumours were rife around Eastsea that Britain would soon be going to war.

On the fourth of August, Keir Hardie was making a statement to a packed Parliament, speaking thus: 'On the thirty-first of July, France refused to stand aside from the conflict. For this reason, on the third of August Germany declared war on France. The Anglo-French rapprochement of nineteen hundred and four – the 'Entente Cordiale' – was not a formal treaty. Therefore, talks between British and French staffs, discussing the dispatch of a British expeditionary force are not binding. Belgium neutrality had been guaranteed by a treaty to which Britain is a signatory. German violation of this has made it difficult for Britain to stand aside. Germany has declined to withdraw from Belgium. I am now declaring Britain at war with Germany.'

There was a hushed silence as the assembly took in the announcement, which sent shockwaves around the country.

As Wallace Hart had predicted, young male civilians were called to arms. Wallace was appointed the recruiting officer for Eastsea, just as towns around the country had made similar such appointments.

Young men deemed to be fit were taken from all walks of life, to join the army. Womenfolk replaced them on farms, in factories, drove vehicles and took to any other vocation that could release the young men.

Wallace kept the garage business going, with the help of, from time to time, Austin Dawlish, who at fifteen had tried to enlist but was refused due to his age, and his son, Julian, who at twelve was learning the trade. The garage business waned. Priority for fuel was given to the military for their vehicles.

Around the country metal fences, redundant machinery and any scrap metal that could be utilised was being collected to make field gun carriages and rifles. Forests were cut down, wood being a vital commodity.

Meanwhile, in Eastsea, recruiting was proceeding, Wallace Hart inspecting the prospective troops and Dr Cedric Lewis carrying out the medicals, assisted by the now elderly although experienced Dr Stanley Moore.

Since the declaration of war, Jessica and Cedric had moved from London to Eastsea.

The recruiting process completed and the time for leaving became reality. Eastsea proved to be a haven for a large number of men eligible for the army. This particular day saw the railway station heaving with families seeing their sons off for training and subsequently to the battlefields in France and Belgium. There was much sadness among the families, not knowing when they would see these young men again, and tentatively thinking whether they would.

Emmeline Pankhurst took advantage of the circumstances regarding employment of women during wartime, commenting, 'Surely women cannot fail to achieve the vote now.'

France, Marne, River Aisne – mid-September

British forces attacked, causing the Germans to retreat. The environment was flat open land. Trenches had to be dug for cover, prompting Field Marshal John French to remark, 'The spade is a great a necessity as the rifle.' Men were exhausted, encountering Germans retreating. Fierce battles raged. Casualties were high, caused not only by the fighting. Food was scarce and conditions were unhygienic, resulting in dysentery.

Eastsea

The doorbell had been rung at Town Green House. Amelia Hunworth entered the drawing room, where Lord Daniel and Lady Helene were having afternoon tea.

'Telegram for you, My Lord,' said Amelia hesitantly.

Daniel took the piece of paper with trepidation, and after reading it, a look of bewilderment came over his face.

Lady Helene watched his reaction and feared the worst.

'What does it say?' she asked.

'Don't worry; it's not what you think. I have been summoned to London to meet the War Cabinet. That is all I can tell you for now,' he replied.

Lady Helene was relieved, saying, 'We live each day fearing a telegram.'

Three days later, Lord Daniel returned from London.

Lady Helene greeted him with apprehension.

'What was the reason for the need for you to go to London?' she asked.

He kissed and embraced her.

'After dinner, explanations. I'm tired and hungry after the journey,' Daniel replied. He then went to freshen up and take a nap.

Later, in the evening.

'I really enjoyed that venison and vegetables and the apple pie. A brandy now, and I shall tell you of my call to London,' said Daniel.

He and Helene sat at the fireside, and Daniel spoke.

'A flying machine, an airship, unlike anything the Wright brothers had invented, has been produced by Germany – a large balloon filled with a gas to keep it airborne, driven by engines. Its function is to bomb our factories in the industrial cities manufacturing equipment for the war effort. Drummond and Ashwell, near neighbours of ours, were there in London as well, together with other Lords of the Manor. The Government wants us to organise locally groups of men to monitor the progress of these airships, day and night, and to alert the authorities of any activity. Belief is the targets are the factories, and not rural areas such as ours. However, if at any time you see any, do not worry too much. As a precaution, underground shelters will be prepared around the town and the surrounding area. Meetings are being convened to organise the groups and explain the situation to the townsfolk.'

CHAPTER FORTY-ONE
1915

Somewhere in France, August 10th – early morning
'GET YOUR HEAD DOWN,' was heard further along the trench as gunfire was heard from the German lines.

Hope was that when war had been declared in nineteen fourteen, the conflict would soon be over. However, it had been raging for almost a year.

'Anyone with their head up must be mad, especially with this heavy rain and mud,' said Simon Baines.

David Hunworth, Cedric Matthews, Dominic Longfield, Lancelot Courtenay, Simon, Marcus Morris, Michael Hughes, Martin and Drew Alexander, along with several other young men from Eastsea, ages ranging from sixteen to thirty-six, had responded to the call to arms.

They were in the East Coast Infantry. Regiments from other areas had been formed, known by the name of the county or district, such as the West Midlands Infantry, Hampshire, Sussex, and so on. Millions were now fighting in France.

Eastsea Harbour – Morning
'Heard anything from Dominic?' asked Percy Baines.

'Not for a couple of months,' replied Archie Longfield.

The pair were walking around Eastsea. Archie at fifty-two and Percy at fifty-four had come out of retirement, reverting to their respective roles with the Constabulary and Customs Service when their sons went off to war. Constables Alexander, Palmer and Dawlish were still serving.

'Nothing from Simon either,' said Percy.

'The only messages that seem to be getting through are telling families around the country that their loved ones are either missing or have been killed,' said Archie.

Families in Eastsea were equally concerned, as others were around the country, dreading the day when a telegram would be delivered.

Such was the mood at Town Green House.

'To think we could receive bad news concerning Lancelot or David, and the rest of the Eastsea boys, for that matter, really worries me. I know Amelia and Max feel the same,' said Lady Helene.

'No news is good news. Myself and Charlotte are just as concerned. She is doing a good job working on the estate. Learnt to drive a pony and trap, ride a horse and milk the cows,' said Lord Daniel.

France – Christmas Day morning
An eerie silence covered the battlefield. There was snow on the ground, and the temperature was below freezing.

'Sergeant Baines,' called the sentry Martin Alexander.

Simon Baines came out of the shelter.

'What is it?' he asked.

Martin pointed across No Man's Land.

A person carrying a white flag, accompanied by two other people, had appeared above the German fortifications and were walking towards them.

'Be wary; it could be a trap,' said Simon.

As the Germans got closer to the British lines a voice shouted out.

'Please, trust us. We are unarmed and come in peace.'

Simon gathered his thoughts. 'Has anyone got a piece of white rag?' he asked.

'Sir, a tall order in these filthy conditions,' said Martin as he gave Simon a handkerchief. 'My mother gave me some, telling me I would find them useful some time, and she was right,' he added.

'Longfield, accompany me and Alexander,' said Baines.

The trio went over the top and walked towards the Germans, and met more or less in the middle.

'Good morning, gentlemen. I am Captain Hans Mueller, and these are Sergeant Wilhelm Strauss and Private Jan Jutner.'

Simon Baines reciprocated.

'Good day, Captain Mueller,' said Simon, and he nodded courteously at the other two. 'My escorts are Privates Longfield and Alexander,' he added.

The six of them were of all same ages, give or take a year or two.

There was silence as the two sides warily eyed each other.

Mueller broke the silence.

'It is true we are unarmed,' he said.

'As we are, and I must commend you on your English,' said Baines.

'Thank you. I was at Cambridge University studying biology,' he replied.

'Why have you made contact?' asked Baines.

'It is Christmas Day: a time for peace,' replied Mueller.

The Englishmen whispered among themselves.

'A time of peace? First of all, our Captain Hughes is badly wounded, unable to join us,' said Baines.

This remark seemed to anger the Germans, and they turned away for a discussion.

'We are sorry to learn of your Captain's injuries. As I said: a time of peace. During the time here we have gained a football and suggest there is a match. England versus Germany,' said Mueller.

'We'll return to our lines and get the opinion of our men,' said Baines.

Back at the British lines, the proposal was put to the men. A heated discussion ensued, with reasons for and against given. Finally it was decided that it would be good to play the match, to release the frustrations of fighting.

An hour later the teams were lined up for the kick-off.

The day had become brighter and the snow melted, making the ground muddy.

There were many players on each side. As time went on the conditions proved to be energy sapping. Most of the players were physically tired due to the previous fighting and marching. In time, both sides decided to call it a day. The result of the match? No one seemed to know or care.

'I suppose the peace will be shattered tomorrow, though this was welcome relief,' said Baines.

'We fight on. Both of us have allegiances,' replied Mueller.

On their return to English lines, the British soldiers learnt of Captain Michael Hughes' death. Later that day, he was buried in French soil.

Eastsea – Christmas Day

The German High Command, it appeared, were not of the same attitude regarding peace at this particular time as their troops on the battlefields were. The Civil Defence Force was reporting German airships heading inland.

'The reports have been acknowledged,' said Daniel Courtenay.

The Civil Defence Force had been born out of the meeting in nineteen fourteen when Daniel, Drummond, Ashwell and others had been asked to form groups in their localities to monitor enemy air activity.

'M' Lord, the authorities are still warning that any bombs not released on the factories could be dropped on their way back to

Germany. Also an airship has been brought down by artillery guns in Birmingham,' said Henry Matthews.

A cheer went up from the rest of the group.

'That is good news. The planes being built now – the Sopwith Camel and the Tiger Moth – are soon to be in service. Royal Flying Corps personnel are being trained. Then we can retaliate,' said Daniel.

France – Boxing Day – early morning

The silence was suddenly broken by the sound of gunfire.

David Hunworth was on watch. He had no need to shout a warning; the noise had alerted them.

Simon Baines had taken up the mantle of captain due to the death of Michael Hughes.

'How quickly attitudes can change. Fraternise yesterday; now out to kill us,' said Simon.

As he spoke a shell landed in their shelter.

CHAPTER FORTY-TWO
1916

THE WAR HAD escalated, with fierce fighting in France and Belgium. The Tiger Moth and Sopwith Camel planes had taken to the air, combating the airships, and with some success.

Eastsea – February
Two weeks into the month, telegrams began to arrive in the town.

Families had news they hoped would never be received, that sons including Cedric Matthews, Dominic Longfield, Simon Baines, Marcus Morris, Michael Hughes, Martin and Drew Alexander, had been killed in action. In a short while Sybil Longfield and Laura Baines were both widows.

At Town Green House the mood was one of anxiety. Having learned of the tragic deaths of those other sons of Eastsea, the Courtenays and Hunworths had not received any news of Lancelot or David.

Daniel Courtenay contacted the War Office only to be told by a clerk, 'There is no record of Lancelot Courtenay or David Hunworth being killed or missing.'

Thus there was relief for the time being.

War continued through the following months.

The Somme – July

The Battle of the Somme proved to be one of the biggest and bloodiest battles of the war, with millions of casualties on both sides.

There was no let-up as battle after battle was fought right up to the end of the year.

CHAPTER FORTY-THREE
1917

Eastsea – March
TOWN GREEN HOUSE had, to a degree, an upbeat atmosphere. News had been received that David Hunworth was now with the Sussex Infantry. After some of the East Coast Infantry had been killed, David had joined the Sussexes. However, in one of the battles, he had been injured and lost his left leg. He was to be invalided out of the Army and would soon to be back home.

On a low note, they were still awaiting news of Lancelot.

David Hunworth arrived home in May. Obviously the Hunworths and Courtenays were at the railway station along with most of the families who had lost family, this being the only experience of having a loved one returning from war.

Initially, the crowd were quiet, and an air of shock was felt on seeing a young man who had left to go to war fit and healthy and with two legs, alight onto the platform, downcast and on crutches.

The mood suddenly changed as they realised that here was a young man, the manifestation of all those they had loved and lost, and tumultuous cheering and applause broke out as David was taken to a waiting pony and trap.

Back in Town Green House, David, looking gaunt and tired, was given a good meal.

'David, have you any news of Lancelot?' asked Lord Daniel.

'Please, not now, M' Lord. He is weak and tired. Give him a chance to recuperate. David has been through a traumatic period of his young life and needs time to adjust. At the moment we are joyful to have him home. Both Max and I are mindful of yours and Helene's anxiety regarding Lancelot. We pray each day that good news will be forthcoming,' said Amelia.

June
A resounding victory for the suffragettes. The protesting finally paid off. Women had won the right to vote.

August
On a daily basis the Hunworths and, from time to time, the Courtenays, were trying to get David to open up. Before going off to war he was an outgoing young man, but had returned withdrawn and sad.

Amelia and Max were sitting in their living room at Town Green House, looking concerned and deep in thought.

'I'm worried about David. He's had time to adjust to life here again,' said Amelia.

Suddenly she collapsed in tears.

'Whatever is the matter?' asked Max.

'What have I done wrong in my life to have these crosses to bear?' Amelia asked.

There was one matter that Susie Matthews could have told her.

Max tried to console her, for Amelia could hardly speak, being so upset.

Composing herself, Amelia continued, 'I lose my first husband and son to the sea, find happiness again with you and then lose a grandson… and another son, a broken man, due to the war,' she explained.

'But I do agree. It's as though he's harbouring an inner secret. We should get Doctor Lewis to have a chat with him,' replied Max.

'It would be good for David to have the doctor to talk to,' said Amelia.

The next day Doctor Lewis arrived at Town Green House.

Max and David were in the living room. Amelia brought the doctor in. David flatly refused to talk, and stormed out.

A few days later, Max confronted David.

'What is troubling you, David? Why won't you talk to Doctor Lewis?' he asked.

David went on the defensive.

'Cannot tell you; I am too ashamed,' he replied.

'Ashamed of what? Did you desert in the face of the enemy?' asked Max.

David sat deep in thought.

'All right, I will tell you. Explain to Mother, but you must really promise not to tell Daniel or Helene,' said David.

'I must tell them. They are just as concerned about you without the worry of Lancelot,' replied Max.

David looked hard at Max.

'You really must promise, or I will not tell you,' said David.

Max thought for a moment.

'All right, if that is what it takes, I promise on your mother's life,' said Max.

So David began. 'Boxing Day nineteen fifteen. There was heavy shelling from the Germans. Lancelot cowered, went berserk, and ran out of the shelter. I followed, to reason with him. Behind us a shell hit our shelter. That is how our colleagues died, although Michael Hughes was already dead from earlier injuries and buried. The shock of the hit threw us both to the ground. Lancelot got up and ran like a madman. It was then I realised he was deserting. Feeling so angry with him, I shot him and buried him. A corporal came by as I was burying Lancelot, and asked for his name. I told him I did not know as there was no name tag. That is why you cannot tell Daniel and Helene, not so much as what I did, but let them think he is missing, presumed dead, a brave man.

Max looked shocked and taken aback as Amelia entered the room.

'What is wrong?' she asked.

Amelia received the news with total bewilderment, and was told she must keep the promise. She understood.

'I came to tell you a name tag belonging to Lancelot has been found. Further, the telegram said that Lancelot Courtenay was missing or killed in action,' she said.

Daniel and Helene then entered the room.

'Amelia has told us about the tag,' said Max.

Daniel was ashen faced. Helene and Amelia were in tears. Max had his head in his hands. David was in despair.

'Although upsetting, it is a relief to know the outcome,' said Daniel.

The war raged on through the summer. Civilian males were still being conscripted, and women carried on working in factories and on farms.

A few weeks after the disclosure on Lancelot Courtenay, David Hunworth had not settled down. He was still introverted and withdrawn in his manner.

Due to having only one leg, David often used a wheelchair. On this occasion, Max was pushing David around the garden of Town Green House.

'I thought after the matter of Lancelot being finalised, you would have been more settled,' said Max.

'Feeling so guilty at what I have done will never leave me. Daniel and Helene are so kind to me. I wonder if they would feel the same if the truth were ever to be known,' replied David.

Max hesitated before speaking, unsure whether to declare this particular thought.

'David, please hear me out on something that has been puzzling me,' he said.

David looked apprehensive, wondering what his father was about to bring forth.

'All right, I'll listen,' he said.

'That name tag of Lancelot's suddenly turning up,' said Max.

David interjected. 'I was wondering if any of you found it strange. You've brought the subject up. No one else has said anything,' he said.

'With the relief of knowing what had happened to Lancelot, I don't think the others have given it a second thought,' replied Max.

David continued, 'Remember me telling you about that corporal questioning me? My answer was not completely true. I had cut Lancelot's tag off and put it in my pocket. After burying Lancelot, I did the same with the tag, some distance away. Heavy rain must have washed it to the surface. I am pleased this has happened as it has put Lancelot in a new light. He is at peace, which is much more than I am.'

Two days later, David Hunworth was found hanging from a beam in an outhouse at Town Green House.

November

An inquest was proceeding in Eastsea Town Hall under the jurisdiction of the present coroner, Joseph Stevens.

Earlier, the inquest had heard Lord Daniel Courtenay recount how, during a shoot on Eastsea Hall Estate with a party of friends, Max Hunworth had gone missing. Still, two hours later, there was no sign of him. A search party was formed and in a copse, His Lordship found his body, with a gunshot wound in it.

Inspector Archie Longfield was now giving evidence. 'At about four o'clock on Saturday, tenth of October, nineteen hundred and seventeen, I was summoned by Lord Daniel Courtenay to Eastsea

Hall. Upon arrival I was taken to the area where Max Hunworth's body lay. The corpse was then transferred to the hospital, where an autopsy was performed.'

Doctor Cedric Lewis gave his findings. 'The fatal shot had penetrated the heart of Max Hunworth, thus causing his death. No other wounds were found that would have contributed to this.'

Amelia Hunworth was too upset to give evidence. Inspector Longfield spoke on her behalf. 'Of late I have had discussions with Amelia Hunworth and feel able to give a reasonable account of her thoughts. As heard at David Hunworth's inquest, the verdict was that David Hunworth took his own life due to being unable to deal with his injuries, physically and mentally. This had a profound effect on Max and Amelia Hunworth. I know the effects of these matters, as many of you will, having lost loved ones. People deal with their grief in various ways. Amelia is devastated, having had experience of this in the past. Max Hunworth gave me the impression there was something more than the loss of his son. Was it a concern shared by both David and Max? We shall never know; it has gone with them to their graves.'

Joseph Stevens announced, 'I can only bring in the verdict of accidental death. There are no witnesses, therefore no evidence.'

A week later, Amelia Hunworth died suddenly at the age of sixty-four. The inquest verdict: pining, withdrawal from real life, and a broken heart. Life had given her too much for any human being to be able to contain within their soul. Amelia's first husband, Nathan Cartwright, had drowned aged forty-six; son Billy drowned at twenty-three; there was parental discord regarding Mary, who ran away and married Dick Matthews, who later proved to be her half-brother; grandson Cedric Lewis was killed during the war, aged twenty-one.

Ypres, Belgium – December
Another fierce battle. The British are pushed back by the Germans.

CHAPTER FORTY-FOUR
1918

January
WAR RAGED on through the year. Millions were still fighting and being killed on the battlefields.

At home, women were working tirelessly in the factories, producing munitions.

Towards the end of the year the Allies were gaining the upper hand with victories in various parts of Europe although at a heavy cost, with countless casualties and fatalities.

The German war machine was in turmoil.

11th November – 11.00 a.m. – Paris
The High Commands of the Allies and Germany were meeting. The Allies were accepting the German Declaration of Surrender.

12th November – Eastsea
There was relief in the community, the country and around the world. However, there was sadness too, for many would not see their loved ones again.

The task of rebuilding the infrastructure of the towns and cities could now be implemented.

Four years of war had changed the lives of people, prompting a politician to declare, 'Although we were victorious, there was no winner.'

The Courtenays had mixed feelings. Lord Daniel said, 'We have freedom, but at a tremendous cost to us all. We now have to be able to cope again and we shall, considering what has manifested and occurred in and around Eastsea and in people's lives, over the last twenty or so years.'

CHAPTER FORTY-FIVE
1919

January
FAMILIES GRADUALLY came to terms with the consequences of the Great War.

Towns and cities were being rebuilt over the following years as life returned to as normal as possible.

As landowners and farmers reclaimed land, bodies were still being discovered on the former battlefields of Europe. Some of those without name tags led families to assume they were their loved ones, as was the case at Town Green House regarding Lancelot. Susan Matthews at first never gave up hope. However, she later faced reality and continued in service for Lady Helene.

March
A war memorial was erected in Eastsea town centre to the memory of the fallen – their names being engraved on the structure.

April
Life at Town Green House was returning to normality, though occasionally a sombre atmosphere prevailed.

Lord Daniel Courtenay and Lady Helene now had the task of getting their thoughts on estate and house matters on course again after the turmoil of previous months.

'I have put off long enough the matters that dealing with estate and house require. Losing Lancelot, Max, Amelia and David in such a short period of time has left a huge gap in our lives and there is work to be done,' said Daniel.

'That has concerned me of late. Let me have your proposals,' said Lady Helene.

'Firstly, an estate manager needs to be appointed. I believe Dick Matthews is the man for the job. He has the experience and, although an estate worker, he took on the responsibility of running things when we were unable to do so. I shall offer him the position,' said Daniel.

Lady Helene considered this suggestion for a while.

'Yes, a wise choice,' she replied. 'Now, the position of housekeeper. One or two of the serving girls would be suitable, but I think Susan, Dick's daughter, could do the job. She has an old head on young shoulders. Amelia taught her well. Sadly though, she is still having difficulty accepting the loss of Lancelot, as we all are. The job will occupy her mind.'

'There are one or two positions for estate workers still to be filled. Should not be too much of a problem though, as we can recruit from Eastsea,' said Daniel.

Mary Matthews was absolutely delighted to hear of her husband's and daughter's ascendancy in the ranks of the Courtenays' dynasty, as were Henry and Susie.

This prompted Mary to remark, 'About time this family had some good fortune.'

There were some snide comments regarding Susan's promotion, such as 'got the job because her father was the estate manager'. Lady Helene got to hear of them and soon put a stop to such idle gossip.

May – Rotterdam

Two men, one older than the other, apparently uncle and nephew, were chatting at an inn.

'Uncle, I'm fed up working on the docks. Both Agatha and me want a change of life. Unfortunately, we cannot afford to do it,' said the nephew.

'I'm sure you can. You've been working long hours of late, have you not? And I may be able to help you,' said the uncle.

'Where would we go?' asked the nephew.

'I know just the place. Both of you will like it. Good for the boy as well. Leave me to make the arrangements,' replied the uncle.

Eastsea

Lord Daniel and his new estate manager were on the estate, surveying the grounds.

'I would love to build another hall,' said Daniel.

'You most likely would have succeeded the first time had it not been for the earthquake. I understand men worked hard, and two died at the time. It's a tragedy that there is nothing to show for it,' replied Dick.

'Myself and Lady Helene are pleased that Susan has agreed to continue as the housekeeper after her trial period. We are both pleased with her work. Also the lad from the town is proving to be a good worker,' said Daniel.

'They are, and thank you and Her Ladyship for the trust and confidence shown in both me and Susan. The rest of the family are grateful too,' said Dick.

'We were both sure neither of you would let us down,' replied Daniel.

June – Town Green House

Lord Daniel and Lady Helene were in the drawing room when the front door bell rang.

After getting the command to enter the room, Susan appeared.

'Sir, someone is enquiring about the job on the estate. They saw a notice in the town,' she said.

Daniel thought for a moment.

'I'll see them in the library,' he said.

Later, Daniel returned to the drawing room.

'What happened?' enquired Helene.

'Strangely enough, he is a countryman of yours,' said Daniel.

'A Dutchman?' retorted Helene.

Daniel continued, 'His name is Marcus Bourdin, young strapping chap, small son, wanted a new life. Talked to a few sailors. Got the impression Eastsea was a good place. Took their chances. Staying at the Cockleshell. Told him I would let him know.'

A week later, Dick Matthews was at the Cockleshell talking to Marcus Bourdin.

'The job is yours, Mr Bourdin,' said Dick.

Marcus shook Dick by the hand.

'Thank you,' said Marcus. 'When do you want me to start?' he asked.

'Hold on. One or two things to sort out first. There are quarters at Town Green House you can occupy. We must get you moved in, and you can start work after that,' said Dick.

A few days prior to this, Lord Daniel and Lady Helene had discussed the possible employment of Marcus Bourdin.

'Enquiries will have to be made into Marcus Bourdin's background. If it is satisfactory, he will be employed. There is still the need for one more worker. They can move into the Hunworths' former rooms. Best not tell them the history surrounding them,' said Daniel.

'That seems to be all right. Sound thinking, Daniel! One matter that rather concerns me,' said Helene, 'Why Eastsea?'

Daniel then related to her the explanation Marcus Bourdin had given him for being there before continuing, 'Don't forget that fate brought you here.'

Within the next few weeks, Marcus and Agatha Bourdin, with son Anders, were firmly ensconced in Town Green House, Marcus proving to be a good worker on the estate, with Agatha working in service within the house.

Lord Daniel and Lady Helene were comfortable with how the arrangement had proved to be suitable.

Charlotte enjoyed babysitting and playing with Anders.

CHAPTER FORTY-SIX
1941

SAUL SMITH and Doreen Hughes married in nineteen hundred and six. Toby and Miranda Hughes retired from the Cockleshell in nineteen hundred and twenty. At this Saul and Doreen left the estate work and took over the running of the inn. Both now in their sixties, they were teaching their grandchildren the trade.

Due to age restriction at the time, Saul Smith and Drew Alexander were unable to go to war in nineteen fourteen. Drew was soon to retire from Hart's garage.

February
Lord Daniel Courtenay contracted tuberculosis. He was attended to by various consultants and town doctor Maurice Simpkins. His brother-in-law, Doctor Cedric Lewis, now retired and aged seventy-one, weighed in from time to time with advice.

Within a week or two Lord Daniel's health gradually deteriorated. Lady Helene and the rest of the family were deeply concerned.

Third of March
Sadly, on this day, Lord Daniel died, aged seventy-two. A sombre atmosphere prevailed around the estate and town, such was the esteem in which Lord Daniel was held.

Fifth of March
Lady Helene, at the age of sixty-six, took the demise of Lord Daniel with great sorrow and foreboding. The rest of the family were of a similar demeanour. Messages of sympathy and cards of condolence were received.

Twelfth of March – noon – Eastsea Parish Church
The Church was full for the funeral service of Lord Daniel Courtenay. The service proceeded in much the same vein, with hymns and tributes, as that of his father, Lord St John Courtenay on the twenty-fourth of September eighteen ninety-six. Officiating were the Bishop of Bishops Lynne and the vicar of Eastsea, Reverend John Murdoch.

After the service, Lord Daniel's body was conveyed to the family tomb.

The wake in the town hall gave an offering of fine fare provided by the purveyor that had catered at the time of Lord St John Courtenay's funeral forty-five years earlier. Fond memories of Lord Daniel were spoken as sympathisers chatted with Lady Helene and the family.

Thirteenth of March – afternoon – Town Green House
The solicitor, Frederick Harrison, was in the drawing room with Lady Helene Courtenay, Lady Jessica Lewis, Doctor Cedric Lewis, Lady Charlotte Hart and Mr Julian Hart.

Frederick, the nephew, became senior partner in the practice after Gilbert died.

'Your Ladyships, gentlemen, as you are aware, the will of Lord Daniel Courtenay will now be declared,' said Frederick.

This proved that Lady Helene had been bequeathed most of his possessions. Other items were left to various immediate family members.

'Now – a most important issue. The death of Lord Daniel

leaves a void, due to the fact there is no male heir apparent,' said Frederick.

There came a knock at the door.

'Not at present. I am dealing with important family business,' he told those outside.

'Who is it?' asked Lady Helene.

'Your housekeeper, estate manager and an estate worker,' replied Frederick.

'What do they want?' asked Helene.

'The estate worker has something really important to tell you,' replied Harrison.

'Then you had better let them in,' said Helene.

Harrison appeared agitated.

'Your Ladyship, this is most inappropriate,' he said.

'Please let them in,' said Helene, with authority in her voice.

The estate manager and housekeeper took their leave.

Marcus Bourdin entered the room.

'What is the reason for this intrusion?' asked Harrison.

'Thank you for seeing me,' said Marcus.

He handed Harrison some documents.

'What are those?' asked Helene.

Harrison studied them carefully.

'Birth certificates, Your Ladyship,' he replied.

Lady Helene had a look of disdain.

'What do you mean, birth certificates?' she asked.

March Fifteenth – Rotterdam

Inspector Hans Doring and Constable Klaus Jorgen of the Constabulary were studying some documents.

'These and our enquiries show this fellow as a law-abiding citizen,' said Doring.

'I do agree,' replied Jorgen.

March twenty-second – Town Green House

Once again, Lady Helene and the rest of the immediate family were in the drawing room, with Frederick Harrison and four other gentlemen.

'Your Graces, I would like to introduce Inspector Hans Doring and Constable Klaus Jorgen from the Rotterdam Constabulary. Inspector Colin Hanley and Constable Sid Beaumont, you already know,' said Harrison.

After salutations were exchanged, Harrison continued.

'Inspector Doring has startling news for you regarding the heir apparent to the Eastsea earldom. I got in touch with Inspector Hanley to contact counterparts in Rotterdam, who are the Dutch officers with us, to get to the bottom of Marcus Bourdin's claim,' he said.

Inspector Doring then explained, 'Prior to meeting you, Lady Helene, Jonas de Smits had a relationship with a Sophia Bourdin, resulting in the birth of Marcus. Whilst sorting out Jonas' affairs following his death, Herman de Smits discovered another birth certificate apart from Jonas' own, which was the one he used on the occasion Herman attempted to pass himself off as Jonas. That particular one had Jonas' surname correct as de Smits, mother Alexandra de Smits, father Lord St Courtenay. The second certificate was for Marcus Bourdin. On this one the mother was named as Sophia Bourdin and the father as Jonas Bourdin. Realising there had been an error, Herman then took Marcus' certificate to the registry office in Rotterdam to point out the mistake. Using Jonas' birth certificate, he persuaded the authorities of the error. The matter was rectified. Another certificate was issued showing Jonas de Smits as the father of Marcus. Then, after a further administrative error by the registry office, the original certificate was retained and the corrected one was destroyed. Upon the request of Lord Daniel Courtenay in nineteen hundred and nineteen to look into the background of Marcus Bourdin, the then officers in

Rotterdam saw the original certificate showing Jonas Bourdin as Marcus' father. Social and working issues were checked, and as far as they could see, Marcus Bourdin was a law-abiding citizen, just as myself and Constable Jorgen have recently discovered,' he said.

'Where did you get all that information, and why is Herman de Smits not with you?' asked Lady Jessica.

'Herman has admitted to the plan being his brainchild as revenge for the way he was treated by the Courtenays when he attempted to impersonate Jonas and his banishment from England. He is in his seventies and quite frail anyway,' was the reply from Inspector Doring.

With this revelation, the family were devastated.

'You are telling us that this makes Marcus Bourdin the heir apparent to the Eastsea earldom. He obviously took his mother's surname. St John Courtenay is not with us any more, but his past is still haunting us. I remember saying to Daniel at the time the Bourdins arrived here, "Why Eastsea?" Another thought I've just had, rather hard to bear: Agatha Bourdin is now the Lady of the House,' said Lady Helene.

Lady Helene was by now quite agitated, and Doctor Cedric Lewis was concerned.

'How are you feeling, Helene?' he asked. 'All quite upsetting,' he added.

'I'm all right,' she replied.

The issues surrounding the Eastsea earldom had leaked out into the community. The estate workers were really concerned for their jobs. Dick Matthews assured them he would have a meeting with Marcus Bourdin, if indeed he was the next earl, as soon as the Courtenay family affairs were completed.

Thirtieth of March – Town Green House

Frederick Harrison had assembled Lady Helene and the immediate family members, together with Marcus, Agatha and Anders Bourdin, in the drawing room.

'You can appreciate that the issues surrounding the Eastsea earldom were complex, and will be aware that the Constabulary officers of Eastsea and Rotterdam meticulously scrutinised those birth certificates and other matters regarding the Bourdins. The investigations revealed all was in order for the handing over of the earldom to Marcus Bourdin,' said Harrison.

'This is a nightmare. Please tell me I am dreaming,' said Lady Helene.

Jessica interjected. 'Mr Bourdin, I shall address you as such, until proven you are the rightful heir to the Eastsea earldom. The deceitfulness, for twenty years or more, knowing that one day, possibly, you could be the next earl. When Charlotte gave birth to two daughters, you realised that the time had been worth waiting for.'

Charlotte took personally the remarks surrounding her daughters' births.

'Well, I'm sorry if my body did not work for the good of the family line. Anyway, you're a good one to talk, Jessica. You did not provide any children at all,' she said.

At this Doctor Lewis interjected.

'This is no time to quarrel amongst ourselves. We have had a tremendous shock, and it is upsetting Helene,' he said.

Frederick Harrison took charge.

'Come, all of you; time to deal with legal matters,' he said.

He produced some documents which proved to be the deeds to Town Green House and a charter for Marcus Bourdin to become Earl of Eastsea.

The signing of the papers followed.

Marcus, about to put pen to paper, hesitated.

'You're right, Lady Jessica. I have no right to the earldom. I cannot do this. Working twenty years on the estate, I cope with. Being Lord of the Manor is another matter. You have to be born to the aristocracy to know the way of the world. I know Lord St John Courtenay was my grandfather, but in an improper manner,' he said.

Agatha and Anders Bourdin were clearly surprised, as were Lady Helene and the rest of the Courtenay family gathered there.

'I thought we had succeeded,' said Agatha Bourdin. 'Why do this now?' she asked.

'Yes, Father, what have you done?' asked Anders. 'We had a good life in Eastsea, about to get better. Herman will have something to say about your actions,' he said.

'I have explained my reasons. We shall return to Rotterdam in due course. Do not worry about Herman. He is no longer part of our lives. Forgive me, Lady Helene. I understand you became a member of the Courtenay family by fate,' he said.

'Don't be insolent, but it is true: fate did play a part. But mainly by love, not deceit. You were here by human error and deceit,' she replied.

In more ways than one, Frederick Harrison thought to himself.

Harrison explained, 'Well, we have proved two can play at being deceitful. First of all, when the Bourdins arrived here some twenty years ago from Rotterdam, there were misgivings. Lord Daniel had them checked out. Following investigations, approval was given to employ Marcus. Recently, when I was shown those birth certificates the reality was they were stupid, or thought we were. Jonas' was legitimate. However, Jonas Bourdin is recorded as being Marcus' father. The evidence of the two certificates did not prove that Jonas de Smits and Jonas Bourdin were one and the same person. I must congratulate you, Lady Helene, and the rest of you for your performances and the part that the four officers played. Marcus Bourdin didn't sign as I had forewarned him, and he agreed not to.'

At Harrison's revelation, Agatha Bourdin seemed to have a modicum of sense, declaring angrily, 'I told you it would never work.'

The Bourdins returned to Rotterdam within the week.

The Courtenay hold on to the Eastsea earldom had been secured, and as to the future, what did that hold?

EPILOGUE

HIRAM JAMES OPENBINDER, fourth Earl of Eastsea. A surname unfamiliar to the English aristocracy classes. To explain, we need to rewind.

Following the deaths of Lady Helene Courtenay and Lady Jessica Lewis, Lady Charlotte Hart became matriarch of the Courtenay dynasty in nineteen forty-three.

Hiram arrived in Eastsea from Texas in mid-nineteen forty-seven, with his wife Isabella, both archetypical of Texan culture: him a sixteen stone, six-feet-six hulk and her an attractive blonde. The Openbinders were wealthy oil, cattle and gold barons. The advent of the motor car, courtesy of Henry Ford, in the early nineteen hundreds prompted the need for oil. Brewster George Openbinder, Hiram's grandfather, capitalised on this, thus becoming the first man to drill and discover oil in Texas. Hiram's father, Charlton Eustace, founded the Openbinder Corporation. Oil having made the business lucrative, he invested in cattle ranches. Hiram entered the business, wanting to make his own niche, and took up gold mine rights in North America. By nineteen forty-five the Openbinder Corporation finances were in the multi-million dollar bracket. Feeling success had been achieved in America, Hiram looked for further challenges.

The temporary appearance of oil and gold in Eastsea in the late eighteen hundreds was legendary around the world.

The challenge for Hiram was to find those two commodities, his motto being: They were there then, so must still be there.

Coinciding with Hiram's arrival in nineteen forty-seven, Charlotte and Julian were of the mind to find pastures new. Four years of ancestral responsibilities had rather taken their toll on Charlotte. Although born into riches and good fortune, Charlotte to a degree was the black sheep of the family. Marrying Julian, although he was a member of a family with a respectable and lucrative garage business, was not quite what Lord Daniel had in mind for his daughter. More to his keeping for Charlotte was boarding and finishing schools, and marrying into an upper class dynasty. This attitude had brought out the rebel in her.

By early nineteen forty-eight, Hiram had purchased the Eastsea earldom and estate. Charlotte and Julian, on recommendation by Hiram together with his friendship with Henry Ford, emigrated to America. Julian achieved a position within the Ford Motor Company. Charlotte and their daughters Martha and Delia, were happy with life in America.

In due course, Hiram purchased the Hart garage business from Wallace and Vivien when the couple were both in their late seventies.

Late nineteen forty-eight, Hiram began drilling for oil on the marshes and prospecting for gold on the foreshore. Both proved to be successful ventures in time.

Within seven years, there was an oil refinery at the end of the channel and a gold mining quarry on the foreshore, employing locals and making Eastsea a flourishing community.

Another five years, and a mansion of great splendour had been erected, using the latest automated plant, on the site of the former building on Eastsea Hall Estate.

Hiram and Isabella had two sons, Harvey and Richmond, providing male heirs apparent to the Eastsea earldom.

Had DNA been available, Marcus Bourdin's claims could well have been proven to his benefit.

The pioneering exploits of the Wright brothers inspired others, thus making advancement in air travel.

Computers, in the main, replaced typewriters.

Telephones progressed from landline to mobile.

Following intensive commitment by women, they achieved the right to vote.

The assumption must be that the whaling ship found the Ark and destroyed the *Basilosaurus*.

This tale attempts to illustrate how life could have been, at the same time showing the advancements of social and economic procedures, of which there are many, though only the tip of the iceberg has been touched.

About the Author

Keith Blades was born on the North Norfolk coast which features as a backdrop to this first novel. Aged sixty-nine he was educated at primary and secondary schools. Working life consisted of thirty years as a jobbing printer and twenty-three years as a security officer. He has two stepdaughters and lives in Kings Lynn with his wife Wendy.